In Retrospect

Katherine Luck

IN RETROSPECT

IN RETROSPECT

The door is open.

Cesar is in the master bedroom, hovering over the lump that Anna's body makes deep in the center of the bed. She floats beneath the red-stained sheets like a dreaming fish, a mutilated mermaid.

He paces the soft rug, aged decades beyond his fifty years in just a day. He's on his cell phone, his eyes staring vaguely at the windows where the dark tide undulates on the other side of the glass. His words waver low in the room, denting the silence like gentle splashes in a still pond. He drags his fingers through his graying hair over and over. Strands drift and float on the air in his wake. He's talking to Harborview Hospital in Seattle. They're sending a helicopter. He doesn't look at his wife, lying so peacefully beneath sheets soaked with her own blood. My sweatshirt still tightly binds her wrists.

I slip away from the open door, unnoticed. I'm running away from this disaster that I caused. Cesar will find my scrawled Post-it note of resignation stuck to the vast surface of his desk, if he bothers to look for me later.

I tiptoe silently down the hall.

Another door is open.

I shouldn't pause, but my eyes are pulled to look.

Cesar's brother is sitting on the edge of his bed. He huddles there, his hands clasped tightly between his knees like a traumatized child. He drips cold seawater onto the hardwood floor from his hair and his clothing. A salty puddle shimmers beneath his feet. His two-hundred-dollar business shirt is defaced by vivid swirls of Anna's blood.

He raises his head. His face is ashen. The icy, lawyerly composure that has always solidified his features has vanished.

His cheek sports a muddy bruise where Cesar slapped him.

He looks at me fully, like a real person, for the first time ever. These are little boy eyes, vulnerable and scared. These are the eyes Cesar sees when he looks at him.

"Flynn…we tried to stop. I want you to know that. You shouldn't have told Cesar. She would have died years ago, if it weren't for him. God…why did you tell him?"

I feel so guilty.

"Was it because I didn't pay you off? I would have. Why didn't you ask me?"

What have I done to these people?

I turn and walk away.

Friday, February 23, 1985
10:56 p.m.
The Hung Dog Tavern
Eastern Washington University, Cheney

The bar is murky and jammed with students. Outside, the rain falls half-heartedly, unseen behind windows steamed to opaque mirrors from the body heat.

In a dim corner, Antonio slides into a booth next to Anna.

"Here we go. The bartender put a sugar cube in yours. I don't know why."

Antonio pushes a shot glass sloshing with tequila and Tabasco Sauce across the table. Anna nestles close to him. She runs a fingernail smudged with three hues of lavender over the rim of the glass. She grins up at him.

"He must be trying to get on my sweet side. Does that bother you?"

"Yes."

He's emphatic. He's unamused. He stares at her until she smiles and whispers,

"Well, you're the only one on my sweet side."

He grins slowly, looking like a little boy for a moment.

He picks up his shot glass and holds it suspended in the air where it catches the low light like a floating jewel.

"What?"

"We have to toast something."

"Yeah?"

She wonders if it's a significant day for them. Exactly six months since they started dating, maybe?

"Okay. I finally finished my application for the law school at UC. Took six weeks of hell to put the thing together. I dropped the beast in the mail this afternoon. Cheers?"

Anna's face falls, then clouds over with conflict and trouble.

"UC. California?"

"Anna, let's not start, okay?"

"Are you serious? California. Right?"

"Yes. California. It's one of the top law schools in the country."

"California,

Tony!"

"Jesus Christ, can we please not get into this right now?"

"You know that I don't want some kind of stupid, long-distance relationship! They never work—they never *ever* work out!"

Anna's cheeks evolve from cosmetic peaches to two stinging roses. She slides to the edge of the booth. She balances precariously there, her arms crossed over her chest.

"What am I supposed to do? I have to go to law school, and there isn't one here. I never pretended I'd be here forever

when we got together. You knew. Look, can we just drop this? I

wouldn't be leaving until September, anyway. That's months and months from now. We can deal with it then."

Anna exhales slowly. She drops her eyes to her lap.

"I guess…"

"It'll all work out. Really. We'll make it work. Cheers?"

Anna's scowl ebbs. She picks up her glass to tap against Antonio's.

"Try not to choke on the sugar cube. I can't help you sue the bar yet," Antonio winks, which makes her smile unwillingly.

Anna comes up for air before her shot glass is empty, gasping and shaking her head.

"Oh God, that is so awful! Why do you like these things? They taste like battery acid."

"Because they're just two bucks each. And they're macho."

"Maybe I don't want to be macho. Ever think of that?"

Antonio takes her glass from her hand and drains it. Anna isn't used to hard liquor. She begins to float. She puts her hand on Antonio's shoulder.

"You're right…everything will work out. With us. Won't it?"

"Sure. I promise."

"Really?"

"Have I ever lied to you?"

She replaces her hand with her head, her eyes blurring to a soft focus. As the minutes pass, she believes him. As the minutes pass, she becomes incautious.

"You won't really go to California, even if you get into that school, right? Not unless you can't get into any of the ones in Washington?"

The muscles in Antonio's shoulder snap taut. Anna opens her eyes and raises her head.

His face is a stone.

"I can't believe you just said that."

Anna's heart begins to batter her lungs.

"I mean…it's just a back-up place…isn't it?"

Antonio slowly turns to ice, his eyes frosting over and making her go cold as well.

"If I get in—if I'm lucky enough to get in, of course I'll go there! It's one of the best schools in the country. It would be the worst mistake of my life if I didn't."

Anna opens, then closes her mouth, her breath stolen.

"I…I…so you'd really leave me, huh? Not care if it broke us up. Never see me again, not even feel bad?"

"Anna—"

Hot adrenaline bathes her stomach and lungs.

"My God, you're such a cold bastard sometimes! You'd never even miss me, would you?"

"Don't say that. You don't know how I'd feel."

"Right, that's exactly it, isn't it? I never know how you feel—I just have to assume, and then I end up looking pathetic!"

"I'm not going to throw my entire future away, just on the off chance that you and I are, you know…meant for each other. Or whatever."

Anna's eyes skate off his. She shakes her head and slides out of the booth.

There's nothing to do but push through the crowd at the bar and start flirting with the bartender. Get a free beer, pointedly ignore Antonio. She's profoundly hurt and feels stupid. He's like all the others: just after free sex and bragging rights.

She feels like a whore.

She drinks the comped beer, not looking around to see if Antonio is still in the bar. He'll find a new girlfriend within the week. He's an iceman. He has no heart.

Maybe she'll go home with the bartender, if he asks. Just to show ol' Tony that she can be cold and selfish, too.

She feels a hand grip her upper arm. It's gentle.

"Anna, please, don't be like this."

Antonio is close, his chest forming a wall against her back. She tries to shrug off his hand, but she's too drunk and unsteady on the stool. She turns her head and slides a narrow gaze over him.

"What, don't be like what, Tony? Huh? Don't be a bitch?

Or don't care about you? Well, fine, I won't do that anymore. No problem. Bye."

She expects him to throw up his hands, say 'whatever,' and stalk away, as her previous boyfriends would have done.

Instead, he startles her. He presses his forehead to hers.

"Please, Anna."

His breath is warm and erratic on her face. His hand cups her cheek. It trembles against her skin. His lips are close to hers, but he doesn't kiss her.

"Please, I can't do this. Let's leave, okay? Come on…please?"

Anna is baffled. This has never happened before.

"Um. Well. Okay. Whatever."

Outside, the rain casts a bitter mist over them. Anna shivers in her thin jacket, the paint splatters from her oils class glowing like fireflies under the streetlight. The deserted sidewalk shines like obsidian as they walk in silence.

Antonio's hand is still shaking when he unlocks the door to his apartment. Inside, he flicks on a lamp and locks the front door behind them. Anna shrugs her jacket off, letting it fall to the floor. This sort of thing usually annoys him. He claims it left paint stains on his carpet once. Tonight, he leaves it where it lies and walks to the couch. He sits heavily. Anna steps to the middle of the living room and folds her arms over her chest. She wishes she could sit, but dignity demands that she loom over him.

"So…what? You want to talk or something?"

Antonio shakes his head mutely. His eyes dart along the wall behind her. He briefly presses his palm over his mouth Anna is swamped with the cold certainty that he's going to break up with her, right now, in this moment. He didn't want to do it in the bar. That's what he meant. He wanted to be a gentleman and do it in privacy. God, it will hurt…

"Anna…um…"

He doesn't look at her. He lowers his hand and it becomes steady.

She squeezes her arms firmly around her breasts, embracing herself. She won't cry. She won't let him see that it hurts her.

"Do…Anna, do you love me?"

Her face goes numb.

"Uh…well. Like, what…um, I—"

"Do you?"

His black eyes jump into hers, burrowing at her pupils.

She has to pull her gaze away from his. He'll make her cry, and that can't happen, or he'll always remember her as the pathetic undergrad he crushed one night. She stares at the print of

Matisse's *Yellow Odalisque* hanging over the TV. She gave it to him for his birthday.

"Well, yeah. So what?"

There's a blur of motion from the couch. She lets out a cry of surprise when he crushes her in his arms.

"I love you," he whispers into her hair. "I've never said that to anyone before. I love you so much."

Her body melts, seeking to blend into his.

"Do you really?"

"Please, don't be mad at me…"

Anna is shocked to see tears standing in his eyes. They

don't fall—she knows he'll never let them. But they are there.

"I'm not mad, not really."

She frames his face with her hands and kisses him.

"Tony? Will you always love me? No matter what happens? With us, I mean?"

"Yes," his lips pray the word over hers. "Always."

Saturday, April 10, 1987
1:37 a.m.
The Hung Dog Tavern
Eastern Washington University, Cheney

"This is the last one, really. I'm serious this time."

Anna eyes the bartender over the rim of her extra-sweet Long Island Iced Tea. She only intended to have a beer tonight, but she found that she was lonely, and the bartender was cute, and before she knew it, she was drunk.

"Damn it."

Anna shakes her head, her dark ponytail tickling her cheeks.

"Every guy I've ever dated's been a total jerk. Well, not Freshman year. They were still boys then. They were so nice. Called on the phone. Came over just to say hi after class. Acted sweet. Then. Then. Then the trouble began."

Anna's face falls softly. It goes smooth and too young under the layers of cheap drugstore makeup.

The bartender polishes his eyeglasses on his shirttail.

"The iceman, right?"

She's been over this already tonight. Twice.

"All Sophomore year—I really loved him! And what's he do? Graduates, breaks up with me, and leaves the damned state! Just like that."

Anna stares morosely at her half-empty glass. Even now, remembering pulls at the inner corners of her eyes, tightening her sinuses in a familiar way. It's hard not to cry, even two years later, when she has spent so many nights alone in the isolating hours before dawn doing so.

"He said...said we would make it work. Damned cold liar.

He was just gone one day. Never called since. Just gone. I guess I became inconvenient."

She taps at the glass with chipped nails, the beds grubby with burnt sienna and ochre. She straightens up.

"Who the hell cares? Waste of my time, y'know, thinking

about him. Real life has to be better than this college crap, right?

I'm going to have a real life in a couple months."

Anna downs the last of her drink. She gradually feels lightened. Things will get better. She'll graduate in two months and move out of this hick-town for New York or San Francisco. She will get a job in an art gallery and work her way up. By this time next year, she'll be drinking Dom at an opening, sleek in a designer evening gown. She'll flirt with handsome collectors and become renowned. She'll be so happy.

"Want another?"

The bartender's face is smudgy, or maybe it's her vision.

"No, nah, I gotta get home."

Anna hauls herself to her feet, steadying herself on the bar.

"Gotta study. Gotta finish a paper tomorrow."

"Want me to call you a cab?"

Anna has enough of her wits about her to shake her head. She lives only four blocks away.

She tosses a wadded bill in the tip jar, then hesitates. She thinks that she might pick up this cute bartender, but then she sees that he knows what she's thinking, yet he's pretending not to know in order to avoid her drunken enticement.

She irritably pads out of the bar, gripping the backs of chairs spastically and wishing she hadn't worn high heels.

Outside, the air is mild and smells of clean rain coming.

"To hell with 'em all! Stupid men. Boys."

She aims herself at her street. She can see her dorm from here. The windows glow pale citrus where folks are drinking or smoking or studying. She navigates through the dark, pointed somewhat straight at the front door.

She hears a rustling to her right. She turns slightly, wondering if it's raccoons in the bushes like last time, and something huge and dark rushes at her. A body slams into hers. Limbs envelope her. A hand slides over her mouth, and she is lifted off her feet before she can scream.

Saturday, April 10, 1987
8:14 p.m.
Cheney, Washington

The only light in the dank basement comes from the bare bulb that hangs over the workbench. The man stands beneath the bulb, his forehead shining with a thin sheen of sweat. He makes a small motor whir between his strong fingers. The room smells of mildew and hot metal and rancid wood.

Anna hangs by her wrists from a sturdy water pipe, sobbing weakly. Hours ago, she gave up pleading with him to let her go; to stop hurting her. Now she simply tries to keep breathing, but it's becoming very difficult.

She's naked, her feet skimming over the surface of a deep pool of her own blood. Her breasts lie across the room on a little china dish that the man brought down from the kitchen.

Minutes ago, he tried to cut off her nose, but his knife was too dull to go through the cartilage. In frustration, he sliced at her face wildly, tearing a deep hole in her left cheek. As she shrieked, he sawed at her mouth until her lips hung nearly detached against her chin. Then he gave up and went to the workbench to sharpen the knife on an electric whetstone.

The man sighs and switches off the whetstone, holding the knife up to the bulb to check the edge. He tests it on his thumb.

It's such a normal kitchen knife, good for cutting carrots and apples. She owns such a knife.

He turns and steps away from the bench, crossing the blood-dappled stone floor to stand in front of her.

Anna moans weakly, trying to hide her mangled face against her shoulder. He presses in close to her, watching for a reaction. His breath smells like peppermint.

She gasps as the knife slits her abdomen, carving straight up in a wicked, singing arc. It doesn't hurt for many seconds. Utter numbness wings through her, as if she's fallen into an icy lake.

Then she has the pain, and then it has her, and she can only scream and scream, her body going limp as her heart pumps her blood onto the floor.

Sunday, April 11, 1987
3:56 a.m.
Cheney, Washington

The bright blur at the end of the road intensifies, resolving into a neon rainbow. Arabesques of candy-colored light dance and jump, becoming slogans and familiar product logos. All-night gas pumps and salvation just a few yards away.

Anna staggers down the dark dirt road. Her naked body is dipped scalp to toes with blood. She shines like a red star under the white slash of moon hanging on high.

She can't breathe. Walnut-sized clots of dried blood dress the two shorn holes on her chest. Her abdomen is a gaping cavity.

Ahead, the lights seem to twinkle like a tiny circus. She's beyond pain now, fogging in and out of sensibility.

Soon she'll fall, and she's vaguely aware that when she does, she may never get up again.

The colors glow all the way to the backs of her eyes, dazzling her.

She trips, her knees and ankles veering in different directions. The dusty road comes rushing up to slap her shredded cheek.

Monday, April 12, 1987
10:26 a.m.
Fort Lewis, Washington

I jerk unsmoothly to a stop in front of the whitewashed clapboard office, jouncing the colonel and making him scowl in my general direction. I learned to drive just three months ago. My drill sergeant was appalled that I had no driver's license upon entry into boot camp, and forced me to learn. I'm still awkward and pudgy-handed at the wheel.

The colonel harumps in his throat; the first vocalization he's made since I picked him up an hour ago.

"Well…soldier."

He eyes me, and I see what must be, for him, a rare moment of uncertainty. He drops the shellac of command for an instant to expose a look of raw confusion. He's certainly never been so unsure of another person's gender before.

"The U.S. Army appreciates you driving me here. Report back to your sergeant. Dismissed."

"Yes, sir."

I salute. I'm better at it than I used to be. My hand is solid; perfectly flat and exact in its angle.

The colonel nods, returns the salute, and steps out.

A pale officer is waiting for him at the top of the steps leading to the office.

He stands gleaming in the sun, his eyes a vast land of frost glinting blue under his camo cap.

I rise slightly in my driver's seat.

It's my Commanding Officer. He's in charge of the entire base. This is the first time I've seen him up close. The only other time I glimpsed him was during the first day of boot camp, when he stalked the ranks of our limp-armed selves and proclaimed us unworthy and foul. Seeing him so near catches me off guard; as if I've spotted a movie star at the grocery store. I salute very carefully, very precisely.

My Commanding Officer sees me. He starts to make the same machine-tooled salute the Colonel made; but like the Colonel, he hesitates.

He looks at me again for the briefest instant. Just a little pause; a little extra glance.

He salutes. It's hard to tell, but I think he made a smile at me. Officers never smile at us generic grunts.

It feels good to be individualized, even as an enigma.

Wednesday, March 15, 1989
10:50 a.m.
Avalon Hospital, Seattle

After a year of visiting his mother at Avalon Psychiatric Hospital, all the duty nurses recognize Cesar. He forgets to sign in sometimes, but they never yell at him about it. They smile at him. They never smile at anyone; not even each other. It helps that he donated over sixty-thousand dollars to the hospital last year, of course.

He walks briskly down the hall, as he does every Wednesday. He doesn't enjoy these visits.

The sun is unseasonably bright today. It pours in thick shafts through the picture windows in the sunroom. Cesar glances at the honey sheen and his steps slow.

A young woman with very dark hair is seated by the largest window. Her body makes a slim, finely-etched silhouette against the sun. He's never seen her before. The light is dazzling and hard to see through, yet something about her quietude, her isolation strikes him as wildly lovely. She's like a deer that will bolt away as soon as it perceives that it's seen. He's unexpectedly stirred.

Maybe it's just the sunlight. It's been gray and miserable in Seattle since mid-September.

Maybe it's just been way too long since he's been on a date.

He forces himself to pick up his feet and continue down the hall. He stops at Room Fourteen.

Cesar knocks sharply on the door. Three taps: it always has to be three, or she becomes agitated. Three is a safe number; a holy number.

The angry, bird-like voice shrills behind the neutral face of the door.

"¿Qué? ¿Qué-qué-qué?!"

"Hola, Señora Ortiz. Tengo su medicina."

"Pase," she hollers.

Cesar opens the door gently and enters his mother's room.

"Hi, Mamá. It's Wednesday."

His mother sits in a rocking chair beside the bed. She's clean and fully-clothed today. Her wispy, milky hair is neatly gathered in a pink ribbon at the nape of her neck. Her previous hospitals had been lucky to get her in the shower once a month, and had required heavy sedation to accomplish that feat. He wonders how long this place will be able to coerce her.

Cesar sits, opening his mouth to tell her how beautiful the sunshine is and that she ought to open the drapes that cover her window, but she cuts him off. Her voice rises and falls in the sing-

song mutation of Spanish that she's been speaking since he was a teenager.

"What I want to know is this: why are they engaged in such extremities? It's intolerable, what they're doing out there!"

"Yes, Mamá."

"It's got to be repaired, that's all I know. Have you done that yet, Cesar? Have you sutured the wounds of our Lord and Savior?"

"Yes, Mamá."

She glares at him suspiciously, then blinks three times.

"There are fountains flowing blood in the south, and you're here again, useless as usual. Jesus is watching you, Cesar."

"Of course."

"And where the hell have the legitimate tortillas gone to? What are these nasty, floury things they keep feeding me here? I want corn! Real tortillas, for God's sake! I've earned them. They're Christ's body."

"Okay, Mamá."

"You tell them that. You make them give me normal tortillas."

"Okay."

"And make that damned doctor talk right! She lisps like a damned Castilian. I can't stand it. Make her speak Mexican-Spanish. Stupid woman. Idiot El Salvadorian whores at the front desk. Chattering like chickens in a berry patch. Make them talk right, too."

He nods. He knows better than to argue with her by now.

"I'll do that."

Her fingers, gnarled like old walking sticks, flick in irritable circles.

"The saints are having a conference about me tonight. They're gonna decide what to do with my feet. They're dividing them up. Heaven and hell…what if they get separated? What'll I do then, Cesar? You'd better call them up and tell them to let me keep both. I need them."

"Yes, okay."

Cesar stares at the wall behind his mother. His mind wanders. Nothing ever changes. She is perpetually disoriented, or worse. Sometimes she's violent. When he was a teenager, her delirium was slight and seemed to relax her, like being drunk. After Antonio was born, she began to deteriorate steadily. Cesar's not sure how much longer she'll remain at this level of coherence.

"Cesar, there are two new creatures being born today in the world. Small things; teeny-tiny. Nobody noticed them yet, except for me. They're highly poisonous. Right out there," she jabs a varnished finger at the shaded window.

"Yes,
Mamá."

"They've sent a man to go kill them. But I know they're creatures of God. Daughters of Jesus. Will you bring them to me in a shoebox?"

"Sure,
Mamá."

Cesar has three conference calls to make when he gets back to the office. The Japanese are getting antsy over the land holdings they purchased last month. He has to redraft their property management plan. He needs to get Chicago to fax over the contracts again. God knows how long that will take.

"And then, when the rain comes, the fish keep learning to walk out of the ocean. Soon they'll be living in the gutters, right above me. I ask you, is that tolerable? No! You need to get rid of them for me."

"Okay."

One evening, she sat at their kitchen table, the shiny thrift store Formica peeling near the elbow spots. She was radiant; all 22 In Retrospect ebony hair and ruby lips under the bare bulb speckled with singed fruit flies and grease spatters. She burned bright in a hot pink dress like a Barbie doll would wear, thrift store also, her rosary clutched in one hand.

Cesar was fifteen and bored; sick of TV but too early to go to bed. He went into the kitchen to find out why she had the Spanish radio station playing at full volume. Enthusiastic traffic reports shook the walls of their decrepit house and resonated off the tall glass of milk that sat on the table before his mother.

The radio announcer fast-talked about impending congestion, and she began to smile. As Cesar watched, she methodically cut the shining black beads off her rosary with a meat knife. One by one, she dropped them into the milk. She said a Hail Mary as she let each rosary bead fall, then pricked her index finger and squeezed off a bead of blood. When the prayer ended, she let the blood ooze into the glass like a fat berry. She sat this way for nearly an hour, until the milk was nearly as pink as her dress. He went to bed and locked the door so he wouldn't have to find out what she intended to do with it. Cesar digs his fingernails into his forehead, plowing at the grooves that have developed in recent years.

"There's nothing precious left in this world."

"True, Mamá."

He has a dinner meeting at seven with the CFO of Preston and Hughes. He has to get all the reports verified and approved by the bank beforehand, which might be dicey. He'd better make some calls as soon as he gets out of here.

"And surely there are no more reasons left for the sheep to be killed. It's ridiculous to see such blood in the streets every afternoon. In this day and age. Isn't it?"

"Yes, Mamá."

He'd better check on the reservations for tonight.

He has so much damned work to do.

His mother's eyes suddenly begin to stab as sharp as silver pins all over his face.

"Where's the baby? Where is he?"

Cesar's gaze slams hard into hers.

"The baby, Mamá?"

"Where's my baby? My Antonio?"

Cesar's stomach tightens sickeningly. She never mentions Antonio.

"He's at school, Mamá."

"What?"

"He's in California. He's at law school. Remember? He's graduating in June."

"He doesn't love me."

"Yes, he does. Of course he does."

She shakes her head, her eyes brimming with tears.

"I want Antonio. I never see him. I cry for him, but I can never see him. I try so hard. I strain my eyes out, out, so far. I cry every night."

Antonio used to strain himself out, so far. Every time Cesar came by the house, he'd see him in the front window, standing in little scuffed sneakers on the back of the torn, mold-puddled couch. His palms were always pressed flat to the chilly glass so that they looked like white gloves. His eyes were always huge, black globes in his tiny face, like two dead planets. He was always watching for Cesar, God knows for how long. The final time, Cesar came with a caseworker from Child Protective Services and a court order. No cops, since there had been no threat to Cesar's life; no reason to think she would put up a fuss.

Antonio had strained out at Cesar through the rain-slicked glass, his face going weak with joy when he saw his older brother on the porch. He jumped off the couch and out of sight to open the door. There was a sinking pause, and then their mother opened the door.

She was pleasant, agreeable even, when the caseworker gave her the legal spiel and the court order. The caseworker spoke in halting, too-tidy college Spanish. She was overly accessorized and tarty in her dry clean suit and big pearl earrings. She was the variety of woman that Cesar's mother loathed.

Cesar could see Antonio standing behind his mother's hip, just beyond the smooth bend of her waist. She'd always kept her figure up. His mother was all nods and amiability, but her eyes were so far away. Suddenly she slammed the door. Antonio started to scream on the other side of the chewed-up wood. Cesar had to kick the front door in, not for the first time, which made the caseworker shriek and clap her hands over her face when wood splintered out at her.

There were such sobs and such screams coming from deep within the house. Cesar ran down the dark halls, not for the first time, and found his mother in the bathroom. She was holding Antonio down in the cracked tub, pressing him flat with her body, her fingers forcing his mouth open. Bottles of pills rolled around the rust-browned scoop of porcelain. She managed to shove two aspirins and one of her antipsychotics down Antonio's throat before Cesar pulled her off. He ripped his little brother out of arms that hooked like thorn branches and ran with him.

Cesar sped with the little boy down the hall, out the front door into squinting winter light, toward his waiting car. Antonio clung twig-slim arms chokingly tight around his neck through the silvery rain, sobbing so hard that Cesar could barely keep from falling on the slippery front lawn. He left the caseworker to cower and scramble around the house for the often-disconnected phone to call the police.

That was a first for all of them.

Antonio sobbed in Cesar's car the entire drive to Cesar's apartment. He sobbed in Cesar's arms when he carried him inside and shoved his fingers down the boy's tiny throat to make him throw up. He sobbed in Cesar's bed when he refused, in a childish blur of Spanish and English, to sleep alone that night. It was weeks before Cesar could get Antonio to take his candy-flavored vitamins or to eat anything pill-shaped like peas or beans. It was months before he stopped having hellish, shrieking nightmares every night. It was years before his teachers stopped sending home crayon pictures he'd drawn of huge women with wild hair and vampire teeth and coffin-tight bathtubs and aspirin-shaped raindrops falling from black clouds to crush little stick-figure boys.

Cesar lets out a sigh. He glances at his watch. It's been forty minutes: close enough to an hour.

"I've got to go."

He rises and kisses his mother's forehead.

The only thing he can't humor her about is Antonio. She has never forgiven him for taking Antonio away from her. He has never forgiven her for treating his little brother so brutally.

"I want churros."

Cesar rakes his hand through his lightly graying hair.

"You can't eat churros. You know that. They're very bad for you."

"I need churros! Churros, churros, Cesar!"

"Alright, okay, yes. Next Wednesday. Okay?"

"Okee-dokee."

She smiles at him, minutely, for the first time since he arrived.

"See you next Wednesday."

"Hmf."

She has already turned away to glare at the heavy shade on her window by the time he reaches her door.

He walks out of her room, shutting the door softly behind him.

He exhales hard, closing his eyes briefly. These visits with his mother are getting harder and harder as the years pass.

They leave him feeling worn out and lonely and aging. He has no one else in his life. Just his mother and Antonio. She's never going to get better, and Antonio is moving on with his life. He's twenty-five, no longer Cesar's little boy. He has become his own man, busy with law school and his own goals.

Maybe he won't come home to Seattle after he graduates, even though Cesar's been coaxing and, at times, openly pressuring him to do so ever since he left the state three years ago.

If Antonio doesn't come home, Cesar will have no one at all once their mother dies. His career has kept him busy for years; ambition driving him hard and making it easy not to notice the things that were lacking. But now, he's financially where he's always wanted to be. Now, he can afford to enjoy life. Now, at forty-two, he's powerfully lonely.

He walks slowly away from his mother's room.

The green exit sign flickers at the end of the hall. The bulb inside is about to burn out.

He glances at the open door to the sunroom and his steps stop.

The young woman is still sitting in the chair by the wide picture window. She stares flatly out into the anemic sunshine, her posture lifeless and empty. Cesar's gaze flicks back to the exit sign. He hesitates.

He steps cautiously into the sunroom.

"Hi."

He speaks softly. He has become adept at talking to mental patients over the years. He knows that you move very slowly, you keep your hands neutral at your sides, you don't smile.

"Are you new here? I'm Cesar. I was visiting my mother. Lupita Ortiz. Have you met her?"

The young woman turns to him. She stares at him, blinks, then slowly aims her face back at the window.

He gets quite a good look at her.

Horrible scars coat her skin, clotting her features. Her forehead is bisected by a finger-thick gash, padded with scar tissue like a pink length of linguini. Her left cheekbone shines chalky through bloodless corpse flesh. The cheek is nearly translucent, a bare membrane of skin stretched to cover her jaw. A filigree of red spider webs radiate across her right cheek and her chin. Worst of all are her lips. They look as if they have been torn off, then barely reattached. They shudder and flicker with each of her exhalations.

Cesar's stomach seizes. He steps too fast to her side.

"God, sweetheart, what happened? Car accident?"

She flinches. She turns farther away. Her nose touches the window; her breath fogs the glass.

Cesar slows himself forcibly. He eases into the wicker chair opposite hers and ignores her for three minutes. He has learned that this helps; it always works with his mother. Softly, he begins to speak again. He keeps his eyes off her face so that she won't get agitated. His mother is always agitated by staring eyes.

"You don't have to tell me, it's okay. Do you like it here? This is one of the best hospitals in the state. My mother hates it. She just treated me to a forty-minute lecture about how awful it is. No corn tortillas, only flour. Nobody speaks Mexican-Spanish, just Spain-style or El Salvadorian. Picky woman. Who's your doctor? Dr. Farrell? She's nice. My mother likes her, even though she learned Spanish from the Berlitz academy. My mother says she lisps."

The young woman ignores him. Under her sweater, her chest is flatter than a young boy's. Cesar tries not to stare at it, but he wonders.

"God, it's gorgeous out, isn't it? Feels like decades since we've seen the sun. Do you ever go out in the yard? My mother refuses. One of her things, you know how it is."

Cesar glances at the back of the woman's head. Her hair is severely skinned back in a tight ponytail, which drips like a black icicle down her spine. He wonders what her name is, where she came from. She's much younger than the other patients.

"You know, I'm gonna sneak my mother in some churros next week. Know what those are? Really yummy deep-fried bits of...I don't know exactly. Some kind of dough. You dip 'em in cream or salsa. Absolutely horrible for you. They'll clog your arteries in ten seconds flat. You want me to bring you some? I'll hang for giving them to my mother if the docs find out, so I might as well spread the joy around if I'm gonna get in trouble anyway, right?"

Her fingers move slightly in her lap but she doesn't look at him. Her eyes are reflected in the window. They're dead and lusterless, like pebbles.

"Okay, so I'll bring you some, too. You're gonna love 'em, I promise. I'll be back next Wednesday. I always come on Wednesday. You should try to meet my mom. She's in Room Fourteen. Just knock and say, 'Hola, Señora Ortiz. Tengo su medicina.' She'll let you right in and talk to you for hours if you say that. Just keep nodding at her and she won't realize you don't speak Spanish."

She doesn't look at him. Cesar rises, glancing at his watch. He really needs to get back to the office. He stayed too long today.

"Well, it was very nice to meet you. I'll see you next Wednesday, okay? Don't forget. Fresh churros."

Anna turns her face slowly to his.

Her eyes drift upward. His gaze cups hers like a secure basket. A heaviness hits him full in the chest. Suddenly it isn't charity anymore. Her eyes liquefy, animate with a swift yearning, then focus raw pain on him.

The room is still and golden, exuding a weighty apathy, like deep within the ocean. Slowly, her eyes drift away and return to the window. She becomes inert in her chair.

Cesar wanders slowly out of the sunroom. He won't go back to work yet. He'll stop at the nurse's station and find out her name. He'll read her file. They'll let him.

It's irrational. He's never done anything like this before. He doesn't know her. She's uncommunicative. Given where she is, he can be certain that she's insane.

But.

He feels needed.

It's so dangerously appealing, this sensation of protective altruism. He hasn't experienced this tight urgency, this willful desire to rescue for years. Not since Antonio was tiny, reaching out skinny arms in the thick dark, shrieking Cesar's name over and over from the thresher of a nightmare. Falling back to sleep with Cesar's arms around him, his little head hard and warm against Cesar's collarbone as the TV flicked a silent blue-gray patchwork over them both.

Cesar turns off his cell phone and walks down the hall, his vision so glazed with sunlight that he can't see.

Wednesday, August 9, 1989
Avalon Hospital, Seattle

Cesar sits on Anna's narrow bed, gently brushing her hair. It makes a dark fan over his palm, pulling tension against the bristles of the brush. He leans against the wall, his legs stretched out. Her body is draped over his, her hand on his thigh, her face obscured.

The little room is neck-deep with drowsy shadows. She always keeps the room dim when he comes to visit her; lit only by a small nightlight across from the bed, dull yellow like candlelight in a frontier cabin. The day she found herself wanting him to come, she stopped letting him see her clearly. She smooths his business shirt so the buttons won't poke her thin-skinned cheek.

"You know, you ought to wear your hair down. It's always hidden up in those scraggly ponytails. I like it a lot better this way. It's so soft. Will you wear it down for me?"

"Okay," Anna murmurs, snuggling closer to Cesar's warm, comforting bulk.

The hospital is quiet. She has spent years in this snug room. She has memorized every nub and fissure in the paint. She knows each scuff in the floor; each subtle warp in the window panes. It's her shell. Her cocoon.

Cesar clears his throat. His thick body tenses up slightly. He studiedly keeps brushing.

"You know what? When I was at work today, I got this crazy idea. The more I thought about it, the better it sounded to me. So, I called your doctor this afternoon, and I talked him into it."

"What?"

Anna rubs her mangled cheek against Cesar's chest, relishing the stillness and feeling of security that she only can attain when he is with her. Lately, she lives only for his visits. She longs for him when he's absent.

"Well, I've been thinking long and hard about this. For

quite a while now. I think it's time for two things to happen."

Cesar sounds hesitant. He never sounds hesitant with her. He has a proposal to make.

"What?"

Anna lifts her face, misarranged and distorted with scar tissue. Her silhouette is an aberration only glimpsed and sensed in the dimness; a horrible implication in the dark.

Cesar sets the brush on the quilt and wraps his arms around her. He rubs his chin against the top of her head, kissing her hair lightly. He doesn't speak for far too long.

"Okay. One: you need to get out of the hospital and into the real world for a change. This place is doing nothing for you. Yeah, I know they've kept you from…you know. Hurting yourself. But that's minor. A good sedative could do that. You're in a tomb here. It's not a life."

"But—" she sits up in alarm.

Cesar holds up his hand sternly. She falls silent, lowering her head to his chest again. Now she, too, is bodily tense.

"Number two: you and I need to start spending more time together. Quality time. These visits aren't enough for me."

"But…I like having you…come here…"

Her lips, displaced and loose on her face, mangle the words.

"You like spending time with me?"

"Yes. Yes, yes."

"Would you like to spend more time together?"

Anna grips his arm, digging her nails in.

"Yes."

"Then what do you say to this: your doctor told me that if I sign a release of responsibility and liability with the hospital, you can spend every weekend with me. At my condo. Just you and me, Friday night to Monday morning. What do you think?"

Anna pulls away from Cesar. She sits up. She turns her carved, ruined face to the wall.

"Dunno."

She feels Cesar sigh next to her, though he makes it silent. He has so much more self-control than she does.

"Anna. We've gone as far as we can here. I don't want this to be it."

Anna's ribs are cinched with cool terror. He has an ultimatum. To propose.

"You don't…want to come…see me…anymore."

She draws her knees up to her desert-flat chest, hunkering her chin down, guarding her vulnerabilities.

Cesar doesn't humor her. He doesn't take her in his arms, doesn't touch her.

"I don't want to have to, no. I don't like knowing that you're moldering in here all day. It breaks my heart. I don't like scheduling you in. I want us to have a normal relationship."

Cesar has never used that word with her. He simply comes and brings stillness to her and leaves. Then she waits for him to come again. Her life has evolved into a waiting room, a holding pattern in anticipation of Cesar's arrival. It's comfortable. It's a gentle focus amidst foul memories. She's confused.

She shakes her head. She turns fully to the wall, giving him her back.

"I can't keep coming here, Anna. It's killing me to see you like this. We need to make some changes. We'll never really know each other if you stay in this place."

In the past two years, Anna hasn't once gone out into the real world. She tried at first, after she'd been pieced back together, but it proved too difficult. It was beyond her.

"Too scary."

This is the crucial, honed moment. It's the moment that will ring forever within her: the one where she will lose him. He will walk out to protect himself. Anna can't tolerate change. She crafted this frail shroud, this spindly nest, through lost years that passed like slow centuries. She's inflexible at the age of twenty-three.

Cesar reaches around her hunched body and grips her chin. He rubs his thumb over the wormy scar.

"Baby, look at me. Do you think I'd ever let anything hurt you? Do you?"

"No…"

"Nothing will ever happen to you, I swear to God. I'd die first. You'll always be safe if I'm with you. You know that, don't you?"

"Yes."

"Then why not try it? Come spend this weekend with me. We'll get in the car and I'll drive us straight to my condo. It'll take just fifteen minutes. It's a secure building. Twenty-four hour guard at the front desk, electronic monitoring, tons of cameras in the halls. Safer than the White House. I'll lock us in and we'll spend the entire weekend together. Watch some old movies, eat some huevos con chorizo like my mother taught me to make—"

"I know…about that. She told me. You almost set…the apartment…on fire one time…making them."

"Don't listen to her! She's got no English, and your Spanish is atrocious. You misunderstood. That was a serious misrepresentation of my cooking skills. Uh…help me think of more denials."

Anna crafts what is, for her, a smile.

Cesar grins, twinning his fingers in her hair.

"We'll order in, then. Chinese food, Thai, Indian—anything you want. We'll drink some wine, listen to some jazz. And when you start to get scared, I'll hold you in my arms all night. Keep you safe and warm. What do you think?"

Anna bites her barely-sewn-on lower lip and closes her eyes to avoid Cesar's searching ones. She should refuse. She should lose him. She has been floating in this medicated, meditative apathy for two years. She has encased herself in a narrow world of pure predictability. Cesar is the only erratic element that has managed to gain admittance in all this time.

"Okay," she whispers, her heart thudding hard and making her feel unreal.

She can't believe that she's agreeing to this. But it sounds so safe and normal. She realizes suddenly that she wants normalcy desperately. She wants to retain Cesar and the utter calm he gives her.

She coils into him, cupping his middle-aged face between her hands.

"But don't leave…me alone. Not for a minute. Promise? I couldn't…stand it…without you."

She speaks very carefully and very deliberately so there can be no misunderstanding. It's crucial to her.

"I swear to God. And to you."

Cesar kisses her cheek where it's as thin as rice paper. He pushes her hair away from her face, his eyes warm on hers.

"Oh Anna, I'm so glad! Thank you."

He presses his hand to cover her heart, her breastless chest heaving under his palm.

"You're so beautiful to me. I really am falling hard and bad in love with you, mi amor. I really am."

Wednesday, January 17, 1990
3:43 p.m.
Harborview Hospital, Seattle

Cesar knocks softly on the half-closed door to Anna's hospital room, then pushes his way in. Fluorescent lights glare down on him, painting him swimming pool green.

"Hi there, sweetheart. Flower delivery service here."

He sets the top-heavy bouquet of flowers on the table next to her bed.

"I couldn't make up my mind, so I got roses, some orchids, daphne, hyacinth. I had the florist mix them all together. She thought I was crazy. She told me so."

The loamy odor of the hothouse flowers dresses up the iodine and Pine-Sol smell of the room. He shakes out his arms, brushing at the pollen that dusts his suit jacket. An unsterile yellow cloud puffs up, then disperses.

Tiny in the steel rimmed bed, Anna smiles involuntarily.

It hurts her face mightily, making her eyes sting with tears.

"I didn't know you'd gone."

Her pronunciation of the words is unfamiliar to both of them. She speaks too slowly, enunciating hugely around the consonants. Her lips are trim and efficient now. She will have to relearn how to talk.

"Yeah, you were sleeping pretty deeply. The doctor said you'd be out for a good eight or nine hours. I just went to the office for a little while to take care of some stuff."

Cesar sits on the edge of her bed and places a hand on Anna's knee. He's functioning on no sleep. He waited out the entire ten-hour surgery in the little room off the operating theater.

He sat all night by her bedside watching over her, holding her hand.

"I took the rest of the day off, so I can spend all evening here with you. How are you feeling?"

"I don't know. I'm still pretty groggy, and I keep thinking I'm going to throw up. The pain's not quite as bad, though."

"Did the nurses give you morphine, like the surgeon told them to?"

"No, something else. Codeine, I think."

Cesar frowns.

"I'll talk to them again. I don't want you feeling any pain with this thing. The nausea and grogginess'll have to pass on their own—that's what the chief surgeon told me. She told me you should feel a lot better tomorrow morning."

Cesar laces his fingers into Anna's. He lets himself stare at her new face. It's her former face, resurrected from the ruins. It's a face he has never seen, except in a few old photos that she had been terribly reluctant to show him.

He runs his eyes over the smoothed curves, the new arcs and bends. He lifts his hand. Very gently, he grips her chin where the stitches terminate. He tips her face at an angle. The rough light gleams off her skin between the stitches, quilting her face white and black.

Her features have been entirely reformed. Each jagged scar has been reopened, delicately scraped clean, then reclosed with careful sutures. They're mere pink threads in her flesh now, like capillaries just beneath the skin. Cesar pulled in many favors to get three of the best plastic surgeons on the West Coast to come up from L.A. for the operation. He emptied a fair chunk of his liquid capital in the process.

He hesitates, his eyes dropping to her body.

"May I?"

She goes rigid, resisting. Then she nods mutely.

He reaches behind her back and unties the paper gown. He peels it down from her shoulders to crumple in her lap. She instinctively reaches up to cover herself. He takes her wrists in his hands and gently pries her arms apart.

"Wow."

Goosebumps rise over her skin from the cool air and from feeling his eyes.

"They're very sore, but…compared to those push-up bras I

37

wore in college, it's not too bad."

Cesar lightly touches the black stitches that encircle the recreated breasts. He's seen her naked before, but never whole. They've only made love twice, all hesitance and unerotic gentleness on Cesar's part. He had decided that was what their relationship would have to be about. He had decided that he didn't need her in that way to be happy.

"You look so gorgeous, sweetheart."

He eases the paper gown lower, baring her waist and hipbones.

"Oh, this looks great!"

The scar had cleaved a sprawling, cherry canyon into her abdomen from beneath her navel up to the terminus of her sternum. Now it's just a light pink hair, thin and barely noticeable under the stitching.

"Look at that! That's amazing. Think how it'll look when the swelling's all gone. There'll be nothing left at all."

She closes her eyes, since it hurts to feel him looking at her.

"Have you seen yourself yet?"

Anna shakes her head, clenching her jaw as the motion brings a flash of pain from her bones out to her corseted cheeks and forehead.

Cesar gets a hand mirror from the bathroom.

"Ready?"

He shows her.

Anna is unprepared for what she sees. Her eyes widen and widen.

She begins to cry.

Cesar's face falls.

Anna quickly puts her hand on his. He has been so good to her. He has given her so much. She can't hurt him.

"It's good, I—I'm happy. It's just a shock. It's so much like the first time. Waking up in the hospital, seeing my face all swollen and bloody, all sewn up. But, but, God, I'm happy, Cesar, I am! This is what I used to look like. Before it happened. God, how could you ever stand to look at me?"

Cesar's eyes stroke her face, his hand squeezing hard on

hers.

"Amor, baby, you've always been beautiful to me. They really did a great job. We'll have to wait until the swelling's all gone and the stitches are out to see if it's perfect. If it takes another surgery or two to get you back to exactly the way you used to be, that's not a problem. I'll get you as many as you need."

Anna is trembling so hard she can't hold onto the mirror. She lets it thump onto the blanket that covers her knees.

"Not right away, okay?"

"No, it's too hard on you, baby. But in a year or so, if you want."

She must calm down. She must think. She can't descend into a panic attack.

"Okay."

He presses his lips gently to the top of her head, careful to avoid the stitches. So many possibilities are spreading seductive, dusky vistas before him. She'll be able to go out into the world now. She'll no longer want to hide herself away, willfully caged in with her solitary fear. Her intricate terrors will fade. They can get married. He can introduce her to his brother. The three of them will be a family. They will be so happy together.

He rubs his cheek lightly against her hair, kissing the long strands that flow in dark streamers over her shoulders.

"You're perfect again. You're amazing. Do you like it?"

Anna is dissolving inside, the familiar panic soaking into her entrails. She forces a smile that rips crimson pain through her face.

She touches his face with a hand that shakes, her eyes growing wet.

"Yes. Thank you so much, Cesar. I can never thank you enough."

"Do you love me?"

"Yes—so much."

"That's all I need, then. I love you with all my heart, baby."

She can wrap her arms tight around him now and feel him

absorb her. She starts to cry silently.

Her face and body have been repaired, but she hasn't returned to being the same woman she was before.

When her face and body had naturally looked like this, she had been so different.

She thought she would wake up from the surgery with the solidity and unthinking inner strength that had been hers before her flesh was ruined. She had liked that person. She wants that purest self back so badly. But, if it's not here now, it must be lost forever.

Cesar kisses her throat gently, his own eyes filling with tears.

"I'll make you safe, sweetheart. You'll forget, I promise you. One day, it will be like a movie you saw years and years ago. It won't be part of you anymore."

Saturday, May 19, 1990
11:37 a.m.
Seattle

At any given point in her past, Anna would have been hellishly intimidated by the exclusive boutique in downtown Seattle. She has never before set foot in a place that sells blouses costing six hundred dollars and up. She's never even heard of such things.

Cesar wends between the spare, elegantly-wrought brass racks with a fearlessness that she can't make herself feel. He holds her hand, which helps, but not quite enough. She feels as if she's continuously falling. Her stomach has climbed to roost near her tonsils.

This is the first time she's been in a store in over three years.

"Bailey says this is the only place his wife'll shop in Seattle. She spends the rest of his money on Rodeo Drive and over in Milan. She learned Italian just to shop better there. Uh-huh,

right. I'll bet she's got some cabana boy set up over there. Exactly how many Italian evening dresses can a woman really need?"

The sunlight slices a knife-edge along the dull marble floor. Anna fears to step on the bright beams. They will cut her feet, straight through her shoes to the bone.

"What you need is a good selection of clothing for different occasions. Casual stuff, but also nice things for dinner parties and entertaining and whatnot. Matronly things."

"Matronly!"

Anna would giggle if they were at home. She swipes her eyes across the cool room, covering the space with vigilance. She must keep alert, or something awful will happen to her.

The racks loom around her, shiny and bony. The over-priced clothing sways at her as she passes. Sleeves and hems snag lightly on her hands and jeans. They grapple at her with soft, empty limbs, trying to ensnare her and drag her into their smothering folds.

The saleswomen near the front doors are haughty with french twists and die-cut faces that will crack if they smile. They eye Anna dryly from behind the glass table where only a crystal vase and a small pad of paper lay. There's no cash register or shopping bags to be seen.

Cesar stops walking. He kisses Anna's cheek, then her neck. He presses his lips into her hair and whispers, "Are you doing okay?"

"Uh-huh."

She digs her fingernails into his hand.

"You sure? If it starts to be too much to handle, you tell me right away and we're out of here."

Back at the condo, it had taken an hour and a half to get her out the door. Then came five failed attempts to climb into the car. Cesar finally gave up and held her sobbing in his arms on the bathroom floor, forcing her to choke down three sedatives. He's only supposed to give her one every six hours, at most. Anna is aware that she's in the midst of a very bad panic attack, but her body and brain are so slackened that they can't muster the power to react.

"I'm okay."

Cesar releases her hand and cradles her shoulders, drawing her close to his thick-walled body. This is better and more secure. Her muscles release a bit. He kisses the top of her head, then her temple.

"I love you so much, sweetheart."

"I love you, too."

Cesar smiles and turns to the racks of clothing. He shakes out a long white skirt and holds the fabric at arm's length.

"Hey, look at this. Nice, huh? You'd look beautiful in this."

Now that Cesar is touching the merchandise, the Japanese saleswoman glides with supernatural speed to his side.

"How may I assist you, sir?"

Anna shrinks against Cesar, half of her body vanishing under his suit jacket.

"Well...we're shopping for my fiancée's trousseau. I'm thinking linen, silk, very light wool—no synthetics. Skirts, dresses. Flowing stuff, nothing clinging or tailored. White, or very close to it. Can you start us off with a few things?"

"Marie is our modiste. I will tell her your requests and she will bring you a selection to start with. Would you care to be shown to the dressing salon?"

Anna glances at Cesar. Surprise cuts through the buzzing fear and makes everything pause.

"No colors at all? No red or blue or anything?"

Cesar shakes his head dismissively.

"Nah, you look so beautiful in white. Like an angel. Call me old-fashioned. I never like when women wear bright, flashy clothes."

Anna herself is a creature of bright, flashy clothes. But that's not what bothers her. She has bound herself to color, worshipping pigment and shade all of her adult life. She once wished nothing more than to make a career of the play of color on a two-dimensional surface. She wanted to own an art gallery, she wanted to create hues never seen before, she wanted to be renowned. She knows seventeen names for yellow.

"Okay," she says.

Cesar looks at her carefully.

"Do you mind? Will you wear what I want you to?"

Long ago, she would have rebelled massively if put in such a position by a man. Now, she shrugs. Nervously.

"Okay."

Things have changed so much in the past three years.

"Great. Want me to come with you girls to the dressing rooms?"

"Yes, please. I've never worn stuff like this, so I don't know what looks good on me."

The Japanese woman hands them off to a steely blond with the body of a darning needle.

The woman, the modiste, rubs her eyes down the length of Anna, then back up again. Anna crushes herself against Cesar, the trembling beginning. The modiste is striping off Anna's skin to peer at the underlying bone and fat and muscle. Anna's body is turning to water.

"You are a size six."

Cesar's fingers are firm on Anna's shoulder, grounding her. She can't run or fall apart. It would upset him. She has to hold herself together.

"N…no."

The modiste raises a thread-thin eyebrow.

"You are a couture size six. Follow me."

The modiste guides Anna and Cesar into a small room with many mirrors. The walls are tinted a warm apricot. The furniture is the color of old lace. The space is soft and encompassing, like a bosom. It's like the spare bedroom back at Cesar's condo. When she came to live with him, he gave it to her for her own.

She put all her old art textbooks on the window sill. She never paints these days, but she likes to sit within the nest-like room, surrounded by the props of her old ambition and feel the secure inertia. She likes to look at the paintings in the books and breathe in the brushstrokes, drowning in the color.

Anna drifts away from the mirrors, standing awkwardly with her arms crossed over her breasts. The paintings on the walls are of very high quality, she can tell. They're originals. She steps forward to examine one, but stops when the blond woman raises her eyebrow. Anna jerks away like a caught thief.

"Damn, this place is nicer than my living room."

Cesar sits on a late-Victorian teak settee and grins at Anna.

"Want a couch like this? Very classy."

"Sure."

The modiste glides in and out of the room, her head held high like an ice skater. She retrieves hangers upon hangers of flowing white clothing, which she deposits on delicate hooks next to the mirrors. She stares at Anna, watching for her reaction. Cesar ignores the woman. He leans back on the couch and tugs his tie loose.

"We need to start thinking hard about what kind of

furniture we want. For the house. That crap in the condo's just hit-or-miss pieces I picked up as I needed 'em. Having a dinner party, better buy a dining table. Doing a lot of work at home, better get a desk. No theme, no cohesion. Bachelor-style. We gotta upgrade. I won't have anything in our house that my wife has to apologize to people about."

Anna grows still. A peculiar enervation swamps her each time she hears him use the word 'wife.' It's a submersion. She'll lose a great chunk of her identity. This pleases her. It eases terror.

The modiste closes the dressing room door and clears her throat. She approaches Anna, her arm draped with a mass of water-cool fabric.

"A casual dress first? Appropriate for afternoon wear, club luncheons. Egyptian cotton, designed by Maritani."

Anna glances at Cesar. He flaps his hand at the modiste.

"Sure, that's fine. Hey, you know, I had a thought just now. You should wear a very high-end silk evening gown for the wedding. Something couture. Maybe French. Not one of those god-awful New Jersey-looking monstrosities you see in the bridal magazines. Very elegant, very clean lines. Maybe no veil."

"Okay."

The modiste raises her sharp eyebrows impatiently.

Anna hesitates. It's been years since she's taken off her clothing in front of anyone except Cesar. She closes her eyes and reluctantly steps out of her tight jeans. She reaches out to set them on a chair. The blond woman swoops in and grabs them before they leave Anna's hand.

"I'll wear my tux, of course. I keep telling my brother he ought to get one. Best investment I ever made. I'd have spent ten times the cost of the thing in rentals just during this past year. He's trying to weasel his way onto the board of the symphony, so he's been putting in a shitload of time at openings and benefits. I hate to guess how much money he's already wasted renting."

Anna stands awkward in socks and panties, swimming in

unease. The blond glares, Anna flinches. Anna inhales with the abrupt, deep inward pull of a high diver. She yanks her bright red tank top over her head.

The faint, fourteen-inch scar running from the elastic of her panties up to her breastbone is only slightly visible in the mirror. Delicately pink, it looks like a crease left on the skin from the zipper of the snug jeans. The saleswoman doesn't seem to notice it. Anna relaxes a bit.

The woman abruptly drapes the dress over Anna's head.

A cloud of white smothers her, stealing her heartbeat. The modiste births Anna's head through the neckline with hands that smell of expensive lilac lotion. She begins tugging and fastening. Anna feels inanimate, like a doll being worked upon. Fear begins to percolate up from her abdomen.

"I think you should wear a very classic pearl choker at the rehearsal dinner. Three strands, maybe four. Freshwater, not cultured. I'll get it for you in the next week or so. I'm not going back to that jewelry shop downtown, though. I know that cocksucker screwed me on the setting for your engagement ring. I'll get you something imported from the International District. Japanese, antique maybe. How's that sound?"

Anna is spun bodily around by the blond woman to face the mirror. Her heart drums irregularly.

"It fits you perfectly," the modiste declares in a practiced tone.

Cesar smiles at Anna's reflection, meeting her eyes in the mirror.

"That's nice, very nice! How's it feel? Looks comfortable."

Anna has to make an effort to keep breathing. The sedatives aren't enough for this. The dress is more expensive and lovely than any garment she has ever owned; than any she's ever tried on, or even seen from afar in a store window. It hangs like a glowing ice sculpture from her shoulders. It frames her body, it touches her skin, yet somehow does not make itself felt in the slightest. She feels naked in the dress.

Vertigo tilts her. She looks angelic, unearthly, utterly unlike herself. Like a thing not real, not alive.

This is how she should have been dressed for her burial three years ago.

"Do you want it?"

Her skin glows too much within this snowy, floating garment. Her refurbished features seem like those of a Grecian sculpture. She is leeched of color; only her eyes, her hair, and the many resurrected lines of her face shining through the foggy white. She looks like a stripped canvas; the paint hacked off to leave a ghostly shadow of once complex shades.

It's a shroud, it's utterly beautiful, it's a casual afternoon dress.

Cesar sits up, looking at her sharply in the mirror.

"Should we take it? On to the next one?"

His body tenses, because Anna has stopped moving. She's not blinking, or breathing.

She stares at Cesar in the silvery glass, watching as he blurs away. Her ears fill with a great hum and she grasps her gaze frantically over the whiteness of herself. The ring on her left hand glints rainbows in the mirror that are so gaudy, so smeary like neon lights which flash and shimmy to bring everything in her life to a crashing halt.

Things sink, and then Cesar's hands are on her upper arms. She can hear herself jabbering and pleading insensibly. Cesar wraps his arms around her and lifts her off the floor.

"Charge it to my account, send me the bill," she hears him say, and then the room oozes away, the shop oozes away, and she's outside in the searing sunlight.

She gasps as the harsh light flays the flesh from her bones. Her lungs flap within her rib cage like two fish on a dry dock. She drowns on white light, compressed by the gravity of the brightness.

Then she's in Cesar's car. It's shady and chill. His palms are cool on her cheeks, framing her face securely and bringing focus. She makes herself gasp in one breath, then another. Her body shakes as if with a convulsion.

"We're going home, sweetheart. We're getting out of here, okay? You're safe. Just breathe, baby. Can you look at me,

Anna? Open your eyes, just for a second. I'm right here, please look at me. Please breathe, amor."

Tuesday, May 22, 1990
3:17 p.m.
Fort Lewis, Washington

Our Commanding Officer is a wickedly intelligent man.

He has already narrowed the field of applicants for five highly coveted Army Intelligence Trainee slots from fifty-three hopefuls down to just seventeen of us. He did so within a mere four minutes by dint of a carefully worded set of commands. We grunts were told to double-time it to the nearest weapons storage facility, obtain a rifle, and return to begin our shooting trials. Thirty-three troops immediately jogged off toward the common lock-up next to the mess hall, some three-quarters of a mile away.

The other twenty of us hesitated, glanced uncertainly at each other, then walked briskly to the small portable weapons shed against which our CO was leaning. We grabbed rifles and stood at attention. We waited to see if we'd been impertinent and would be failed.

The CO eliminated three hopefuls for obtaining ammunition. He hadn't ordered us to obtain ammunition.

Now the CO jerks his head at the remaining seventeen of us. We fall in behind him, our muscles coiled up and our eyes blazing with heightened alertness. The CO is crafty. This process isn't going to be simple or straightforward.

The sun is gorgeous and evil as we take positions on the firing range. It glints stabbing shards of silver off of every reflective surface, rendering the grassy field an arctic-bright nightmare. The targets at the other end of the field are utterly obscured by the glassy bursts of light. I suspect the CO has secreted bits of tin and polished mirror in strategic places in order to disable us.

I squeeze off my twenty-four rounds in the prescribed sixty seconds. My eye sockets ache from squinting so hard into the light. I lower the rifle. I don't like it. It's unfamiliar and is poorly calibrated; the sights are sadly low.

The CO stalks our line after ceasefire has been called. He points four times: bang, bang, bang, bang.

"Thank you for your effort."

I'm spared.

Now there are thirteen of us. Unlucky thirteen.

The CO prowls fluidly up our line. We stand rebar-straight, rifles at rest, our faces immobile. He glares into each of our eyes. We must not flinch.

"The capital of Peru, Corporal!"

The young woman's eyes shift slightly.

"Sir?"

"Out. Thank you for your effort."

Oh God. I'm no good at this. I've never been book-smart. High school was a disaster, and I never went further.

"What is the current time in Saigon?"

"Uh, um…oh-eight-hundred, um—" the corporal fumbles.

"Out. Thank you for your effort."

Oh Jesus. I'm screwed.

"What do the letters in KGB stand for?"

"No idea, sir," the private barks, without hesitation, his face rigid as a newly dead man's.

"Remain."

"This is bullshit!" Saigon-time shouts on our periphery.

"You were dismissed, Corporal."

The CO's words thud like four boulders. I would be crushed if they were directed at me.

I want so badly to look, but I must not. I must remain at attention. Those were my orders.

I cheat and flick my eyes at the corporal. He is red in the face.

"This is prejudicial, sir! This is a bullshit process!"

"Corporal, will you remove yourself, or will I have do it?"

"To hell with you, sir!"

And oh my dear God, the corporal raises his rifle and there's a blast. The CO goes down.

The field becomes a blur of camouflage as I run to him,

and others rush the Corporal to wrestle the rifle away. Everyone else stands frozen with shock.

I rip at the red front of the CO's shirt, desperately trying to recall my first aid training. The red on my hands is cold and smells wrong. It smells like paint.

The CO raises his head off the grass. I am shocked when he winks at me. He sits up, shoving me aside. He stands.

The Corporal's arm is being bent to dislocation by four of my cohorts. The CO points five times. At the Corporal's attackers and at me, his rescuer.

"You soldiers remain. As for the rest of you: thank you for your effort."

We straggle into line, ratcheting our quaking, adrenaline pumping bodies more or less to attention. The CO glares at the five of us.

"Training begins at oh-six-hundred hours tomorrow. Lay hands on one of my officers ever again, and I'll ream you out personally with a two-by-four. Dismissed."

He brushes at the paint spatter on his shirtfront and walks away from us. And I swear to God, as he passes, he winks at me again.

Friday, May 25, 1990
7:09 p.m.
Seattle

"Why are you so nervous, Cesar?"

Anna sits on the couch in the sunken living room with her feet tucked under her, as Cesar rushes around the condo. He's erratically tidying up.

"Is he a neat-freak, or something?"

"No, no, of course not…"

Cesar carelessly shoves Anna's copies of *The New Yorker*, *Gourmet*, and *Seattle Bride* under the couch. She's been studying all three like college textbooks for a midterm. She's constrained to master a large amount of new information in too short a time. She's never tasted foie gras in her life; she has managed never to read Salmon Rushdie or see a Cocteau film. She hadn't realized she was so deficient. She needs to improve herself quickly if she's going to be Cesar's wife. He is a man of the world.

"I'm just excited about the two of you finally meeting. I want it to be perfect. I haven't told him about the engagement yet. He's probably figured it out, though. He's a sharp one. I bet he won't even bother to pretend to be surprised, that little jerk!"

Cesar sweeps her new Swarovski crystal earrings off the coffee table. He bought them for her the previous weekend; achingly expensive things, and too heavy to wear for more than ten minutes at a time. He jingles them in his hand like loose change.

"He hasn't been in this place for almost a year. Not since right after he got hired on at Burgess, Jackson and Harrison. They're usually impossible for a young lawyer to break into. I threw him a party. Really upscale: cocktails and hell-of-influential guests. Invited all the partners from his law firm. Introduced him to all my business contacts. Five of the City

Councilmen showed up. The mayor couldn't come, but he sent some flunkie that turned out to be two degrees of separation from the governor of Washington. Every major judge in King, Pierce, and Snohomish Counties came. *Seattle Magazine* wrote it up. Antonio got himself an excellent client base from that evening. This damned place was so—so *clean* that night. Flawless. Now…it's like a demilitarized zone."

Anna feels the instinctive pang of domestic failure; the guilt of a middle-class housewife. She forces it down. Cesar isn't criticizing her housekeeping. Every time she tries to straighten up, he grows exasperated and tells her to leave it for the maid service. He seems offended by her efforts. He doesn't let her cook, either. All she knows how to make are suburban, all-American family dinners. Tuna casserole, pot roast, pasta salad. When she moved in, she studied the recipes of the Culinary Institute of America to no avail. The few times she attempted crème brûlée or hand-packed inari, the taste was as tediously déclassé as her grilled cheese sandwiches and chocolate cake from a box. Anyway, in all the time they've been living together, Cesar has never failed to bring home takeout from one of the best restaurants of Seattle. The café around the corner delivers croissants and lattes every morning for breakfast. There is nothing for her to do.

"Why hasn't he been here for a year?"

Cesar tosses her earrings into the asymmetrical Chihuly glass candy dish that she has warned him to be careful of. The sharp ping makes her flinch protectively. It was a gift from a client of his, and he was surprised that she knew more about it than he did. He still doesn't fully believe that it's worth over thirteen-thousand dollars on the open market.

"Because!"

Cesar throws up his hands, surveying the mesas of faxes on the coffee table.

"Why should he? I mean, what's the point? He works downtown, and there are a dozen great restaurants within walking distance of his office building. We talk on the phone every other day. Hell, I've never even set foot in his apartment."

"Why not? That's weird."

"It's—it's a man-thing. I mean, I don't wanna see where my little brother, you know. Sleeps. Does his private business. You know what I mean."

Cesar picks up his work papers in a jutting, shifting heap and hurries out of the living room. Anna hears the kitchen door swing open, then a thud, then Cesar cursing in Spanish.

She is growing uneasy. Cesar's little brother sounds beyond her. He sounds aristocratic. She's not sure she can handle meeting him. The jittery, panicky feeling that she normally never feels anymore when Cesar is around begins to dodge between her lungs.

Cesar returns with a trio of thin wine glasses and a large decanter. The glasses and decanter are glazed a deep ruby color.

Anna has recently learned that this is tacky.

Cesar sees her looking. He shrugs helplessly.

"He gave me these last year. For Christmas. Hell, he's only twenty-six, he doesn't know any better yet. Though he's catching on. Very, very fast. He was wearing Brooks Brothers suits from some awful retail shop when he graduated law school. It didn't take him long to ask for a hook-up with my tailor. Maybe he'll laugh at these crappy things tonight. It'll be a good ice-breaker."

Cesar flops down on the love seat across from Anna. His eyes are bright with amusement and affection.

"I'm so proud of him, you know. He passed the bar exam on the first try—got an excellent score. He's really taken off at his firm. He's got a real talent for networking. It took me years to get as good. The partners are starting to give him the big cases, letting him stretch beyond junior status already. I can't imagine anyone I'd rather have as my lawyer. He's an exceptional litigator.

Though I am prejudiced in his favor. Oh, hell, everything'll be fine tonight."

Cesar rises and sits next to Anna on the couch. He cradles

her in his arms, kissing her forehead.

"I'm so happy, baby. I never thought I'd ever be so in love, or that everything could be so—so perfect. You've made my whole life complete, you know that?"

The nervous panic fades out in his arms. It dissipates into him. Anna kisses him on the lips.

"I'm happy, too. Very happy."

"Really? Sweetheart, I want you to remember that no matter how much time passes, if there's ever anything you need or want to help you forget, I'll give it to you. No questions asked. I don't care what it costs—"

The security buzzer cuts through the condo, making them both jump.

Cesar leaps up and hurries into the foyer. Anna hears the intercom crackle.

"It's me."

The voice is distorted to tonelessness by the tinny speaker.

"Okay, come up."

Cesar pokes his head back into the living room. His face is tight with nervous anticipation.

"Okay, he's here. Now, he's a little stiff with new people sometimes. A little too formal, but don't let it put you off. I'm sure that in just a half an hour or so, it'll be like we've all known each other for years—"

A knock on the door makes Cesar disappear.

Anna hears the door swing open, muffled masculine voices greeting each other, the thump of Cesar hugging his brother.

She rises from the couch. She straightens her long, white skirt and takes a deep breath. She's never liked lawyers. She hopes Cesar's brother isn't too cold and humorless.

Anna puts a friendly smile on. She makes herself feel open-minded.

Cesar leads his brother into the living room, saying, "So…here she is. My Anna."

Her smile shatters and falls away. She feels her cheeks drain of color and become slack.

Dressed in a crisp trench coat, an expensive suit peeking

out underneath, Cesar's brother comes to a dead stop three paces from her.

Antonio stares at Anna. She sees the flash of recognition that she knows is blatantly gleaming on her own face.

Cold shock flutters lacy wings in her throat.

Silence rings all three for an endless heartbeat.

She has to speak—Cesar must not know.

"Hello. It's very nice to meet you, finally. I'm Anna."

Her voice sounds taut and unnatural to her ears. She forces formality into her eyes.

Antonio stiffly takes a step closer to her. He swallows visibly. He holds out his hand to her.

"I'm Antonio. I'm happy to meet you, too."

Friday, May 25, 1990
9:43 p.m.
Seattle

"Okay, okay, kids: I gotta go to the bathroom. But when I get back, I want an answer from you, Papi. I mean it—I really want you in a formal tux for the wedding. A good one: not one of your damned rentals. I'll buy you a rig. I want to see you in classic-cut tails for once. He'll look so cute!"

Cesar swoops in to ruffle Antonio's hair.

Antonio dodges him and raises a hand.

"Don't—"

"Touch the hair, yeah, yeah. Be right back."

Cesar plants a kiss on Anna's forehead and walks out of the living room.

Antonio and Anna are alone for the first time all evening.

A thick silence smothers them.

Anna stares hard at the rug, then at the abstract painting over the fireplace.

Antonio coughs uneasily.

Anna glances toward the door that Cesar passed through.

"So…how…how have you been? It's been quite some time," she ventures.

"Good. You?"

Anna openly looks at his face for the first time since he arrived. He has gained subtle worry lines in his forehead and at the edges of his eyes, but no scars. She lowers her eyes to her lap.

"Cesar didn't tell you yet, did he?"

"Tell me…?"

"About what happened. To me. He will. Um…"

Anna glances at the door again, then leans close to Antonio, cutting her voice down to a faint whisper.

"Listen, I don't think we should tell Cesar about, you know. Before. Because he's so…"

"He's very protective of you. I could tell when he first started to talk about you."

"But I had no idea—"

"Me neither."

"There's a million guys named Tony—even more women with my name, right?"

Antonio's eyes dart to hers, a bitter smile quirking his lips.

"Cesar never called me Tony. No one did. Only you."

Anna bites her lower lip.

"God, this isn't good, is it?"

"It doesn't have to affect anything. Let's just plan to keep the past to ourselves. All right?"

"Yes. I think that's the best thing."

"Telling secrets about me? Shame on you both!"

Cesar strolls back into the living room, bearing a bottle of champagne.

"Look what I got! Krug Clos du Menil, the quality stuff. Didn't think I'd let you get off tonight without making a toast, did you? You gotta practice, Mr. Best Man! I don't want you using your courtroom voice at the wedding—it's so nerve-wracking! Here, wanna do the honors?"

Cesar offers the chilled bottle to Antonio.

Antonio avoids Anna's eyes and smiles up at his older brother.

"You sure you want me to? After what happened last time?"

"Still can't open it without spilling, can you? Here, let the pro do it."

Friday, December 18, 1992
8:19 p.m.
Ortiz Farm

Antonio drives his BMW slowly up the winding driveway leading to Cesar's new house on Skyhamish Island. The massive outer walls of the structure are covered with clear sheets of industrial plastic that billow eerily in the high wind, like banshee hair. He parks on the muddy stretch of ground that will eventually be the front lawn. As the engine dies, he clenches the steering wheel and gathers his thoughts.

Early on, he parked behind the garage, cautiously stowing the car away behind the bales of hay and brand-new farm machinery. As the months passed, it struck him as a ridiculous thing to do. None of Cesar's neighbors ever comes down the mile-long driveway, and the house itself can't be seen from the road. Cesar's housekeeper, cook and stable manager know exactly what's going on. Antonio has given up on sneaking, and just slips them twenties whenever he comes out here.

Anyway, if Cesar ever were to come home unexpectedly, it would be better for him to see his brother's car openly displayed, rather than find it hidden. A hidden car would cause instant suspicion. A car parked casually out front could be explained.

Somehow.

Antonio climbs the stairs to the unfinished porch, dodges piles of empty flower pots, and knocks on the front door. The wind is drawing dense sheets of slate clouds over the sky. There's no moon. Soon it will start to rain torrentially. He leans his ear against the door and listens. He hears nothing within. He knocks again. He's impatient. He doesn't want to be here.

Behind the thick wood, feet suddenly thrum a beat of desperation. The door is wrenched open.

"A—An—oh, God, thank God!"

Soft light washes over Antonio. Anna flickers within the

doorway, a slim silhouette hovering tremulous on one foot. Her face is maddened, panicked. She grabs Antonio's upper arm and hauls him inside. She slams the door and locks it. She shoves a kitchen chair under the knob and backs up against the far wall of the foyer. She has no shoes on and her hair is wild. Her chest bucks under her blouse, her fingers quivering against her skirt.

"God, God, I'm so glad you're here! Thank you for coming. I just, it was too much, I couldn't…"

Antonio has resolved things for himself in the three weeks since he last came out here. He and Anna already talked about it.

He stands by the door with his coat on. He keeps his face still and disinterested.

"I'm not staying. I've got a return ticket for the next ferry. I just wanted to tell you in person…Anna, we have to stop doing this. I can't keep betraying Cesar this way. I'm done."

Anna's eyes take the space of five breaths to come to his. Her face is bare like milk, her features asphyxiated. Antonio maintains a flat affect. His hands remain in his coat pockets.

Anna sinks to the bottom of the staircase, her legs giving out. But not because of Antonio.

"Oh God, I'm so scared!"

She covers her head with her hands, her entire body trembling. She crumples limply onto the stairs, like a battered fish beached on a shoal. Her chest convulses.

"Anna?"

Her body begins to shake, knotting up like a fetus. She stops breathing. She visibly whitens.

Antonio has seen her do this before, and it always frightens him. He had planned not to touch her, not to come close to her.

He kneels on the bottom stair and puts his arms around her. He makes them brotherly, with no eroticism whatsoever.

That wasn't what she was after when she called him, and the realization stabs him with an odd, blunt guilt.

"Anna, please calm down, okay? Anna?"

She digs her fingers into his back, clinging as if her nails were angler's hooks. She gasps in a breath that sounds as if it's tearing her throat apart.

"How long have you been like this?"

His voice is gentle in the way it only ever is for her.

"Oh…God, Antonio! Every night, every single night since Cesar left on his trip, I dream about what happened! I didn't sleep at all for two nights, but then I started to see it! Really see it, like real life. Happening over and over and over. I saw *me*, right there at the end of my bed, hanging from the ceiling, and bleeding, and….am I going crazy, Antonio? Do you think?"

Her hollow eyes churn with tears.

Antonio won't kiss her.

"I don't know. No."

"It never happens when Cesar's here. Or you. I can't stand it. I'll have to do it. I'll have to do it to myself. I can't go another night like this. Cesar's not coming home for four more days. Oh Christ, four days!"

She bursts into tears, and before Antonio can stop it, her head is on his shoulder and he's stroking her hair, which he shouldn't do.

But he won't kiss her.

"What can I do?"

"Will you stay with me?"

Her lips are wet against his neck, her voice shuddering his skin.

"Anna. No. I don't want to do this to Cesar anymore. You don't either."

Anna pushes him away and leans flat on the stairs. Her arms go out, vulnerable and crucified on the third step. Her eyes stare without seeing, fixating him like a pair of murdered faces.

"Last night, when I saw it happen again, I went to the kitchen and I got the biggest knife we have. I went back to the bedroom and I locked myself in. I held the knife all night. To protect myself. But then, oh Jesus, I started to play with the blade. Started rubbing it up and down my arms. I just scratched...see?

But I'm so scared of what I'll do by myself tonight, Antonio..."

Her inner arms are scored with a network of red hatchmarks. Antonio's stomach grows tight. He pulls her off the stairs, arcing his arm around her waist to hold her up. He turns her wrists up to the light. He wears his dismay openly, his expression utterly unguarded, which is unusual for him.

"Anna, you need to take those sedatives Cesar got you. That's what they're for. Please, will you take one?"

"I can't bear it. I can't breathe here alone. Four more days. I can't, I won't last..."

Antonio lets go of her. She kneels at the foot of the stairs, her body strung taut. Her eyes plead.

He sits back on his heels and sighs wearily.

"All right. I'll stay tonight. Till you're asleep. But we're not going to do anything. Understand? We're through with that."

Anna's breathing deepens and slows. Her eyes soften and her body loses its grinding tension. She smiles hesitantly. It's her old smile: the one that hurts him and brings an ache.

"Okay. Yes. Thank you. Thank you so much. I lov—"

"Don't. Don't do that. Or I will leave, I swear to God."

The rain is falling insistently on the half-finished roof when they walk into the living room.

"Would you like some wine?"

"I don't think that's a good idea."

"Cesar got five cases of a new French Bordeaux from an unproven winery. I think he hates it, but doesn't want to admit it, since he paid a ridiculous amount. He'd be glad to lose a bottle."

Antonio sighs and sits on the couch. He raises a hand noncommittally.

"All right. Just a glass."

Anna brings their wine to the couch and sits beside him.

Not too close.

"Tell me what you think of it."

Antonio tastes, puckers, and raises his eyebrows at her.

She smiles involuntarily at his too-worldly sneer of disapproval. He's getting better at making it. It's almost natural now, though he hasn't yet reached thirty and still makes mistakes.

"Cesar picked this out?"

"Yes. Not me!"

"Good God."

"I know, it's worse than that terrible Chianti they served at our wedding. Cesar can't give it away, since it would reflect badly on him. We'll be stuck drinking it forever."

"I hope to God he doesn't try to give it away! I'd never accept another gift from him."

Antonio sniffs at the wine, then adds, as an accidental afterthought, "It's gross."

Anna giggles, sliding slightly closer to him.

"You know what it makes me think of?"

"What?"

His knee is touching hers now, but he doesn't move away.

"The Hung Dog. Their two-dollar Mexican Prairie Fire shots."

"Oh, Christ!"

Antonio laughs, and his hand is on her knee, but he's not really aware of it.

"There is a similar…something…"

"Like a bite—an acidity. Very macho," her voice sounds exactly like it used to.

Antonio's smile fades. He swirls the wine, aerating it like Cesar taught him to do.

"Do you ever wonder—" Anna begins.

"That's over. I don't want to start talking about it."

"Okay."

They are quiet. He hasn't lifted his hand from her knee. Her hair is light on his shoulder, then her cheek rests there as well.

She's very calm. She's lulled.

"I'm not asleep, so you can't go home. You missed the last ferry, anyway."

"Shit, really? What time is it?"

"Very late. It's raining too hard to drive, and you've been drinking. You'd crash your Beamer."

She smiles to herself. Her hand rests on his chest now, next to her face.

"Anna…"

His voice has lost its firm edge. He's slipping away from his sense of purpose. His hand begins to absently stroke her hair, then her cheek.

"We really have to stop doing this."

"It would hurt Cesar so much if he knew. I don't want to ever hurt him. I couldn't live with it," Anna murmurs.

"You have to help me here, you know. I can't do it all."

"I do want us to stop. I really do. I'm so happy with Cesar. And he loves you so much."

Their empty wine glasses rest on the small myrtle wood end table at the foot of the couch. Anna knots her fingers lightly around Antonio's suit lapel, her fingers petting the soft wool. Her eyes are sweetly lost.

They don't talk.

Antonio stares at the unfinished wall across the room.

The plastic sheeting glows in the low lamplight like unpolished crystal. His face eases to hers so slowly, so gradually that he doesn't realize what he's doing. His lips touch her forehead. Just a touch—not a kiss.

Then he does kiss her forehead, his hand cupping her cheek. She lifts her head and sees a painful sympathy in his eyes.

His fingers trace the hair-fine scar on her forehead, then the nearly invisible one down her left cheek that only she, he, and

Cesar know to look for. She gently pushes his hand off her face.

"Do you still love me, Antonio? I mean, now that we're not…now that we've stopped, will you still care about me? Or will you make yourself hate me? So it'll be easier?"

"I don't know how to answer that."

"You hated me before."

"I never hated you."

"You left me. I hated you for a long time."

Antonio's lips curve down.

"Oh."

"So…how should we feel about each other now? What would be easiest?"

Antonio plays with her hand, staring at her fingers.

"Easy…I don't think…goddamn it, Anna. You know how I feel about you."

Anna's face hangs before his, like a pearl beneath still waters.

She leans in to kiss him lightly, like a sister.

Her lips move across his cheek, then they are on his, and his arms are around her body, and they are kissing each other furiously.

"I love you, I can't help it, you're the only one I've ever…please, for God's sake, make me stop, Anna! We can't do this."

Anna tears at his chest with her fingernails, her lips going over his face desperately.

"Just once more. Just one more time. Then we'll stop."

Monday, March 17, 1997
9:45 a.m.
Fort Lewis, Washington

I'm in full dress uniform. I'm upright and unbending.

I've made my face expressionless, because that's all they will accept.

I'm being dishonorably discharged from the army. I got caught. We got caught.

I had expected the courtroom to have tall, many-paned windows filtering in stale, mote-thick sunlight. I primed myself for dark wood paneling and profound, echoing silence. Instead, we stand in a cramped conference room with industrial gray carpeting, no windows, and bright, schoolroom-style overhead lights. The judge's bench is a collapsible metal table. I sat at such a table every week during briefings.

The colonel, who once was in my passenger seat, makes glacial eye contact throughout the proceedings. I have a military-issued attorney, but that didn't help me any. I took my share of the responsibility. It hadn't been rape or coercion, after all. I wouldn't ruin my CO's name with that sort of lie. Not to save myself.

My CO should have been here today, or at his own court-martial. But they didn't court-martial my Commanding Officer.

The colonel reads my dishonorable discharge orders aloud. They're very long. I expected it to be a much briefer proceeding, like civilian court on TV. Just a gavel and the pronouncement of the word, "guilty." I try to pay attention. I try very hard: this is important. But the discharge orders are so difficult to follow.

My CO isn't on base any more. He's in Tacoma with his family. After we were found out, it quickly became clear that there'd be no cover-up, no sweeping under the rug by the higher-ups. My CO grew very deliberate. I didn't see him. He went to his quarters and cleaned his personal .357 Glock 32 and shot himself in the mouth. The most efficient kill-shot when you're doing yourself.

He'd come to ruin, like me, but he had more to lose. He was career military; had been for twenty-five years. What else could he do to support his family? His wife packed up when she heard about us, promising to take his kids away and tell them all about us so that they would hate him as much as she did.

He had wrecked me as well, which in spite of his reserve, I knew had hurt him terribly. He had great hopes for my career. Before he ever touched me, and even after, he had been my mentor. If we'd never been found out, and had decided to stop on our own, I believe that he would have been satisfied with just that. I know I would have.

He couldn't face the court-martial on top of everything else. His funeral is today, but I won't go. It would be tacky.

And then it's over. There's no gavel. No one says, "guilty." I don't even realize that it's over. My attorney has to touch my arm and murmur into my ear two times.

I follow my attorney out of the courtroom, trembling irresolutely now that I'm no longer military.

My attorney shakes my hand in the hallway. There's no more saluting now. He hands me my signed and stamped discharge papers. He walks down the corridor and leaves me alone.

I stand very still.

It looks like an office building here in the hall: all thin carpeting and neutral walls and anonymous closed doors. I'm numb. I wait for the colonel and the other officers to come out of the courtroom and glare shunning shame at me. They don't emerge.

Eventually, I turn and walk down the hall; the same way my attorney went. My boots don't make a sound on the gray carpet.

The last time I saw my CO was just a few hours before we were called in for questioning. He was conducting a unit briefing on objectives for an upcoming intelligence training scenario. The room was chilly with too much air conditioning, but his sleeves were rolled up and his cap was off.

The last time I spoke to him was the night before. We were alone in his office, but it wasn't like that. He was administering an oral examination on my knowledge of operating system terminology. Terse questions, terse answers. He wrote my score in red ink on the question sheet. He dismissed me. Only for a flickering moment did he glance at me.

"Tomorrow night? Are you free?"

I nodded.

I said, "Okay."

I never questioned anything. If I'd made myself curious about the kind of person he really was, I could have seen his death coming. I could have prevented it. Maybe.

I reach the double doors labeled Exit. My hand sweats into my discharge papers. I must pack and be off the base within two hours.

Career military was all I ever planned to be. It was my purpose, my ideology, my self. Now, I'm nothing.

Friday, January 30, 1998
2:01 a.m.
Auburn SuperMall, Washington

It's painfully late: rawly late. I want to die.

I walk the slow, chicken-footed pace that the security company forced me to practice in front of the hiring supervisor so many months ago. It's not military in any way. Not even police-inspired, I suspect. I have to walk this way, since there are cameras all around the parking lot, and I can be fired for walking normally.

The mall's sprawling parking lot is deserted. Christmas is over and the gift-return season has petered out. There are only four cars in the lot: derelicts that I radioed in to the security company's electronic reporting system back in November. 'To report a trespasser, press one. To report an abandoned vehicle, press two...' They may be towed someday, or maybe not. The twenty-minute training video that constituted my job orientation didn't say that I should call in more than once. I've given up on trying to excel.

I walk slowly, nearly goose-stepping like a Nazi. I turn my head to the left and right every five steps, as trained.

I have no gun, no pepper spray, not even a stick. Just a radio, a plastic flashlight, and a god-awful costume that looks like a cop's uniform if you're really drunk. It took me half a fifth of vodka to accept it. Weaving drunk at the bathroom mirror in my sad little apartment, I couldn't even laugh at myself. I would shoot me, if I saw me approaching.

Tonight it's not raining, which is an unusual stroke of luck. The darkness and solitude are legion. I'm smothered by a lack of stimulus. It forces itself, as dry as old lint, straight down my throat where it chokes me. I feel like a prisoner of war, blindfolded and gagged in the hole. I've been kicking around the idea of learning to smoke, just for something to do while I walk around and around the exterior of this mall, over and over and over. I pass Sears, I pass Abandoned Vehicle Number Three, I pass the main entrance to the mall for the eighth time. I will pass them nine more times. I will study the burned out A in the Sears sign each time. I'll wonder numbly when it will be repaired.

I didn't get a military prison term for my transgression, but I realize full well that I'm imprisoned nonetheless. God or the CO or someone put me here, since it was justice. This is my punishment. This is my own hell.

I used to analyze complex military security systems. I used to sharpshoot for my company's sniper competition team. I ran ten miles a day and could take down anyone on the close-combat deck, except the CO. I drove the tank during drills. I was in charge of my platoon's rifle maintenance inspections. I had over two dozen people I could count as my friends. Another thirty casual acquaintances. An entire five thousand comrades-in-arms on the base. I had a career. A promising future.

Now, I am responsible for ensuring that drunks aren't peeing in the parking lot. I have no friends, no acquaintances, no 82 In Retrospect comrades. My shift starts at ten each evening. I walk the walk until seven in the morning. I watch saccharine morning shows alone in my tiny apartment. I go to bed.

Sometimes I take the bus to this very mall during the daylight hours, when I should be sleeping. I crave human interaction. I get nothing but customer service courtesy, rote phrases, and phony eye contact. I soak it up nevertheless. I haven't had a genuine conversation since August.

No one else will hire me. Not even McDonald's. I put pride in my pocket and asked, when the solitude and the boredom became too much to bear. I was turned me down, along with all the other folks who checked the Yes box after "have you ever been convicted of a crime?"

Sometimes, the worst times, I'm invaded by memories of my CO. Regretful, fluid memories that pull me back in time to fantasize about how I could have fixed things through the power of hindsight. Oh God, I wish he was still here. That's the worst thing of all.

Tuesday, July 28, 1998
12:14 p.m.
Seattle

I'm wearing my only nice pair of khakis and a very clean black turtleneck. I never dress like this. I feel constrained and false, but today I must look professional.

The bus lets me off a block from the madly expensive restaurant downtown. Its name is foreign, with lots of vowels in odd spots. I don't know how to pronounce it. I don't even know what language it represents. I'm devastatingly nervous. I shake.

I pull open the frosted glass front door and step inside. I'm immediately chilled by high-power air conditioning. A weighty crystal chandelier as big as a refrigerator swings overhead, waiting to fall on me. Flowers choke the small space, their scent overpowering and cloying. I toy with my wrist like a child, making myself small. This is unlike me.

A man in a tuxedo stands behind a podium draped in stiff silver silk. I take a brief second under his eye to tug things straight, then I approach.

"Hi."

"May I help you?" he counters.

I never say "may." This is a sign of the upper-crustiness of the restaurant. I'm way out of my element.

"Yeah—yes. I'm supposed to meet a guy named Cesar Ortiz here. For lunch."

The man should consult the leather-bound book lying open on the podium, but he doesn't.

"Mr. Ortiz hasn't arrived yet. May I seat you now?"

"No, thanks, I'll wait."

The man says nothing; he merely cocks his head ever-so-slightly. I twitch my eyes around. Where will I wait? It's just him and me and all these flowers in the foyer. This is not like the Outback Steakhouse with benches for the "just another

fifteen
minutes" masses.

Awkward now, I cough.

"Okay, sure, I'll take a table."

The man hands me off to another tuxedoed fellow, and I'm led into a high-ceilinged space like breathless heaven. Seltzer-light music plays. I'm dazzled by glowing white tablecloths, wallpaper, and carpeting. Nothing about this place suggests the dim, oily grubbing of the food joints I'm used to. I'm intimidated by cloth napkins, glassware that pings like orchestral chimes, the sight of business suits on men and women alike. Thank God I didn't wear my usual jeans and T-shirt, as I'd considered doing.

I'm seated at a round table, rioting with linen and silver and crystal and blossoms.

"Would you care to order now?"

"Um...no. Can I wait? Till Mr. Ortiz gets here?"

"Of course. Anything to drink?"

"Water?"

I pray that he doesn't inquire what type. I have a feeling that this is the kind of place that has more than one water. The man seems to realize my discomfort and departs.

I fiddle with my silverware. There's too much of it. My napkin is folded into a strange shape, like a bird. I poke at it, and it flops flat over my plate.

I glance surreptitiously at the other tables through my screen of glassware and florals. I can't identify any of the food I spy. Across the room, a platter bursts into flames that lap at the waiter's face. No one is alarmed.

I don't belong here.

I must get collect my thoughts. This place has to be a test. Mr. Ortiz must want to see if I can blend in here. The CO used to test us like this. He periodically sent his recruits on strange scavenger hunts off base. Unbeknownst to us, senior officers with far more assimilation training were sent to spy on our progress. Early into my training, I was sent to find "banh mi" in Little Saigon on the bad side of town. It took me three hours of blundering around with no-English refugees and teenage chop-shop gangsters to figure out that I was hunting for sandwiches, and easily-acquired ones at that. I was taken severely to task for giving myself away to the entire neighborhood. I can blend far better now. I've had so much training.

Mr. Ortiz could be here already, checking me out.

I eye my neighbors and adjust my posture, striving to sit as they do. No one else is dining alone, however. No one is desperate like I am.

After twenty minutes, which span several uncomfortable lifetimes for me, I see a slightly overweight man of about fifty hurrying into the room behind one of the tuxes. When he sees me, he beams a harassed, impersonal smile.

"Hi there, Cesar Ortiz. You're Flynn, right?"

"Yes."

Should I stand? I don't know, so I don't. He doesn't attempt to shake my hand. The tuxedo-man seats Mr. Ortiz across from me, then makes off with his light overcoat, leaving us alone.

I scan Mr. Ortiz. He looks Mexican. He has a very light accent. He's extremely well-dressed, like a reporter on TV. I like his tie.

"Very sorry, terribly sorry. There was a horrible traffic jam on I-5. I thought I was gonna lose my mind. My cell phone lost all charge after I spent forty minutes on hold with my lawyer. Cocksucker!"

Mr. Ortiz pauses, smiling with slight embarrassment.

"Sorry. But I can call him that, since he's my brother."

I force a smile and a laugh. My desperation must not show. To get a job, you must seem not to need a job.

"So, did you order yet?"

"No."

He picks up the enormous menu and glances at it.

"Let's see…nothing looks good, does it? I want a sandwich. None of this wet, sloppy stuff. Something quick."

Magically, spying from somewhere close by, yet another

tuxedo-clad waiter appears. He looks at Cesar, not at me.

"The scallops are very good today. Prepared w—"

"What've you got in a sandwich? Normal sandwich—no knives or forks?"

"The chef can make you a po'boy with shrimp and oysters."

"Those things always ooze all over the place, don't they?"

"He'll make it very dry."

"Okay, sounds fine. How about you, Flynn?"

I can't turn the fifteen pages of the menu. I can't focus on the scripty letters and multilingual offerings. My ill-fated bahn mi might be amongst the unfamiliar words.

"I'll…I'll take that, too."

"You sure? This is on me, keep in mind. Get anything you want."

"No, that sounds really good. Not messy."

"Hm, okay. Two."

The waiter takes our menus away and leaves us to our solitude.

This interview is not beginning well.

Mr. Ortiz leans back in his chair and eyes me. Not intimidatingly exactly, but curiously. My heart begins to go hard and jittery.

"Okay. I'll let you know that I reviewed quite a number of resumes for this live-in security position I've got available. A whole lot of resumes, actually. But yours jumped out at me. I was very impressed with your training in the army."

Now he sweeps his gaze over the sum of me, not just my head. I hope that he's even more impressed, due to my physique. Everyone expects an Olympic athlete, a martial arts movie star, when they learn about my training. However, he's probably just baffled by me. Everyone always is.

"So…can you tell me about what you did in the army? Some details?"

I draw in a solid breath. This feels better. This I can do.

"Well, some of it's classified, of course."

"Sure."

"But I can tell you about my training, and how I used it later in general."

"Fine."

"I have extensive training and experience in the recognition and identification of hostile targets, as well as the transmission of position to battlefield commanders during heavy attack scenarios. I have participated in the review of functional equipment prototypes within simulated armed reconnaissance missions, involving changing operational environments, measures and countermeasures. I have been trained to establish covert tactical communication systems intended to locate and neutralize a variety of hostile enemy devices, including anti-personnel and anti-tank mines. I can calculate optimum force deployment, zero and engage targets during combat mobility, counter-mobility, and survivability test cases. I have operated within, and maintained communication equipment for, radio net and GPS linkage. I have extensive experience processing and analyzing captured documents in a range of media formats."

I gasp for a quick breath. I forgot to inhale during my signification. I'm too nervous. I really want this job. It's a unique opportunity that will never come again.

Mr. Ortiz's eyes are half-closed, as if lulled by a bedtime story. He perks up slightly when I fall silent.

"Very solid background. I'll be honest: I'm impressed. However, the only thing is…"

He will make a comment on my body. It makes people uncomfortable. They usually couch it in a seemingly neutral query, all roundabout and hesitant, pussyfooting around the real question of what exactly I have in my pants.

My CO was forthright. When I applied for admittance into the Military Intelligence Training Program, he said to me, 'Corporal, you've consistently made your fellow recruits of both genders uncomfortable, given that they tend to think you're either a homosexual person, or are cross-dressing your way into their unit in order to prove something. How do you intend to counter these assumptions?'

Instead, Mr. Ortiz says, "Why, with all of that experience, are you working at the Auburn SuperMall as a night security guard? Why did you leave the army?"

Oh. The other big question.

"I. Well."

I have to force myself not to glance around or play with things on the table.

"I was dishonorably discharged. For fraternizing. You understand? With a superior officer. I haven't been able to find anything better than my current position, due to the army record. The dishonorable discharge always comes out in a background check, but not the reason for it. People always assume it was for drugs, or assault, or something. But it was...incurred by very normal stuff. In the real world, at least. It just wasn't acceptable in the military."

Mr. Ortiz nods thoughtfully.

"So there was no question of loyalty, or anything? Did you give the other person up?"

"It all came out due to discovery. When I was court-martialed, I had to confess. I wouldn't lie. But I didn't betray him. I was never accused of misconduct or seriously reprimanded for anything prior to that. I just...fraternized."

Mr. Ortiz nods again, rapidly this time.

"Ah, food's here."

The waiter places our plates very carefully in front of us. Mr. Ortiz dives into his sandwich. Thank God he uses his hands like a normal person. I couldn't deal with a knife and fork right now. My hands are shaking atrociously. I've never discussed the discharge in such an open way before. I feel depleted.

"How are you liking this weather?"

Mr. Ortiz's eyes have become impersonal, as they were when he arrived.

I sink. It's the big brush-off.

"It's nice. Warm."

"Out on the island, we've had a straight week of over eighty degrees. That's pretty unusual out there. We're right in the wind path from Alaska, so it's usually fairly chilly. Not really cold, though. Last year we got some snow in January. But that's rare."

"Really?"

"Yeah. The horses hated it. Freaked them out. My stable manager let them out into the yard pens to see what they would do. I think he was bored and wanted to mess with them just for the fun of it. They kept sticking their noses down in the drifts, like dogs, then they'd snort and run off like they'd been bit. He had a hell of a time corralling them afterward, so I guess they paid him back good for teasing them."

"Yeah."

I try to eat, but my guts are constricted. I want to leave, since there's no hope.

Mr. Ortiz wipes his mouth with his napkin, most of his sandwich gone. He gives me his gaze.

"Tell you what. If that's all you did, the fraternizing, that's fine by me. If you'd ratted out, or, you know, deceived someone who had trusted you, that'd be a problem. But, hell, people fraternize. Human nature. I need someone who can be completely loyal to me. Someone I can trust without having to think about it. I feel like I can trust you. You've got a good face. It's honest."

I smile at this. It's something I've never heard about my face before.

"Can you start within the next week or so? I realize it's a big move to ask so fast, but I really need someone as soon as possible."

I am awash in light. I am dizzy.

"Yeah, yes, sure, no problem. Thank you. Very much."

Oh. Thank. God.

Cesar Ortiz has liberated me from hell. I owe him everything.

Monday, August 3, 1998
9:19 a.m.
Skyhamish Ferry

"Here we go. About time."

Cesar sits on a vinyl seat the color of dried blood across from me. The ferry's massive engines have finally, weakly, kicked to life after a twenty-five minute delay. Cesar looks personally hassled by the delay. He shoots his cuffs and tightens the knot in his tie.

"Marine Machinists Union's a bunch of idiots! Bastards don't know what they're doing."

"Ah."

I'm not sure what he's talking about, and am unwilling to look stupid on the first day of my new job.

"I don't care how old these damned ferries are—I've had my yacht's engine machined before, and I know that these things never crap out without a reason. You gotta maintain them. If you're spending all your time in bullshit collective bargaining, you don't get around to doing your job."

Cesar forces his scowl to resolve into a more or less cheery smile.

"So! How are you holding up? Hungry?"

I shake my head, though I am.

"Have you spent much time in the San Juan Islands?"

"No."

"Well, the island we live on is one of the most remote. It's only got a population of about five hundred people. There's just one town, where the ferry docks. The only way on or off is the damned ferry. Makes it hell if they get closed down due to bad weather. Or if the bastards go on strike. But the island itself is incredibly beautiful. Unspoiled. I've got an amazing piece of land. Huge. I had my house built from the ground up, exactly the way I've always wanted. I love it. My wife does, too."

The suspect engines buzz through the soles of my shoes. The ferry heads out into open water. Tiny islands, barely more than a hill and a tree, rise out of the water on all sides. Gray things are swarming all over the dun, unfertile coasts of these weensy islets. I start as I realize that they are rabbits.

"Why…"

I point, and Cesar turns to look.

"Oh, yeah, they're not native. I used to think that some, I don't know, some crazy rich guy had imported them to hunt. You know? Some rich nineteenth century lordling in exile out here on the Pacific, pining for home. Turns out the bastards can swim."

I had a bunny when I was four. I don't recall swimming being one of its skills.

"Really?"

"Yeah. Saw it myself one night—freaked me out. I was sitting at that window over there on a Friday night, exhausted beyond belief, totally dying to be home, know what I mean? I looked out, and the little monsters were swimming right alongside the ferry. I asked the first mate about it. She was buying coffee at the food bar, and I'm being all careful, so she won't think I'm drunk or something. She didn't even blink when I told her I'd seen at least fifty rabbits swimming by. She said that they migrate that way from island to island. They eat up all the green stuff, then swim on. The deer do it, too. She said it's hell if one of them gets sucked into the engine turbines."

Cesar glances at the food bar, the ghost of a scowl still hovering over his features.

"It's an hour and a half trip, you know. God, I need a drink. You want some wine? They have a really awful red. The damned bottle's been open for months, since I'm the only one who ever buys it. But it's better than nothing."

Should I accept? I don't know if I can handle booze so early in the morning.

"Um. Okay."

Cesar gives me a pleased grin, the corners of his mouth

flickering with mischief.

"It's gotta be after five o'clock somewhere, right? Just don't tell my wife."

I breathe easily for the first time all day when Cesar leaves me alone. I'm not used to this level of intensity; not anymore. In a way, it's wonderful to be so watched and scrutinized, after months of anonymity. I have to re-accustom myself to human contact.

Cesar acquires us the wine and sits, pushing a plastic cup at me. The dark liquid swishes against the sides like a monarch's velvet robe. I never drink wine. Beer, mainly, and the occasional hit of vodka and Tang when things seem too hard and depressing. Not so occasional in recent months. None of my unit-mates from the army will talk to me. Not after what happened. They disapprove, and they are folks inclined toward venery of all varieties. Prior to my discharge, they thought I was all obedience; all straight 'n' narrow. I shocked them, so they cast me out. I saw my staff sergeant in Wal-Mart three weeks ago. I was glanced at so fast, like the darting sting of a yellow jacket at a picnic. Then I was nothing; I was unseen, even though I was standing next line, my grooming products and toiletries lined up blatantly on the black rubber belt.

"If I'd been smart, I'd have brought a flask of good Irish whisky for coffee. That would be more appropriate this time of the day. Oh well: cheers."

Cesar downs half his wine, staring absently out the window into the bright sunshine and watery emptiness.

"It's a gorgeous day, isn't it? Perfect weather. I wish I could go out on my yacht. Pretend to fish. No such luck. Too much to do. Mountains of paperwork."

I watch the tiny scraps of land slip away, then small humps of earth just barely above water, then there's nothing. We're marooned in an oblivion of water.

I taste the wine. I don't like it, but I'm unable to tell if it's good or bad the way Cesar can.

"It's pretty awful, huh?"

Cesar's eyes are all over my face. I won't be able to hide

things from him: he's unabashedly perceptive.

"Yes."

I set the plastic cup aside.

"I always seem to wind up with bad wine. I swear, at least once a month when I'm out with a client at a really high-end restaurant in Seattle, the wine steward tries to foist some corked, musty garbage on me. Maybe the sommeliers have got themselves a union: maybe they've blacklisted me. Goddamned Steelworkers Union and their Marine Machinist buddies tipped 'em off."

I force a tight laugh, because Cesar is chuckling to himself.

I stare out the windows at the plains of water surging around the ferry. It's all nothingness, inhuman wetness, and merging blues. I've never traveled over water before. In this empty clarity, I feel that I'm truly gone from my life now.

I glance at Cesar as he rubs his hand over his gray hair and reaches for his cell phone with a bare trickle of wine on his lower lip. I want to stay gone.

Monday, August 3, 1998
11:41 a.m.
Skyhamish Island

It's a thirty-minute drive from the ferry docks on Skyhamish Island to Ortiz Farm. Cesar insists that I drive, which is fine with me. I've always learned the lay of the land better when I'm in the driver's seat than as a passive passenger.

The island is very beautiful, choked with enormous pine trees that stretch higher than office buildings to scratch the sky.

The ocean flashes blue and gray between the branches and needles, smelling briny and promising fish. There's a profoundly rural lack of houses on the island. I strain to see power lines or airplanes tracing a powdery track overhead. The sky is achingly blue and unbroken.

"Feel free to take the Jeep out anytime. It's basically our staff vehicle. I don't like to drive it. Anna doesn't drive. She might ask you to run some errands with it now and then."

I spy an enormous brown dog standing by the side of the road. It jumps away with a flash of white ass, and I realize that it was a deer.

Cesar points to where the deer was.

"I almost bought that stretch over there. But property taxes started shooting up, and to be honest, I've got more than enough land to keep me busy as it is. The farm's nearly twenty-five hundred acres, did I tell you already? That's almost exactly one-sixth of the entire island that I own. There's an Indian reservation up north—they've got that land locked in so no one can touch it. And there's the National Forest in the center of the island. It takes up something like half the total area of the island. Don't go in there. You'll get lost, guaranteed. I went in, just for a little stroll, when we first moved out here. I couldn't find my way out for five goddamned hours. No lie. Thought I was gonna die in there. It's very poorly maintained."

Cesar scowls sourly and taps his finger against his window.

"That's one of my two neighbors over there. White trash family, total rednecks. Hope I don't offend you; it's not a racist thing or whatever. They really are. I think they're growing pot out on their land and selling to the Indians. I called the Island County cops on them four times last year for firing shotguns into my property. Shotguns! They said they were hunting deer. Yeah, and what's sad is that I believe them. How else'll they get their hands on some red meat?"

A mud-laden tin can trailer flicks by, mired in the middle of a dull brown field. A confederate flag flies, a pickup rusts on cinderblocks, a 1980's era satellite dish the size of a minivan lists against a tree trunk.

"The other guy out this way is only here in the summer. He's from Tacoma, I think. He inherited a little shack from his granddad. He just uses it as a vacation cabin. Roughing it, fishing, camping out, that sort of thing."

We pass a brown, humpty slap of clapboard that just breaks through the dense greenery. Cesar abruptly sits up very straight. His face brightens by degrees, like a rheostat easing a light bulb on.

"Here, turn in,"

He points at a smooth bend in the road. I jam in the clutch and the break barely in time to avoid a tall iron fence closing off an extremely long cement driveway. The fence is high enough for a prison, wrought in sturdy iron with fanciful spear-points atop each post. Cesar fiddles with a remote activator attached to the sun visor.

"The opener's erratic. That'll be your first job. Fix this thing."

The gate slowly swings open. I cautiously put the Jeep into first gear and release the clutch. I must not stall the engine, as was my unfortunate habit in the army. Not on my first day.

The driveway is paved much better than the public road we drove in on. A flawless, precisely mowed lawn rolls outward on both sides, loping lazily over gentle hills and dips like a golf course.

I drive us a good mile in. Just when I'm getting antsy, an enormous house rears out of the green landscape. My breath stops completely. My hands clutch the steering wheel.

Cesar grins with obvious pride.

"Mi casa y mi corazon. Like it?"

"It's so big," I stammer, unable to think of anything better to sum up such a place.

The house is unreal. It extends and towers. It's as big as the barracks back at Fort Lewis. Pale golden wood shines everywhere, even the roof. The building seems to float on its own luminescence, riding smoothly like a Viking ship on a green sea. Hundreds of windowpanes reflect the sun like chrome. Myriad flowers blow in the wind.

This must be a legitimate mansion. The front door is twice as tall as a normal door. The porch wraps the house with miles of bright tile and curling railing and complicated potted plants that I've never seen in the gardening section of the Home Depot. I ease the Jeep slowly to the end of the driveway, awestruck.

Cesar hops out of the Jeep the instant I apply the brake.

"Come on, let's meet my wife. She'll be extremely glad we're home."

Cesar grabs his suitcase, then my duffel bag as well, which I find awfully courteous of him. He impatiently strides ahead of me up the front steps, which sparkle with imbedded quartz. He goes right in: the front door is unlocked and has no alarm system. That is dangerous.

"Anna? We're home!"

Cesar's voice echoes away into the glowing stillness of the sweeping foyer.

I'm overwhelmed. I know nothing about architecture, but I can tell that this place is a masterwork. The ceiling looms dozens of meters overhead. The floor is as bright as an NBA court on TV. The walls are honey-hued wood, pure and unpainted. Geometrical black and red paintings suggestive of bears and wolves hang over amazingly delicate little tables bearing tall Chinese vases crammed with live flowers. The silence here is so rare, like in a holy place. I fear to speak aloud. My voice is unrefined and will damage things.

Cesar casually plunks our luggage down on the virgin floor as if he were in a hotel lobby.

A tumbling of feet rolls above us. I look up at the enormous spiral staircase, which coils up to a balcony-style landing on the second story.

The feet thud closer, at a dead sprint, and then I see them. They're pale, bare woman-feet.

Cesar doesn't move. He blatantly restrains himself, with obvious difficulty.

"Cesar, oh God, Cesar!"

A very young woman runs wildly down the stairs. I feel a sharp thrust of unease when I see her fully.

She's crying.

She throws herself headlong into Cesar's arms, pressing her thin body close to his and breaking into harsh sobs. She's wearing a floating white dress, sleek like silk, which shines mutely against her body. Her arms are bare and white, like the dress and her feet. They twine at Cesar's neck, clutching like a pair of bloodless weeds. I get an impression of black hair, long and cottony-soft, but no face. Cesar holds her tightly, his eyes closed. She crushes her face against his chest, vanishing into him.

Cesar didn't mention having a daughter.

Or…is this his wife?

She's so young. She looks to be my age; maybe younger. Cesar is easily old enough to be my dad. I stare, though I shouldn't. I had expected a dignified, slightly overweight woman in her mid-fifties. Very Hispanic. An imposing doña with silver-shot hair in a bun, crow's feet, and too much ruby lipstick. Someone slow to show true emotion, but highly courteous. Someone polished. Someone like Cesar.

"I couldn't stand it, I missed you so much, I thought—"

"Shhh, shhh, sweetheart, please. I've brought our new security officer. Can I introduce you? Are you okay, baby?"

Cesar doesn't lower his voice. He's speaking for the benefit of all three of us.

The young woman draws in a shuddery breath within his arms. She becomes very still, like an animal sensing an unheralded human presence. Slowly, she wipes her face with both palms in a childish gesture, then nods against his chest. A moment passes as she gathers herself together.

She raises her face and turns it to mine.

"I'm sorry. Very sorry. I...maybe Cesar told you that I don't do well at all when he's away on business? It's...it's a phobia. Some kind of garden-variety neurosis. I'm very glad to meet you...?"

"Flynn," Cesar supplies softly, his arm curved protectively around her waist. He's trying to send me a message with his eyes, but I can't decode it.

"I'm Anna. I'm happy to have you here. I'll feel so much safer, knowing you're working for us."

"Good to meet you," I murmur.

I feel her studying me, as everyone does when they first encounter the likes of me. But for once, I'm gazing back just as intently. Her face is so odd. It's unreal; it's surreal. She has perfect features. Too perfect. Her nose is precisely sculpted, her forehead is utterly smooth, her lips lack the natural shaping of time and expression. Her skin is so radiant and flawless that it seems wrought of plastic. It's like a small child's face. It's disturbing atop a grown woman's body.

I wonder if she's had a facelift already. She must be in her late twenties or early thirties, at most. There's no hiding that kind of youth. It's obvious in the way she of holds her arms and head, her posture, her overall presence. She seems to float in the foyer like a tropical butterfly,

nervous and light on her bare feet. Cesar doesn't release his hold on her. I realize that I'm staring openly and force myself to stop.

"How was your trip out here?"

Her eyes are very red, but no longer leak tears.

"Fine."

"Engine problems on the ferry again; that's why we're late.

I'm gonna buy a prop plane next spring, I swear to God. I've had it with those damned boats."

Mrs. Ortiz giggles, which is unexpected. It's endearing. It makes me smile unbidden. The sound is natural, unlike her face.

"Would you like a tour of the house? Or would you prefer to settle into your room first? The ferry is so wearing."

I opt for the tour. It takes over an hour. I try not to ogle, but it's impossible not to. I've never so much as set foot in such a place, and now this is my home. I feel like a complete hick. The kitchen is enormous and has professional chef accoutrements. That's the word Mrs. Ortiz uses: "accoutrements." Not appliances. Maybe they aren't appliances: I can't divine the function of any of the gleaming steel things in the room. I puzzle over the three stoves with bizarrely-shaped burners, two cave-sized refrigerator units, a wall of wickedly bright knives, and racks upon racks of copper pans hanging from the ceiling. My mom had three pans when I was growing up. I count thirty-nine before Cesar moves me along.

"This is the best place of all. The showpiece."

Cesar ushers us through a pair of parquet doors. The living room stuns me. I stop in the middle and can't move. The entire far wall is composed of massive floor-to-ceiling windows that look out over the ocean. The view makes me gasp out loud. It's wrenchingly beautiful. I could go without TV for the rest of my life if I could look out these windows instead. Gulls circle silently behind the clean panes. The water surges agonizingly blue, bounding under the huge sky, dazzling me with its glassy enormity. The sun burns a brilliant gold coin in the sky, seducing me to stare at it and go blind. A glossy, white yacht bobs and humps with the tide against a small dock far below.

"What do you think? Do you like it?"

Mrs. Ortiz has composed herself fully now. Her voice is remote and careful on the vowels, like that of a rich woman on a soap opera. She speaks the way a person like me would think a rich woman should. I wonder if it's real or an act. It's elegant.

"Yes…"

I have to rip myself away from the windows; an operation as painful as pulling my own tooth.

"It's so…wow. It's…."

I'm not very articulate; not very witty. I flap my hands helplessly.

Mrs. Ortiz's fine lips arch up. Cesar jerks his head at me.

"Wanna check out your room?"

Up the spiral staircase of blond wood lie the bedrooms. There are six guest rooms, a huge suite for Cesar and Mrs. Ortiz that I'm not allowed to see, and one for me at the end of the hall. Mrs. Ortiz names things as we walk: Etruscan vase, David Hockney painting, Chippendale table. I thought those were naked guy dancers, but I say nothing. They conclude the tour at a tidy bedroom snugged in at the end of the hall. My room.

"I've got a shit-load of calls to make. My office is just three doors down: feel free to knock if you need anything."

"And if you get hungry, let me know. I'll be downstairs.

The cook will fix you anything you want."

They shut the door, shutting me in. The room is small, but not unpleasantly so. It's the perfect size. Any smaller would be claustrophobic, any larger would encourage introspective lingering. It feels like a nest. There are nice pictures on the wall: neutral watercolors like at a doctor's office. Nothing experimental or difficult. I'll be able to gaze at them at night and not feel troubled.

I set my duffel bag on the tightly made bed and feel military for a moment. A quarter would almost bounce off this quilt. I can make it drum-tight; I can make a coin bounce as high as my nose. My jeans, T-shirts, and sweatshirts come out of my duffel bag neatly folded and stacked. I refold and restack them. I fill the dresser next to the bed. I line my shoes up on the floor of the closet, the toes exactly one centimeter from the wall, like the CO taught us. I lay out my comb and deodorant on the top of the dresser. I shove the empty duffel bag under the bed.

Now what?

Should I sit here for a bit? It's so quiet. The stillness presses at me.

I consider going downstairs. Should I impose myself? Make friends with the boss's wife? I wouldn't dare disturb Cesar for all the world.

I sit on the bed.

It's so quiet. The house seems to lurk around me. There should be dozens of people living in so vast a space. I wonder if Mrs. Ortiz works. Is she just Cesar's wife? What does she do all day? I doubt she keeps house in the traditional sense. The place has the mark of professional cleaning. It's unnaturally odorless and dust-free, like a hotel. The bed is narrow and firm. A preteen bed; a narrow, sex-free bed.

The CO had a bed like this in his quarters. He called it his cot. The bounce-back of the springs as I shift remind me of things. He liked the firmness.

I wonder what the CO would think about this enormous house, and about my working here. He would probably approve, given my circumstances. It's respectable work. I wish he could be here to give me advice. It's going to hard to live with my boss. To this day, I don't know how my CO and the other officers maintained such perfect self-possession and aloofness from us grunts 24/7.

Well. My CO didn't manage. Not with me. I was the flaw that spoiled it all. Still, I think he would tell me that, since I can't belong to the military ever again, this place must be my country. I'll have to see Ortiz Farm as my home-base from now on.

Utter loyalty: That's what Cesar wants. That's what I have to strive for.

Monday, August 3, 1998
1:35 p.m.
Ortiz Farm

Cesar swoops the Jeep along the dirt path leading from the house to the green-on-green fields. He handles the vehicle with the elaborate shiftings and wheel jerks of a stock car racer. He's a spectacularly bad driver.

"I hate manuals, gimme an automatic any day,"

He grits his teeth as we jounce halfway into a field filled with migrant workers. He draws hard on the parking break and we jolt to a stop in time to avoid the workers. Barely. Dirt showers them.

"There: that's the carrot field, and out that way's the spinach and romaine. I've got squash, potatoes, and I think we're trying tomatoes in the greenhouses this year. Amazingly rich soil on this island; great environment. You can grow anything. Except tropical stuff—no lemons, no oranges."

The migrant workers ignore us, bending and stooping rhythmically between the rows of carrots. Their bodies are rounded and thick from bad food and misdirected exercise. No one is supervising them.

"Everything's organically grown. We produce basic cash crops every year and sell 'em in Seattle at higher prices than the corporate-farmed produce fetches. Great profit versus production cost. Hippies in Seattle will pay the most ridiculously inflated prices for lettuce grown in horse shit. Still, no one on the island could ever make a real living off of farming. It's just a way to get the acreage to earn its keep."

The acreage expands out to the horizon. Green and profound, it's a thousand emerald waves straining to infinity, like a fantasy of Ireland. Cesar jerks the Jeep into reverse and shoots us out of the field. My stomach soars backward between my vertebrae as he humps us back up onto the roadway.

"This next area is a bit more profitable."

Cesar rockets us along a beaten dirt path. John Deere machinery litters the edges; earth-browned blades point skyward with clods of potato clinging. We bounce over furrows and rain ruts toward a steel building. It stretches out and out, elongated and rambling, like a bus garage.

Cesar slams down on the brake and the clutch and points.

"Horses. Not thoroughbreds, but very fine animals. The cousins and bastards of race horses, mainly. I have Secretariat's grandnephew, you know. He's just a yearling. Who knows, maybe he'll prove out and win me a Kentucky Derby," Cesar chuckles.

I stare through the sunlight shattered windshield at a fenced-in area next to the stable. Several men who look Mexican are leaning on the fence. They are watching a huge cloud of dun dust whirling within the thick metal slats.

"Seriously, though, this is where some real money comes in. Not spectacular money, but it covered the property taxes last year, so I won't knock it."

I squint into the brightness for several seconds before I realize that inside the clay colored cloud is a large horse. It bucks and jumps as if the ground is covered with stinging tacks. Its legs shoot up and out like spring-loaded battering rams, kicking up the dirt furiously. A man is on the back of the horse. His body flows with it, as if welded to the saddle

"That's Kell. He's in charge of the horses. Very skilled guy."

I'm transfixed. I've never seen such a thing before. The man has his shirt off, his arms bolted into right angles as he grips the horse's mane. His hair is very long and tosses black and

ribbon-crisp behind him. His chest and arms strain with the ropy muscles of real strength, gleaming brown in the sun just like the horse's coat. The horse leaps onto its front legs and kicks the fence with its back hooves. The sharp clang makes me jump, even with the windows rolled up and the air conditioner gushing white noise.

The Mexicans scatter off the fence, then return slowly, shaking their heads with nervous laughter. The sour spike of adrenaline eases into a jittery pounding under my shirt.

The man hasn't fallen.

The horse rears, clawing the air like a cat going after a songbird.

"I hired him several years ago, when I acquired my first three horses. I guess his family or tribe or whatever used to be in the horse trade back in the early nineteen-hundreds. Till the ferries started to run cars out here to the islands. They bred and sold for the entire San Juan chain at one time, from what I hear."

The horse rears up again, then slams to earth and begins galloping in an enraged, bee-stung circle. The man rolls with it, his face locked in a fierce yet work-a-day expression of determination. He clings on effortlessly, though it seems that he ought to fly off into the berry-blue sky as the dull dust drives up in a haze all around him. He looks infinitely competent and brave without effort.

For me, competence and bravery have always required such an effort.

Monday, August 3, 1998
10:12 p.m.
Ortiz Farm

Cesar has thrust the world's most unendurably vile drink on me. I will never trust him again.

We are sitting in his office upstairs, the lights low and confidential. The close dimness brings to mind illegal gambling and racketeering.

Cesar laughs at me when I gag.

"It's cognac. You've never tried it before?"

"No. Oh, God," I wheeze, setting the round snifter glass on his desk.

Cesar smoothly slides a coaster under the glass and grins.

"That's six hundred dollars a bottle, you know."

I thought that after my time in the army, I could handle any form of alcohol. My unit-mates and I used to go drinking in the town just off the base as our primary form of recreation. I drank real moonshine from a still once.

Cesar steps behind his desk and floats his large snifter on its side in a glass of hot water, to warm and fortify the wicked cognac.

"So…what do you think of the farm? Think you can stand to live out here?"

I wish for a piece of bread or a glass of water to leech the burning taste off of my tongue.

"Sure. It's very beautiful out here. The air's so clean. It's quiet."

"Yes, very quiet. That won't bother you? You're used to the city."

I shrug.

I may have lived in the city prior to this job, but silence and loneliness were all I had at home in the tiny apartment, and all I had at my terrible job. I've had more human contact on this island in just a day than I could get in six months back on the mainland.

"I like it."

"Good."

Cesar sits on the edge of his desk, drawing his snifter carefully out of the water. A drop falls on his knee and turns the fabric black. He rubs the snifter between his palms and inhales the fumes.

"My wife seems to like you, which is very important. A large part of your role here will be to keep her feeling safe. I have to leave the island quite frequently on business, and Anna doesn't deal well with being alone. I want her to feel protected."

I nod.

"Beyond that—just being a presence, patrolling, that sort of thing, I really need a redesign of my entire security system. It's utter crap right now. The last person who was in your position installed some high-tech piece of shit that's never worked right. I was very impressed with your credentials, and I have a feeling that it'll probably take you just a few weeks to get everything up and running properly. I worry about theft more than anything else. We've had a few fairly expensive items go missing over the years. And one of our neighbors lost an entire car out of his garage last month."

"I can start on that tomorrow morning, if you want."

"Good."

Cesar sips at his cognac, his face smooth and blissful.

He's not faking his enjoyment of the taste to tease me.

"Just off-the-cuff, could you give me an analysis of what you think this farm needs for security? Without getting into that other messed-up system."

"Okay."

I inhale, gathering my thoughts a bit. It feels very good to be doing this again. It's been so long.

"You've got too many employees working independently. The field-workers, I mean. Who's in charge of them?"

"Kell. The one you saw breaking the stallion."

"He's not supervising them. He's got other things to do, it looks like. You need to have someone watching over them at all times. They've got no stake in your well-being. I think one of them is responsible for the thefts."

"Mm. Go on."

"Meanwhile, your house itself has no security system. I don't know anything about art or whatever, but I'd guess the stuff in your living room, and that painting over there, and the statue-things in the dining room aren't from Wal-Mart, so you need alarms on them, as well as a general house-wide system. Then there's the stable. I assume the horses are valuable in and of themselves—expensive to replace. They could get out, or someone could remove them, and you'd never know till they were long gone. You need to tighten that place up. Um, let's see, the garage is detached, so it needs a separate system. You have how many cars?"

"Three."

"The Jeep, and…"

"There's a Lexus and a Mercedes. Oh, and an old Lamborghini that doesn't run. 1971 Miura P400 SV. Worth a fair amount as is, but if I ever get around to having it restored, it'll be a pretty impressive nest-egg. So, four."

"They need an independent system. And how about your wife—any jewelry? Do you keep your investment records or bond certificates or whatever in the house? If you have a safe, it needs to be highly protected. Let's see, what else…"

Cesar smiles wide and pleased. He holds up a hand. His palm is very pink from the warm snifter.

"That's fine, that's great, Flynn. Very, very impressive. I'm glad I hired you."

Warmth swells to fill me. I shouldn't respond so fast to compliments from a new boss, but it's wonderful to be appreciated again.

"Now, here's the other thing I need. First of many opportunities, if you handle it well."

Cesar removes himself from the desk and slides into the high-backed wing chair next to mine. He's changing the mood;

placing emphasis on this next phase of the conversation. I sit up to show that I understand.

"I am currently trying to solidify a financial deal to buy a fairly risky piece of commercial property with a group of high-profile investors from Seattle. I'm going to need you to serve as a consultant to me on this venture. For two reasons: first, to keep me from getting screwed. I'm not sure what the security needs of this property will be, so I need you to give it a number of goings-over. A few quick assessments, then a very in-depth analysis, and then hopefully, implementation of a highly complex security system."

Cesar leans close, providing a sense of secrecy and trust. Only the CO got to resort to this quiet technique. The lower officers could only order and rant at us. I prefer this method.

"Second of all, I want you to accompany me occasionally during the deal-making process to provide, shall we say…a look of strength to my position."

"You mean intimidation?"

"No, no. No, of course not. Well. Yes."

Cesar glances at me and smiles rather sheepishly. He swirls the cognac in hypnotic circles.

"I need you to be there, looking tough or whatever…but also I'd like you to help keep the process from crossing the line. Do you understand? I don't want you to be overt. I…sometimes I lack good judgment in knowing how far is too far. I'm really just a low-level salesman who managed to claw his way up in the world. Sometimes I can come across as tactless. Or overt. Know what I mean?"

I nod.

I have great experience with discretion. The CO called me into his office once like this, when I was entering the Water Evacuation segment of my Military Intelligence Training. He asked me to spy on my cohorts.

'Flynn,' he phrased it, 'high command takes an active interest in the performance of intelligence soldiers, and wishes to assure universal completion of this training exercise.'

I nodded. The room wasn't dim like Cesar's office, but a

sunny sepia. It was a late autumn afternoon with thick sun and shadows as wide and deep as ponds.

'To that end, we wish to seek internal intelligence about both the performance of the training soldiers, as well as that of the supervising trainers. Do you understand?'

I nodded, though I did not.

The CO sat stolid and impenetrable behind his desk, his fingers interlaced on the surface. His eyes were like sea billows.

'I don't need to tell you what an extreme level of discretion this duty implies.'

This I understood. I was always comfortable with discretion. I was proud to be chosen.

'Meanwhile, it's of equal importance that absolute circumspection be maintained by both of us regarding what transpired last night.'

I nodded.

The CO's veneer despoiled very slightly as he inhaled through his nose, made real eye contact, and laced his fingers a bit tighter.

'It can't get around. To anyone.'

'No.'

'Was it okay?'

I looked at him with bafflement, and he was naked in the face, like last night. It felt so disquieting to see him like that. His eyes searched as they never needed to.

'You didn't like it.'

He wouldn't take his eyes off me. They strained at my face.

I couldn't let it be like this, so uneasy and strange, when all I wanted was to talk more about gathering intelligence and to feel trusted.

'It was okay. Really.'

The CO ground his eyes into mine a moment more, then eased back in his chair a fraction.

'All right. You can go, Flynn. I'll want a full verbal report on tomorrow's training at seventeen-hundred hours.'

'Yes, sir.'

I stood. He turned away to his paperwork. His pale neck

was bent in a firm arc; his scalp shone through his crew cut.

'You can stay afterward, if you want to. With me.'

Cesar finishes his cognac and sighs. His face is tired, but just barely shows it on the surface.

"I usually rely on my brother very heavily in situations like this. He's an incredible lawyer. That man, he'll be a full partner of his firm by forty, mark my words. He's brilliant: he's got an unbelievably analytical mind. And he's a lot better at subtlety than me. He went to college, went to a very good law school. He got to mix with the upper crust informally and at a much younger age than I did. I refined him young, so he would never have to struggle on the way up like I did. He's coming out here tomorrow. When you meet him, you'll see what I mean."

Cesar sets the empty snifter on the gleaming little table that lies between us.

"I'll be so glad when he's here. I miss Antonio terribly when he's not around. He's the only person I really trust in the world. Besides Anna, of course."

I park the Jeep and get out, slamming the door to keep the air-conditioned chill inside. The sun glares off the ocean in fat, luminous sheets, threatening to fry my skin. I scan the horizon for the ferry and am gratified to see that it's only a bare five minutes away, chugging slowly over the water from Seattle.

I'm very curious to meet Cesar's younger brother. Cesar rolled his eyes dramatically when he asked me to pick him up this morning.

"He's terrified of dinging his damned Aston Martin on the ferry. He won't drive it on, so when he visits, we gotta chauffeur him around the island like royalty. I keep telling him to quit it with the luxury cars. Very bad investment. I mean, he drives them! You gotta store 'em if you want to make money off them. Oh well, he's impressing the gold-diggers, at least."

The ferry eases to the loading dock. I become alert. The gates of the automobile deck open and cars start to roll slowly off. On the deck above, the walk-on passengers debark single file down a slender ramp. I watch several families lead small children down the ramp. Then a few weary looking Mexican migrant workers follow, probably returning from the free clinic at Harborview Hospital in Seattle. A small knot of guys dressed in outdoor clothes and toting huge backpacks tramp my way, undoubtedly headed for the National Forest to hike and camp.

Then a dark figure appears on the ramp, suspended between sky and earth with all the menace of the angel of death. In the airless interval of his descent, I strive to stem the flood of intimidation that washes over me. The man bearing down upon me is wearing a perfectly tailored black suit that even I, who have remained ignorant of rich things all of my life, can tell is by a prestigious designer. The kind of designer who doesn't have a catalog, who sells suits that cost more than a small car, and whose name I wouldn't be able to pronounce. His tie is a severe navy blue broken by a brittle mother-of-pearl sheen that probably indicates that it's made of rare silk woven by children in a Far-Eastern sweatshop. There's not a hint of whimsy or humanity in that tie. He's wearing reflective sunglasses like the Secret Service prefer. His face is hard, handsome, and unamused. He looks to be at least twenty years younger than Cesar. He walks up to me without hesitation. He has no luggage: he carries only a sharply-tooled leather briefcase.

"Cesar Ortiz sent you?"

Antonio's voice is unfriendly and lacks warmth. I expect him to have a slight Hispanic accent like Cesar, but his enunciation is razor-perfect, like a radio announcer's.

"Yes."

Antonio says nothing more. Without a second glance at me, he climbs into the Jeep. He's careful of his suit, jerking his lapels straight as he sits. I jump into the driver's seat. Antonio radiates impatience. My nerves jangle audibly—I can hear them as a faint ringing in my ears. It's worse than when my future-court-martialing colonel was in my passenger seat. I'd better get going fast, or Antonio will become hostile. I start the engine.

"Do you want me to take you straight to the house?"

"Yes."

I pull out of the parking lot. The town slips by, and we gain the road that circles the island. The silence within the Jeep is tangible. I should say something.

"Is it cool enough in here? Do you want me to turn up the air conditioning?"

"No."

Antonio's face is rigid behind the assassin sunglasses. A mile creeps by, then another. He reaches into his breast pocket and pulls out a cell phone. He dials fast, with his thumb.

"This is Mr. Ortiz. Fred Weinbach's office, please. Fred. Yes. What did his client say? No. Unacceptable. No. Then tell him that if he doesn't sign, we will liquidate all his holdings and put his mother out on the street. No, I'm serious. Understand? Good."

Even over the gusty air-conditioning, I can hear the voice on the other end squawking desperate protests. Antonio hangs up.

Oh God, I do not like this man! He rattles me worse than any screaming, cursing, fist-shaking Drill Sergeant. They were all bluster and mean comments, but they couldn't actually hurt you. This guy is a fucking hitman.

I must persevere. I must be professional.

"It's…it's been good weather lately. Here. On the island. Has Seattle—"

"I'm not interested in having a conversation with you."

I'm so astonished that I take my eyes off the road for an instant, which I never do. Antonio shoves his cell phone back into his breast pocket and tightens his lips with what can only be deadly vexation at my petty chatter.

I shut up, as ordered.

A raw, four-year winter evolves between us in the chilly Jeep. At last, when my T-shirt is about to reveal the nervous sweat oozing its way down my back, I pull up at the front door of Cesar's house. I've never been so glad to arrive anywhere in all my life. Without a word of thanks, Antonio gets out and walks to the front door. He turns the knob and goes in without knocking. Clearly, he comes here often and feels very much at home in his older brother's house.

"Antonio?"

Anna's voice wafts into the foyer from the living room. She steps into the hall with no shoes on, her finger stuck between the pages of a book.

"Oh, good, you made it."

Antonio removes the CIA sunglasses. His eyes are as black as his suit, and just as sharp at the edges.

"Hello, Anna."

Stiffly, perfunctorily, he kisses her cheek.

"How was the ferry ride?"

"Nothing new. Tedious as usual."

Uncomfortable silence hangs over them, drawing me into its awkward circle.

"Can I get you anything to drink?"

"No. Thank you. I have some calls to make."

"Okay. Cesar's tied up on a conference call with some investors right now, but he'll want to talk to you when he's done."

Antonio nods and walks out of the foyer, pulling out his cell phone for another dial-a-threat.

Anna glances at me.

"The iceman cometh," she says softly.

Then she winks at me and walks away, leaving me alone to mop up my cold sweat.

Tuesday, August 4, 1998
8:37 p.m.
Ortiz Farm

The four of us are having a good ol' fashioned family dinner. The stained glass chandelier overhead casts cheerful oranges and soothing apricots over us to encourage calm and easy conversation. I can't take my eyes off the table. Its surface shines with a severe polish through which a rich wood grain gleams. I count the tree rings. I can see more than a hundred years back just beneath my plate. I cannot converse or raise my eyes because Cesar's younger brother is sitting directly across from me. He radiates such palpable hostility.

"Try the mung beans. They're sweet. Have you ever had them before?"

Anna's voice is low so as not to carry around the room.

"No."

I don't look at her. If I lift my eyes, they might inadvertently stray onto Antonio. If that happens, I'm certain that he will bark harsh reprimands like my Commanding Officer used to do whenever my eyes wandered while standing at attention.

"I think they're Vietnamese. Or Korean. The cook orders them from an Asian market in the International District in Seattle."

"See, I really want to get it off the ground by the end of the year. The whole deal signed, sealed, and in the vault. Then the next couple quarters can be spent bringing the place up to code. By this time next year, it'll be churning the raw diñero, know what I mean?"

At the head of the table, Cesar is oblivious to my discomfort. He works his fork rapidly and efficiently, tearing off economical bites of fish.

Anna leans close to me.

"The wine is good, too. It's actually a dessert wine. Cesar

won't usually drink it, but it pairs very well with the sole and the mung beans. It's called Sauternes: Are you familiar with it?"

"No."

"It's French. Quite expensive. Cesar picked it up at an estate auction two years ago, for my birthday. We have three cases in the cellar. Has Cesar shown you the wine cellar yet?"

"No, not yet."

"That's an area we'd definitely like to have some sort of security system set up in. We seem to lose at least one bottle out of every case we buy. Maybe some sort of alarm system— sensors, or motion detectors, if you think that's possible."

"And the thing is, the investors are all very enthusiastic about this deal. Total buy-in. I've worked with all of them before, so that helps."

"Cesar's going to buy himself a steel recycling plant. For some reason."

Anna's voice is louder, no longer just for my benefit.

"Tax shelter! Not 'for some reason.' Antonio, can you believe this? Good lord."

Anna is smiling, and so is Cesar.

"How's the wine, darling?"

Cesar wrinkles his nose at her.

"Gag."

I allow myself a quick sip of a glance at Antonio. He is eating with great focus. His movements are precise, like a machine's. He seems to be ignoring both Anna and Cesar intently. I must not look at him. He will pounce.

"So, Flynn. What would you say is the total security risk of a steel recycling facility? I don't think they get robbed all that often, do they?"

Cesar is peering down the table at me.

I swallow my food fully and wipe my mouth. I have to be socially graceful. We're not in the mess hall.

"That depends on whether you're going to recycle industrial steel—like actual tonnage, big hunks of it—or if you're doing small things. Old cars, stuff that's light enough to remove and that someone might think they can sell or use."

"Actually, I'm gonna try to get a Navy contract. Old ship hulls. That's long-term. For now, it'll be building materials. Girders, mainly."

"If you take military decommissions, you'll have to show that you have a very good security system in place. In case of espionage."

"Hm. Will that be expensive?"

"No. You just need to be extremely thorough, and have documentation on hand at all times proving your system's sound. You'll have to follow the procedures the Navy asks in receiving

and disposing of the stuff. It'll be time-consuming, but not expensive."

"Could you set up something like that?"

"Sure. The Navy will want to have one of their people inspect they system and maybe suggest changes, but the design and implementation's something I can do, and any corrections they order. They're pretty anal."

Maybe I shouldn't use the word "anal." Is it a dirty word?

Cesar points his fork tines toward Antonio, stabbing at him triumphantly.

"See? I knew there was an easy way to do this. It's a perfectly defensible business, right Flynn? It sounds like the security system would be cost-effective, making the venture a damned good risk. Like I told you."

Antonio swallows and pats his lips with his linen napkin. Like a pair of obsidian scythes, his eyes slide at half-mast to Cesar.

"I never said it wasn't. I told you to have the cost and risk analyzed versus potential profits. Apparently, you just did."

I glance from Cesar to Anna. Her left eyebrow quirks up slightly in a way that I can't read. Contempt, or amusement, maybe.

Cesar waves his hand dismissively at Antonio. He grabs the wine bottle and fills his brother's glass to the rim.

"Don't be a prick, Papi. Here, finish this shit for me. I can't keep up with that one down table."

Anna's lips curl up pink and deadly, like spun sugar confections laced with cyanide.

"Oh, Antonio's never been able to keep up with me, dear. But maybe Flynn can. Maybe someone in this house will finally try to get on my sweet side."

Anna is addressing Cesar, but her eyes are on her brother-in-law. Antonio swivels his head on oiled castors and his gaze locks with hers, like the sights on a missile launcher. Anna tilts her head girlishly, insolently. To my dismay, Antonio's eyes slip off Anna and come to rest on me. I can feel my skin turning blood-bright. The army trained me very well in the skill of keeping stonily at attention, however. I force myself to maintain neutral, unblinking eye-contact with Antonio.

"So. Since we're on the subject. Could you explain your experience for me, Flynn? Cesar hasn't enlightened me yet."

Cesar rolls his eyes elaborately.

"Come on, Papi. Later. You want some more salad?"

Antonio holds up his hand, not removing his eyes from mine. I want to look away so badly. This must be Antonio's courtroom face. Grim and blank and hellishly intimidating. I don't let my eyes move; not a twitch, not a blink. I tell myself that this is just like when the tip of my CO's nose was an inch from the skin of my forehead, bawling me out publicly for an infraction.

"Humor me."

"Turn off the damned cross-examination routine, for God's sake! We're having dinner, here," Cesar mutters, taking a drink of the sweet wine and making a face.

I open my mouth.

"I have extensive training and experience in the recognition and identification of hostile targets, as well as the transmission of position to battlefield commanders during heavy attack scenarios. I have participated in the review of functional equipment prototypes within simulated armed reconnaissance missions, involving changing operational environments, measures and countermeasures. I have been trained to establish covert tactical communication systems intended to locate and neutralize a variety of hostile enemy devices, including anti-personnel and anti-tank mines. I can calculate optimum force deployment, zero and engage targets during combat mobility, counter-mobility, and survivability test cases. I have operated within, and maintained communication equipment for, radio net and GPS linkage. I have extensive experience processing and analyzing captured documents in a range of media formats."

My voice is dead and toneless. I'm in uniform again, standing on the drill grounds the first week of boot camp, reciting the chain of command, or something similarly elementary and rote.

Antonio raises his eyebrows a fraction.

"Impressive. Then why exactly were you working at the Auburn SuperMall as a night security guard when my brother hired you?"

"Antonio, for Christ's sake! Enough!" Cesar snaps, dropping his fork onto his plate with a clatter. Things have ratcheted up a notch. I can smell it in the air. It's not so cheery in here; not so oranges and apricots.

"Did you tell my brother already? Or didn't he bother to ask you? Maybe you'd care to share with all of us right now."

Antonio's voice resonates with threat; strident and too loud for this elegant dining room.

"I'm warning you, Antonio…"

Cesar raises his index finger at Antonio. He shakes it lightly and ineffectually, like an irritated dad on a sitcom.

Suddenly, clarion-clear, Anna's voice cuts through the room.

"Antonio. This is my dinner table. Do not harangue our guest."

A silence as weighty as in the deepest ocean trench presses down on all of us. Antonio turns to Anna very slowly. I duck my head so fast, ten years of military training lost to the cold, wordless glare he turns on her.

"Flynn is your employee, not your guest."

Anna meets Antonio's eyes firmly. She leans an elbow on

the tabletop and turns her face fully to his. She eases toward him languidly, like a sun-warmed lioness zeroing in on an antelope.

"And you are our family, but you're a far worse guest than Flynn. Shut the hell up and eat."

Antonio glares at her. He glares and glares. Then he drops his eyes.

Stiff stillness drapes itself over the table.

Cesar bursts out laughing. It's a forced, false laugh that strives to bring relief of tension.

"Ah, Papi, don't be like that! We're all just having fun here right? Relax, lighten up. We've got that chocolate thing you like for dessert, right Anna? Come on, drink up…"

Cesar forcibly puts the wineglass into his brother's hand.

"I was going to save this for later, but I've got great news for you. Remember those tickets to the opening night of Mahler's Fifth you wanted? Sold out for months, right? Well, never say your big brother doesn't have connections! I got you eight of them: right up front, dead center. That'll impress the partners at the firm, eh? Come on, cheers! Anna," Cesar gestures with his fingers and glances pointedly at the door to the kitchen.

Anna rises lightly. She bends down close to my ear.

"Come help me get the dessert, will you Flynn?"

Her breath is so soft. Her voice is so soft.

I stand and follow her out of the dining room. My shoulders ache from holding them so stiffly back. My body has lost its ability to stand at attention. Anna's heels click through the big kitchen. She opens the enormous refrigerator and pulls out a pink box. She sets it on the marble counter and begins to root through a drawer. She turns to me, a frown creasing her too-perfect face.

"I apologize for that, Flynn. Antonio takes things too far sometimes. It makes me so mad."

"It's okay."

Anna shakes her head and pulls a slim knife out of the drawer. She slits the sides of the box and spreads them open

109

on the countertop, like the petals of a flower.

"He's so protective of Cesar, and he doesn't trust you yet. He hates feeling insecure. He can't stand it when he doesn't understand every little detail of what's going on. He gets scared, and he hides it by acting like an asshole."

I find it hard to believe that anything could ever scare Antonio.

Anna carefully slices something that looks like a chocolate cake, but which has the consistency of pudding. She pulls four delicate china dishes down from a shelf and eases the slices onto them.

"Antonio thinks Cesar brought you here to spy on him."

"That doesn't make any sense."

Anna meets my eyes, the knife drifting to waver in the air above her left wrist.

"Exactly! Cesar would never do anything like that.

Antonio's just…well, he drives me crazy sometimes."

She smiles and sets the knife down. Her eyes are appealing and seek to make me agreeable. She touches me for the first time: her ring finger fleetingly grazes my wrist. Her nail is needle-sharp, the flesh around it so cold.

"Don't tell Cesar what I said about Antonio, okay? It'll just cause a fight."

Wednesday, August 5, 1998
10:55 a.m.
Ortiz Farm

I've never been in a stable before. I step out of the burning sunlight into the musty dimness and immediately start to cough. The air is a soup of floating chaff and dust. I can sense the hulking forms of the horses on all sides, barely hemmed in by the thin plywood stalls that line the walls.

"Hello?"

My voice reverberates deep into the stable, riling the unseen, imprisoned beasts. Things nearby begin to whicker and thud. I don't want to wander around in here. I don't trust these horses. I suspect that, like monkeys, they are clever and can get out of their feeble cages. I'll come upon one wandering free, and it will attack me.

"Hello? Anyone?"

"Over here," a male voice calls.

Tentatively, I walk deeper into the stable.

"I'm in Perro's stall."

I read the painted signs that hang over the stalls as I walk. They're strange names, not quite like the ones I've seen in horse races on TV. Caliente, Pelota, Juguete, Coche. I find the name Perro and stop. Brass lettering for this one; scripty and elegant. There's nothing but a web of electric blue bungee cords to block the opening into the stall. I don't want to poke my head in. The horse will bite me; of that I'm certain.

I tap on the outer wall of the stall.

"Excuse me? Mrs. Ortiz sent me to find Kell."

A man, just a haze taller than me, pokes his head out. He smiles, then steps over the bungee cords. His skin is profoundly brown, richly so, like the husk of a ripe nut in autumn. His black hair gleams down his back in a loose ponytail. He's an Indian; the Native American kind. He's wearing tight jeans and a white tank top soaked with sweat.

I've seen him once before. The man pulls off his leather gloves and drops them onto the cement floor.

"I'm Kell. Who're you? Wait—you're Cesar's new security guard, right?"

"Yes."

The man's smile widens and he glances me over, as everyone does when they first see me. He sticks his hand out.

"Nice to meet you, finally. You've been here about a week already, right? What's your name again?"

"Flynn. Not a week; just two days."

I shake Kell's hand. It's warm and very hard. It's a working hand.

"How are you liking it here so far?"

"It's fine. Mrs. Ortiz wanted me to find out if you've mailed some documents regarding one of the horses. Mary-something."

Kell rolls oblivion-black eyes ceilingward and grins.

"Mariposa. Yeah, yeah, I did that about a week ago. They're just owner registration papers, no big deal. Anna worries too much."

"Okay. She gave me this, in case you hadn't sent them."

I offer the dainty note. It's folded just once, with no tape or envelope to protect it. I didn't sneak a peek on the way over. I'm used to handling confidential communiqués.

Kell instantly scowls and huffs out a breath. He takes the note and unfolds it. His eyes go right, left and right again over the delicate paper, then he closes his hand and crumples it into a ball.

"Oh, give me a break!"

"What?"

"Nothing."

Kell shakes his head, hesitates, then glances at me and takes a small step closer. He opens his fist and smooths out the note.

"Okay. Listen to this…"

He pitches his voice a shade higher and reads,

"Kell. It is very important that all of our livestock acquisitions be registered immediately upon installation on the

farm, for tax purposes. Failure to do so results in a loss that Cesar may consider taking out of your pay. Please see to it the papers are mailed by close of business today. Anna. "

A grin see-saws on Kell's lips.

"Well, fuck me very much. I'm gonna keep this. I'm gonna stick it on the tack room wall. Oh, she of little faith!"

"So, I'll let her know the paperwork is in the mail."

"Yeah, right, you go on and do that."

I turn to leave.

"Hey, Flynn. I hear you met Antonio yesterday."

Kell's grin has become a wise-ass smirk.

I stiffen.

"Yes."

Kell's smirk widens, his lips parting to reveal not-quite-white teeth.

"So…how was dinner?"

"It was nice."

I'm re-learning how to dissimulate with disturbing ease.

"Yeah, sure. I bet it was. Don't worry about it—he did the interrogating-asshole-lawyer routine to me when Cesar hired me. He was feeling you out."

I'm not sure what to think of this.

"Ah. Well…I should get back to work."

I turn.

"Hey, Flynn. Are you really gonna be living out here? Permanently, I mean?"

"Yes."

Kell's dark eyes become larger, and so does his smile.

"You really agreed to that? Sight unseen? This isn't just a trial-period?"

"No. Cesar hired me, and as far as I know, it's a permanent position."

"Wow. You're brave."

"Why?"

"Well, you could have ended up with some psycho family. Like in the movies. Or stuck on a white trash meth lab where they wouldn't pay you for months, and you end up blown to kingdom come when the place explodes. You got lucky. The islands out this way are pretty, but they're dirt poor. Everyone's on welfare. Cesar's the richest guy in the whole San Juan chain."

Behind Kell, within the stall, a horse neighs loudly.

There's a jarring thunk as it kicks the wall. Involuntarily, I flinch. Kell notices.

"You're not afraid of horses?"

I smile helplessly, which is unlike me.

"They kick…"

"Only if provoked."

"I saw that horse you were on the other day. How come it didn't kill you?"

Kell looks surprised and, strangely, pleased.

"You saw me? When?"

"Out in the yard, inside the fence. You were on that horse that was kicking and jumping."

Kell leans against the outer wall of the stall, hooking his thumbs into his belt loops. His thighs are thick and rounded within his jeans from gripping flailing horses in the saddle. For a moment, it seems like he's showing them off to me.

"That was Zapato. He's a new stallion Cesar just bought. I was breaking him. I didn't know you were watching."

Kell is looking at me more than he ought to. More fully, more freely, and not just at my face. I clear my throat and begin the backwards gotta-get-to-work step that colleagues do so as not to be rude.

"I'll let Mrs. Ortiz know about the papers."

"Hey, Flynn. You wanna go grab a drink? Like a soda, or something? It's shaping up to be hotter 'n' hell today."

I shake my head.

"I've got some other things I need to take care of right now. Thanks, though."

"Okay, maybe later."

Kell's eyes are very present on my face. I feel studied, memorized.

"It was good to meet you."

I nod.

"You too."

I leave quickly, striving for the sunny yard and breathing space.

Wednesday, September 16, 1998
7:55 a.m.
Skyhamish Ferry

"We should be back home by five tonight. This is just a day trip. I don't want to drag this thing out."

Cesar sits next to me on the ferry to Seattle. His face is intent.

"We're going to meet with John Stapp and Bailey St. Germain. They're potential capital investors in my steel recycling plant. I need to gain a firm commitment from them before I can buy the property. They've started dragging their feet, now that it's time to put pen to paper and make the partnership legal and binding. They're really starting to piss me off. I can't figure out what their game is. Maybe they're angling for a higher percentage; maybe they're trying to stall me so someone else can buy the thing out from under me. I don't know. I need you to watch them for me during the meeting. Tell me if you pick up anything that gets your hackles up. Also, I like the idea of bringing my hired thug with me. Put a little fear of God in them."

Cesar laughs.

I laugh, too, wondering how much he's actually kidding on this. I know that I'm not physically imposing in the least. That's what impressed my CO when I started the Army Intelligence Trainee Program. He was used to muscle-fattened varsity football guys; six-foot-tall basketball star girls. His recruits usually looked like they could kick your ass clean off, then dust it off and hand it to you without breaking a sweat. I surprised him. I piqued his interest. It's probably what drew him to me in the other way. I was different; he could pretend that I wasn't someone under his command. I was someone who could be approached; someone who could be touched.

I watch as Seattle's tall buildings rise like swords out of the water. After six weeks on the island, it seems futuristic and unreal. I feel unaccountably excited to be going to a genuine Big City with over five hundred people, tens of thousands cars, a billion watts of unnatural light. I must be rusticating on the island without realizing it.

The ferry docks efficiently. Cesar grabs his briefcase and steers us through debarking the crowd.

"We'll grab a cab. It's not far, but I don't want to risk being late. Jackasses would probably up and leave."

We ride several blocks downtown in a grimy, incense-fogged taxi. The sidewalks are clogged with office drones in suits. They're fleet on their expensive leather shoes that have been professionally shined. They're busy with their briefcases and cell phones. I think of Antonio and feel a prick of unease.

We pull to a stop in front of a large steak restaurant located on the ground floor of an extremely tall office building. Cesar thrusts a twenty at the silent cab driver and jumps out.

"It's early for food, but they insisted on meeting here. Idiots. They act like this is an FBI sting or something. Gotta meet in a public place, God forbid we go to one of their offices, such bullshit."

Cesar brushes a hand over his graying hair and walks past the red-coated doorman without thanking him. I thank him. I'm still awkward. I haven't learned the finesse of wealth yet.

It's only a little after eight-thirty in the morning, yet the restaurant is open and smells strongly of hot beef and aftershave. It's a moneyed, manly combination. The décor is brass and dark wood, with heavy New England sportsman furniture. Many of the tables are filled with customers: all middle-aged white men in business suits. Cesar approaches two of them with confident steps.

"Hey John. Bailey, sorry we're late. The ferry was murder. As usual."

Cesar beams a great, false smile. It's extra hearty with no warmth under it.

The two men seated at the round table return similarly cool smiles. Their suits are dark and presidential, like Cesar's. They stick out their hands to Cesar for a shake, and then to me, which throws me off. We saluted in the army. I still haven't gotten used to shaking hands.

"Not a problem, glad you could meet with us so early. Sit, please."

Cesar and I settle in across from the men. They eye me curiously but don't speak to me.

"Care for a drink?"

The man directly across from Cesar has a head that gleams as clean and smooth as a peeled egg. He gestures at a waiter to swing by our table.

"Sure, a Bloody Mary. Anything, Flynn?"

I shake my head, as I know Cesar wants me to. I'm getting better at reading his face. He's very subtle, but he projects what he wants with the level of his eyelids, the angle of his head, the tightness of his mouth.

The waiter departs, silent and unobtrusive. He seems used to dealing with impatient businessmen with little time and the need to talk privately.

"So, your brother faxed over an updated copy of your business plan and your proposal yesterday."

The man across from me tilts what looks like a gin and tonic back and forth on the white table cloth, watching Cesar over the rim of his eyeglasses. He's at least fifteen years older than Cesar, edging in on elderly.

"Good, good. You'll notice that we've included the latest figures from the city tax assessment. The property's going up in value. We gotta get rolling on this deal a.s.a.p."

"A few issues need to be taken care of first. Now, we realize that you've thought this deal out very thoroughly—that's not our area of concern. But the…the very liquid nature of this investment is still troubling to some of us."

"Liquid? What do you mean? What's the problem?"

Cesar's Bloody Mary arrives and he grabs it blindly, not taking his eyes off the two men.

"Cesar, let me make an analogy. It's like asking for a cash payment in full on a car that's never been seen, never been test-driven, and might never be delivered for all we know."

Egg-man's voice is soothing. Cesar is not soothed.

"What the hell are you talking about? You've been out to view the property half a dozen times with me and my brother—and God only knows how often you people have gone on your own."

"It was an analogy, Cesar."

The man is frosty now. Cesar's face is flat and unsmiling. The two eye each other over their drinks.

"Yeah, well, it was a piss-poor analogy. Excuse me, but you're starting to offend me. Liquid? What the hell should you be investing? Time? It's not like you people are new at this. Forgive me, but you're acting like a bunch of twenty-five-year-old start-up punks heading into their first stock offering. I'm starting to think you're gonna up and vanish when it comes time to put up the cash. Leave me holding the goddamned bag."

"Now, let's take a step back."

The older man holds up a white, wrinkled hand. He has a news anchor voice, confident and calming.

"We're interested in this deal. That's a given, or we wouldn't be here right now, correct? We've got what you need for financial backing. And yes, we are willing to share it. However, we need to have confidence that we're going to get a solid return on a very hefty investment of capital."

Cesar plunks his glass down on the table a bit too hard. He lowers his head for a fraction of a second, then he brings up a wide smile.

"Okay, tell you what. You guys need to come out to my place for the weekend. I can see that we're getting stymied by something, and we just need some focus time to get past it. I'll have my brother come out, too. We'll relax, take in some fishing, figure this thing out. How's that sound?"

The older man glances at his hairless companion.

"Well…I can't speak for Kurt or Fred, but I'm available this weekend."

"I can free up my calendar for Saturday and Sunday. As long as I'm back in Seattle by Monday morning."

The bald man smiles reassuringly, but I'm not reassured in the least. These men are reptilian, yet want to seem safe as house pets.

"Good! This will be very beneficial. I'm sure we'll get it all sorted out, get everyone happy. I've got another appointment in…shit, right now. Thanks so much for your time."

Cesar takes a final swallow of his drink and rises. He shakes the men's hands and quirks his head at me. I rise, unsure if I should shake their hands as well.

I don't. I follow Cesar. He walks swiftly through the lobby.

"Cab," he orders the doorman, who hurries to the curb to hail one.

"Goddamn pendejos! What do you think about all that?"

I'm not sure if this is a rhetorical question, or if Cesar really wants me to comment. I hesitate.

"Um. I think they're stalling. They want to buy time, or something."

"Time, yeah, I think so, too. If they wanted more money, they'd be hinting around about the upgrades that we'll have to do to bring the property up to code. Why the hell would they want more time?"

"Maybe…maybe it has nothing to do with the deal. Maybe they want to check you out."

Cesar turns to face me fully.

"What do you mean?"

"Like…like in the army, when we'd do reconnaissance, we weren't always just counting tanks when we were counting tanks. Understand? Sometimes we were really watching each other to check for flaws in the training we'd received. Sometimes we were engaging in subterfuge."

"Hm. Maybe they're trying to sweat me. See if I'm desperate. Looking to swoop in and liquidate me themselves if I am. Bastards."

Cesar steps off the curb and climbs into the waiting cab. He passes the doorman five dollars though the open window. I thank the man reflexively as he holds the cab door open for me.

"Seven months we've been in negotiations. The thing that kills me is, they approached me!"

Cesar leans back against the torn upholstery, the scowl lines in his forehead deepening to gullies.

"They volunteered their backing—I didn't solicit it. I've worked with each of them separately on so many previous deals, I just automatically trusted them. They've got some kinda alliance now, and I don't like it. They're ganging up on me."

The cab breezes us past tall office buildings to a very sleek little café jammed in between a skyscraper and a print shop. Cesar shoves money at the driver and gets out. We pass through the sweeping glass doors and I'm struck by a sense of Europe, though I've never been there. Paris, or Berlin maybe, from a 1930's film. The café is ringed with mirrors. The air is heavy with the smells of strong coffee and sweet pastry. Soft music dresses the room. I like this place better than the steakhouse. It's relaxing. No one here seems to be in a hurry.

Except Cesar.

He sits. He drums his fingers on the small tabletop. He shoves the thin silver vase with its single white orchid aside, then sets it irritably on the floor under the table. He frowns out the window for several seconds, then abruptly pulls out his cell phone and dials.

"Yeah, it's me. Where the hell are you? Hurry up, we're here already. Yes! I'm leaving if your ass isn't here in five minutes."

He hangs up and stuffs the phone back into his jacket pocket. A waiter wearing a very long white apron arrives, pad and pen in hand. Cesar sighs.

"Okay, okay, I'll take a Pelligrino. What do you want, Flynn?"

"I'll take the same thing."

"Have a double espresso con panna ready when our third arrives, okay?"

The waiter nods, deftly snatches up the thin vase from the floor, and leaves us alone.

"It should help, having them out to the farm for the weekend. Get them on my home turf. Hammer out the damned deal till it works. All very civilized and non-threatening, of course. Ah…"

As Cesar looks over my shoulder, his dark expression eases, lifts, and a smile warms his face. I turn to see Antonio hurrying through the front door of the café. He is the embodiment of harried annoyance. He dodges the tiny tables and slides in next to me, impeccable in his expensive lawyer suit. His hair is perfect, even though a light rain has started to fall outside. His tie is knotted as hard as a hickory nut against his Adam's apple. It's blood-red silk today.

I stiffen and scoot as far away from him as possible. He smells of good cologne and wet wool and printer toner. He doesn't spare me a glance.

"Let's keep this short. I have to meet a client back at my office in fifteen minutes."

Antonio thunks a large briefcase onto the small table and pops the shining clasps open. The waiter arrives with our drinks. He carefully puts the espresso into Antonio's hands to avoid spilling on the briefcase.

To my surprise, Antonio goes completely still.

He lifts his eyes to Cesar's face. The first smile I've ever seen from him softens his entire face. Vulnerability and pleasure ring his eyes. For this brief moment, his mean, cold features rearrange themselves into a younger version of Cesar.

"How did you know?"

Cesar grins and smacks Antonio lightly on the cheek.

"Come on, your big brother knows everything. Buck up, Papi. Don't say I don't love you, huh?"

Antonio takes a sip of his coffee and begins to root through his briefcase, his expression slowly icing back over. His eyes, however, remain lit from somewhere deep within.

"Did you meet with the investors already?"

"Yep. Sure did. What a train wreck."

Antonio pulls out a thick manila file and hands it to Cesar. He snaps his briefcase closed and puts it on the floor so that he can set the tiny espresso cup on the table.

"This is all the data I could get. The research is solid, but limited in scope."

"How limited?"

"Short of hiring our own outside researchers, which would take six months and cost thirty-thousand minimum—"

"Forget it. I'm sure it's fine. I'll read through it tonight."

Cesar slides the file into his briefcase without glancing inside.

"What were the specifics of the offer they put on the table?"

Cesar smirks.

"None. No specifics. They were very careful. Nothing at all was put forward."

Antonio frowns.

"No contracts? Nothing for me to review?"

"Nope. Just the same vague propositions. Not even in deal-making terms."

Antonio sighs.

"If you have nothing in writing and nothing stated verbally in absolute contractual language, then we've got nothing to work with from a legal standpoint. There's nothing that we can use to put pressure on them at this time."

"Bastards are playing a game with me."

"Be that as it may, you've got to get them to commit in some tangible way, or I can't do anything to move this along. There's no point in drafting a contract if we don't even have terms that have been suggested informally."

"What I want to know is, why aren't they moving forward? They were so eager to get on board six months ago; then for the last four weeks, they drag their feet. I'd kill to find that out."

Cesar glances at me.

"Say, Flynn. Ever done anything…industrial? Any experience in that form of, know what I mean, information acquisition?"

I frown.

"Industrial in what sense?"

I see Antonio shake his head almost imperceptibly at Cesar, who smiles too quickly. He switches gears violently.

"You know, have you ever worked in a factory? That's all."

"No."

"Just curious."

I get the distinct impression that Cesar was about to ask me to do something very illegal. I glance at Antonio. He's sipping his espresso and eyeing his cell phone as if waiting for a call to come in.

"Well, I'm gonna have them come out to the farm this weekend and get this worked out once and for all. Then we can actually get some sleep at night, huh?"

Antonio glances at an ornate gold wristwatch and sighs. He rises, tossing back the last of the espresso.

"I have to go. I'm late."

"Hey, you're free for this thing on Saturday and Sunday, right? I need you there."

Antonio grabs his briefcase, shoving his cell phone into the breast pocket of his jacket.

"I'll clear my calendar. Call my assistant, give her the specifics. I'll get any materials together we might need."

"Great. Call me tonight, if you can, okay?"

"I will."

Antonio turns and walks swiftly out of the café, his dark coat sweeping behind him like a cape. Cesar watches him through the picture window until he vanishes up the street. He turns to me, his eyes shining.

"He's my baby boy, I tell you. God, I love that man! Who else has a brother like that? I'm so damned proud of him!"

Cesar drains his glass, takes a deep breath, and stands.

"All right, on to the next appointment. Go grab us a taxi; I'll pay the tab."

We ride south in our third cab, creeping in grueling traffic down the freeway. The rain falls lightly on the windshield, tapping like insistent fingertips. We inch along behind a moving van, jammed in tight and claustrophobic by featureless

Hondas and Toyotas. Cesar grows impatient and makes several clipped, cryptic calls on his cell phone as the trip drags on. He doesn't handle the traffic well. He resists, leaning forward in his seat as if he's in a saddle and can urge the cab forward like a horse.

We roll across the West Seattle Bridge. The landscape is bleak, littered with old warehouses which are gradually surrendering to rust and decay along the shipping harbor. The air smells sharply of sulfur and hot metal. The cab pulls into a grungy parking lot at the foot of the derelict shell of an old factory. Cesar tells the driver to wait for us, shoves a ten-dollar bill at him, then jumps out into the drenching downpour. He turns up the collar of his coat and shoves his hands into his pockets.

"Don't say a word when we get inside," he growls directly into my ear, like a wary dog.

Cesar crunches over the gravel to a small particleboard portable building with a sign reading "Foreman" over the door. Before he can knock, the door opens and a very tall black man of about forty stares down at us. His body is thick like a bricklayer's, encased in sturdy jeans and a canvas work shirt.

"You're late."

The man sticks out his hand and grasps Cesar's in a slapping handshake like the grunts from Southern California used to do.

Cesar moves up the steps and shoulders his way past the man.

"Traffic. Got any coffee?"

I follow close on Cesar's heels, as instructed. The man eyes me suspiciously, but lets me pass.

"Who's your new friend?"

"Flynn. My security officer."

"Well, that's real friendly. Bringing a body guard with you. Makes me feel great, Mr. Ortiz."

The man curves his lips up into a pissed-off grin.

"So you got any coffee, or not?"

Cesar's speech is clipped, his Hispanic accent more

prominent than usual.

The man grudgingly pours us Styrofoam cups of cold coffee. It smells like it's a few days old. Cesar sits in a metal folding chair near a cluttered desk. The man settles in behind the desk. I remain standing. I study the walls, striving for a neutral facial expression that won't betray my state of general confusion. The walls are covered with fake wood paneling like my dad put on the family room walls when I was a kid. These tacky and homey walls throw me off.

Cesar thumps a plastic stir stick against the rim of his Styrofoam cup, his eyes needling the man.

"So, what've you got for me?"

"Shit, do you know how hard it was to come up with more information? You're starting to pump a dry well, man."

"Rick. What've you got for me?"

The tall man shakes his head and reaches into one of the desk drawers. He pulls out a large manila envelope and tosses it across the desk to Cesar.

"Here. You want more, hire a professional."

The man looks at me significantly and smirks.

Cesar opens the envelope and pulls out a thin stack of paper. He shuffles through the sheets quickly.

"What is this crap? This is useless to me. And this you've given to me already. Jesus Christ, Rick."

Cesar stuffs the papers back into the envelope slaps it onto the tabletop with a crack like a firecracker.

"Hey, Mr. Ortiz, it's like I said. There ain't nothing else I can find out. It's this or nada. You don't want it?"

The man holds out his hand, eyebrows up. Cesar rubs his forehead irritably.

"No, no, I'll take it. Damn it."

"Now, what about those concessions we talked about?"

"We can't move on that yet. I've still got no contract Motherfuckers are stalling."

"We need those concessions, or you won't get shit for union work when the place reopens—"

"Yes, yes, I realize that. Give me one more week."

"The union reps ain't gonna like it."

Cesar rises slowly. He fists his hands on the desk and leans in.

"Fuck 'em if they don't like it! You tell them that for me: Tell them they can go fuck themselves if they can't wait one goddamned week! I will get their concessions, but they need to be patient, understand?"

"Shit, you tell them. Let them tear *you* a new asshole, man."

"I have no sense of humor today, Rick, I'm warning you."

"Yeah, and I don't want to turn up floating face down in the Sound, okay? Those boys don't play."

Cesar straightens slowly and sets his cup of coffee on the desk. Grounds and dark liquid slosh over the rim onto the already grimy surface.

"I don't play, either. Give me one week. Or you can forget about the union boys doing you—I'll do you myself."

The tall man shakes his head, smiling broadly and without amusement at Cesar.

"Whatever, man. You call me when you've got the contract. If I ain't a grease spot by then, I'll set up a meeting with the reps. But if you can't get the concessions, then it's the end of us working together. Always."

"Fine."

Cesar shoves the manila envelope into his briefcase. He turns toward the door, then pauses.

"Just remember this: if I hear about you souring the good faith with any little comments out of school about me, you're going to have a hell of a hard time finding work, shelter, or a pot to piss in for the rest of your damned life. We're gonna keep this between us until next week, got me?"

The man stands.

"Uh-huh. Need me to call you a taxi?"

"I've got one waiting."

They shake hands again. Cesar jerks his thumb at me and we step back out into the rain. Our cab driver is lurking under the roof overhang, smoking a dusty brown cigarillo. He wipes it out on the wet bottom of his shoe and pockets it for later.

"One more stop."

As the driver starts the engine, Cesar sinks deep into the backseat. He rubs both hands over his face, leaving a ruddy trail down his cheeks that is slow to fade. He squeezes his eyes tightly closed, opens them with a sigh, and turns to me.

"How're you holding up, Flynn?"

He sounds so tired.

"Okay. How about you?"

"I'm getting too old for this. It was so much more fun when I was in my thirties."

We creep back across the bridge, bumper-to-bumper with the car in front of us. Cesar is not impatient anymore.

"God, I don't want to do this last one."

We ease down the freeway, picking up speed as we head south. Cesar closes his eyes and grows motionless next to me. His body seems to shrink beneath his skin, as if his interior is cringing.

I watch the buildings that line the freeway grow shabby, then decrepit, then derelict. Saggy two story apartment buildings with grubby kids dangling bare legs between the balcony railings give way to abandoned houses; the parchment-colored boards over the windows illuminated by scorch marks from long-ago fires and gang tags in fluorescent spray-paint. We take a poorly marked exit off the freeway and wend through ranks of public housing units. Ramshackle gas stations with no pumps and the word "Tienda" over the main doors form hunting blinds for lurking police cars. Out in the open, dozens of Mexican men stand against fences, waiting for construction bosses to come looking for day laborers.

The cab drifts to a stop in front of an aged brick building. It's surrounded by a high iron gate. A sign over the front door reads, *La Casa de Mi Abuela.* Behind the gate is a sodden courtyard littered with weeds and cigarette butts. Cesar pays the driver, gets out, and the cab pulls away. The rain is falling fast like a squall on the coast. He draws me close to him. His hand grips my upper arm as if he's trying to crush it.

"Stick close. Some motherfucker tried to mug me the last

time I was here. I managed to scare him off by cursing him out in Spanish. Got your gun?"

I don't have a gun of my own. The Ortiz family handgun, the one that I carry when patrolling the farm in the evening, is locked in my desk back at the farm right now.

However, I nod. It's easier to lie.

Cesar looks relieved. He steps to a small box welded to the gate and pushes a button. His other hand is still firmly locked on my upper arm.

A voice crackles through the intercom.

"Bueno?"

"Cesar Ortiz."

"Pase."

I hear a metallic click, then Cesar pushes on the gate. It swings inward with a painful shriek. He steps into the wet courtyard and I follow, leashed by his hand. Cesar's shoulders are parallel with his ears. He pauses at the front door of the building, draws in a hard breath, lets go of my arm, and slowly turns the knob. A universe of shining, cracked linoleum and shaky incandescent lighting meets my eyes. Directly facing the front door is a tall desk behind a scarred sheet of Plexiglas. A woman with a suspicious face is seated there. Cesar approaches her with visible reluctance.

"Buenos días. ¿Puedo visitar a la señora?"

"Sí. Claro que sí."

The woman slides a little window open and pushes a clipboard at Cesar. He writes rapidly and shoves it back through the window. The woman steps out into the hall with us and begins to walk. It smells like bleach and urine. We pass numbered doors on both sides of the hall, all tightly closed. The woman stops at number fourteen. She knocks: three firm raps.

"Hola, Señora. Tengo su medicina," she calls at the closed door.

"Pase," a dry, unsteady voice replies from behind the door. The woman opens it, gives us a brief nod, and leaves. Cesar presses his lips together and steps inside.

The room is very dim. I can just make out a bed, a dresser, and a TV on a rickety table. A tiny old woman is seated in an easy chair by the window, which is decisively shaded. Her frost-white hair is bound tightly into a small bun at the base of her neck. She wears a perky turquoise sweatsuit, but her face radiates nothing like perkiness.

"Buenos días. ¿Cómo estás?"

Cesar voice cracks slightly around the edges. He doesn't sound like himself.

The woman glances at Cesar, snorts slightly, then turns her dark gaze to the window shade.

Cesar draws up a chair. It scrapes loudly over the linoleum, making me wince involuntarily. He sits. He folds his hands between his knees, his face creased and uneasy. I station myself beside the bed, trying to be inconspicuous yet ready for action should Cesar need me. I can't imagine that this wizened old creature poses a threat, though.

Cesar begins to speak very quietly to the old woman. I don't have to pretend not to listen, since he's speaking Spanish and I can't understand a word. As my eyes adjust to the dimness, they drift to a gaudy wall calendar depicting the Virgin Mary with a flaming, disemboweled heart on her shirtfront. She looks very placid in spite of this surely fatal injury, pointing to it daintily as if she's a modeling a brooch on a jewelry-selling TV show.

The old woman suddenly begins to bray rapidly and stridently in Spanish. I snap to full attention, my arms hard at my sides, my head up and my neck rigid. She sounds like a combative crow guarding its nest. Did I do something I wasn't supposed to? I glance at Cesar. His head is bowed and he is nodding, repeating over and over,

"Sí, sí. Claro que sí. Sí."

Her little arms trace wide, wrathful gestures in the space between them. Her dead leaf lips form profound circles and gaping knife slashes. Her eyes squint at Cesar, then widen to stare at him as cold and black as the moonless December sky. They're exactly like Antonio's eyes. I don't dare look directly into them, and neither does Cesar. He drops his gaze to the floor, and there it remains, fixed on the linoleum, for then next half hour. He keeps nodding, keeps saying, "Sí, sí."

At last, in the dead heart of her tirade, he glances at his watch and rises.

"Ya me voy. Hasta luego, okay?"

The old woman snaps her mouth shut abruptly, cutting herself off. She turns her face back to the window shade. Cesar, his face worn and troubled, kisses her forehead gently. She makes a disgruntled little growl in her throat, and he straightens up fast.

"Flynn."

He motions with his hand and walks very quickly out of the room. He moves to the front desk, scrawls on the clipboard, and shoves his way out the front door into the courtyard. The rain begins to soak his hair, but he doesn't seek shelter. He pulls out his cell phone and dials fast. His hand trembles.

"Yeah, can I get a cab? Now. 134 Miller Avenue South. Right. Thanks."

He hangs up.

"Let's wait here. It's safer."

He jams his cell phone, then his hands, deep into his coat pockets. His face is lined with trouble as raindrops slide down his cheeks like tears.

Twenty minutes pass. Cesar says nothing. The rain thuds down on the scrubby shrubs and half-dead rosebushes that line the courtyard. It flows in cold sheet from the gutters onto our heads. I'm accustomed to waiting for orders in wet conditions. At last, a taxi pulls up in front of the building. Cesar hurries out the rusty gate, holding it open for me with an impatient gleam in his eyes. We jump into the cab and bang the doors shut behind us.

"Ferry docks. Quickly."

The cab pulls away from the building. Cesar deflates. He slumps into the seat, his body going slack. I see him rub his thumb into his eye very quickly, then he turns his face to the streets that slip past behind the rain spattered window. The traffic is light, flowing downtown like a colorful river. The cab drops us at the ferry terminal. Inside, Cesar sags onto a mucky bench to wait for the ferry to arrive. His hair and his coat drip steadily. I sit next to him. Our rainwater puddles mingle, then merge to surround our shoes. He bites his lip, fidgets, then turns to me.

"That was my mother," he blurts out. "She's very sick. She's been in and out of hospitals for years. Decades. Since I was about seventeen. God, she's so sick, it breaks my heart…"

"I'm sorry."

Cesar shakes his head and rakes a hand through his hair.

"Damn, I need a drink."

He roots through his briefcase and fiddles with the papers there, pulling them out, shuffling them, putting them back. He pulls out his cell phone, starts to dial a number, then switches it off instead. The ferry arrives. Cesar swiftly boards it, giving the impression of a fugitive clawing his way to freedom. I have to jog to keep up. Cesar angles us toward the small galley on the top deck.

"I need a beer. You want one?"

"Okay."

Cesar gets in the short line, buys two beers, and jerks his head at a booth in an isolated corner of the deck.

"Let's sit over there—is that okay?"

"Yeah."

Cesar hands me my beer, sits, and wraps both hands around his. He stares into it, utterly immobile, until the ferry engines kick to life. He lifts the plastic cup and drains more than half the beer in a single swallow. He sighs: a long and shattered breath that ruffles my hair.

"She just…absolutely refuses to stay in any of the better places I've found her over the years. She can't bear to be away from that awful old neighborhood of hers. And she doesn't speak English, so…that's the only place. It's the final option. God, it's so horrible there. I hate going to see her."

Cesar looks at me.

"That's a terrible thing to say, isn't it?"

"I don't know."

Cesar shakes his head brokenly.

"She gets so lonely, but she won't come live with us on the island. Well…that's for the best. Anna would never be able to take care of her—there's no way she could handle it. Mama would run away again, get hurt. She's safe at that place, and I guess she's as happy as possible. Still, it just kills me!"

He drinks again, and there's only a finger-width of beer left in the cup. His face darkens.

"But…the thing is, Antonio lives just fifteen minutes away, and he hasn't been to see her in three goddamned years. The last time he visited her, it was only because I literally forced him to. I'm serious—I had to physically drag him there, and he fought me the entire time. Cursing me, swinging at me. I'm surprised no one called the cops. He just can't bear to leave his perfect, ordered world. If that had been my attitude, I would never have met Anna."

This last part strikes me. I open my mouth to ask him, but he cuts me off.

"Well…okay, I guess it's understandable. I mean, Mama didn't really raise him; not in any sense of the word. She took good enough care of him till he was two, but then…"

Cesar shakes his head, playing with the nearly empty cup.

"I was nineteen when it got to be too much for her. I had a decent job by then. Not great, but I could afford an apartment, a car. There was usually a little money left over at the end of the month. It was like being a teenage dad, though. I taught Antonio how to tie his shoes, read, ride a bike. I used to bring him to my place to spend the night when things at home were bad. At first, I'd fix up a spot on the couch, but when he had to start staying for longer and longer, I got him his own bed. Little toys, clothes. I kept shuffling him back to our mother, then she'd get too sick and I'd come by and find him all filthy and freaked out, hiding in the back room of their house, eating raw chicken or hot sauce outta the bottle or some shit like that. Christ. Then he'd be back at my place for another couple weeks. It went on for years like that. He just kept staying at my place longer and longer, until pretty soon…he was all mine. He was six when he came to live with me permanently. I took him to the first grade on my twenty-third birthday and had to explain to his teacher that I was his permanent legal guardian. What a nightmare!"

Cesar sighs and drains off the last drops of his beer.

"That sounds very hard. Complicated."

I still don't understand just what's wrong with Cesar's mother. I don't know how he will react if I ask.

"Yes, very complicated. You can't even imagine. I just wish…I don't know. I've given up wishing she'll get better. After, what, almost thirty-five years, you kinda lose hope, y'know? But I wish Antonio felt something for her. He pretends that he doesn't remember living with her. Bullshit. I know he does. I wish he could forgive her for being too sick to be a real mother to him. Then, it's selfish, I know, but then maybe he'd help me with her. I have to do it all. I visit her and make sure she's doing okay. I buy her new clothes, talk to her doctors, go to her yearly Social Security reviews. It's so hard for me to get off the island every other week to see her. But I do. I do it all. I'm alone with her."

Cesar taps the plastic cup on the table. Tic, tic, tic.

"I think I'll get another."

He glances at my cup, sees that it's still full, and rises. I watch him wend through the line; a wealthy man in his fifties who radiates that particular power of true financial security. A man dressed far better than anyone else on this ferry, hunting for cheap beer that usually he wouldn't have ingested on sheer principle.

The sun is beginning to back its way down to the horizon, tingeing the sky a crisp crimson, when Cesar slides into the booth. He laces his fingers around his second beer. He points his face pensively across the room where the windows lie.

"Shit, do you know what bothers me the most? Every time I go see her, you know what I think about? Not about her, not about how old she's getting, or if she's unhappy. My mind always, always goes back thirty years to when Antonio was four and I was driving over to check on them at this house she used to have in South Seattle. Down five or six blocks from the house, I just happened to glance out the window, and I saw Antonio huddled up against a stop sign. He was hunkered down on this muddy parking strip—no coat, no shoes, no shirt. Just a little pair of shorts. It was the middle of November, raining like hell. The little guy was utterly drenched, like a drowned puppy. Completely terrified. To this day, I still don't know what happened to him, or why he was out there. He was shaking so hard it made the pole ring like a bell. I could hear it in the car with all the windows up. It stopped my heart. I remember hollering, 'Holy shit, what're you doing out here?' He didn't really speak English very well back then; not when he was upset. So I shouted as loud as I could, '¡Entre el coche, Antonio!' He started crying when he saw me, and he was too cold to get up, so I got out and picked him up and put him in the front seat. All these El Salvadorian women poked their heads out their apartment windows to see what was going on. They started yelling how they were gonna call the cops—they thought I was kidnapping him. Bitches. Why didn't they show any goddamned interest when he was freezing to death out there alone in the rain? Huh?"

Cesar shakes his head, pressing his lips together. He is still for a moment, then gulps down his second beer without coming up for air. He shoves the plastic cup aside. It falls off the edge of the table, but he doesn't notice.

"Christ, you know what the first thing he learned to say in English was? 'I want to go to Cesar's house.' Why the hell do I have to always think about that, every single time I see her?"

Cesar falls silent. He doesn't look at me anymore. After a few minutes, he pulls out the file that Antonio gave him and starts to read. I watch the sky and water fade to blue like old jeans, then blackness blots out the view through the windows. I sip at my beer, which has grown warm between my hands.

When the ferry lands on Skyhamish Island, Cesar slowly stuffs the papers back into his briefcase. It takes him a long time to rise, find his cell phone, gather himself together. The other passengers press toward the exit. Cesar glances at the night-darkened windows, then at me.

"Hey Flynn. How would you feel about…hell, I really can't go home yet. I'm all knotted up inside right now. What do you say we grab a quick drink at the bar? Just to unwind."

"It's been a very long day," is all I say, because I don't know what else is appropriate in these circumstances.

Cesar nods vigorously and claps me companionably on the shoulder.

"Great! Just a quick beer, or something. Maybe a burger, if you're hungry. They got a decent menu, for a hole-in-the-wall."

Cesar leads me two blocks up from the ferry dock to a small tavern next to the liquor store on Main Street. It's dusky and warm and filled with locals. Good ol' boys eating burgers and thick hero sandwiches; Indians downing pitchers of beer with buddies after a hard day's work. Cesar slides us in between the thick-gutted men at the bar and secures us two stools. Tap handles gleam by the dozens: all variations on Pabst, Rainier, and Miller.

Cesar applies a forcedly cheerful smile and lightly pats the shining surface of the bar.

"Now then! What would you like?"

"Another beer's fine."

"Okay. Miller? One Miller, and one shot of tequila."

Cesar takes his shot slowly, without salt or lime. I'm impressed and slightly disgusted. The sight of him downing that acrid nastiness makes me think of the cognac he forced upon me the first evening I was in his employ. I hope to God he doesn't try to get me to drink shots with him tonight. I've never liked tequila. Cesar wipes his lips with a finger, glances at me, then orders another shot. I tense up, but he drinks it himself, with relish.

"Ahhh, very nice. Good stuff, but not great. I've had great: a very high-quality variety from Jalisco. Know where that is? It's one of the states in Mexico. Big time tequila producer. Got fields and fields of blue agave for as far as the eye can see. I went down there once on business. Is the beer good?"

"Yeah, it's fine."

"You know, I think maybe I'll have a Corona. Why not—we're slumming tonight, right?"

I wince at this. The locals might take exception. But it's loud in here, and no one seems to hear.

Cesar takes up his bottle, disdaining the wedge of lime that the bartender tries to jam inside. His face is pinker than usual; his eyes bright but not perceptive.

"Cheers."

He slams the beer back hard. I peck and sip at mine. One of us has to keep it together.

Cesar rolls his eyes at me with a grin that's floppy at the corners.

"God. I don't look forward to telling Anna about this weekend. She's gonna be mad. Maybe I'll let you do it for me."

"You mean because you're having those men come?"

Cesar lets out a very loud laugh; too loud. People glance at us.

"No, no, God, no! She won't mind that. She enjoys entertaining. It keeps things lively out on the farm. No. Nooooo, it's the other person involved in this deal that she won't be at all happy to have as a guest."

I stare at him, not getting it. He grins, cups his hand alongside his lips, and mouths hugely,

"Antonio."

I frown.

"I don't get it."

"Oh Flynn, Flynn, my God, those two cannot stand each other."

"Really?"

"Didn't you notice? When he came to dinner last month? Christ, nobody but *nobody* ever tells Antonio Gabriel Ortiz, Senior Corporate Attorney at Burgess, Jackson and Harrison LLP, to shut the hell up and eat! Oh, my dear God! That was pretty typical of every conversation those two ever have, at least in my presence. I hate to think what they say to each other when I'm not around."

Cesar's smile begins to slip. He takes another drink of beer. The bottle rattles when he sets it down, nearly tipping over.

"It was worse when Anna and I first got married. I don't know what happened. She and Antonio just took a—an absolutely instant aversion to each other. From the very first time they met. That was one of the most uncomfortable nights of my life. They just kept staring at each other, like…like, they were horrified with each other, or something. They actually refused to be in the same room for almost a year after the wedding. Can you believe that? Like they'd come to a consensus about it. One would come in, and the other would go right out. They wouldn't let me set up family get-togethers for the three of us; not even Christmas. I asked them both why. Privately, you know, so nobody would get embarrassed. I got nothing but the same polite crap from both. 'It's just better we're not around each other—it'll cause problems.' What the hell does that mean?"

I can sympathize with Anna. I'd never be in the same room with Antonio if I could help it.

"Well…some people just can't get along. No real reason. Some people just don't like each other."

"Yeah, yeah, I guess. But they're my family. The only family I got. Except my mother. Anna doesn't feel close to her family at all. She hasn't communicated with any of them since before the…well. It's like she just wants to seal herself away from the world; stay safe and hidden at home. Given what happened, that's understandable. Still, I wish she and Antonio could get along."

Cesar kills the bottle and lets his forehead fall into his hand.

"They fight all the time when they're together. Always exchanging snide little comments that I can't follow. It's so childish! I feel like I'm their dad sometimes, trying to keep the peace between a couple teenagers. I wish…I just wish that they loved each other."

I nod slowly. I feel sorry for Cesar.

"What do you wish most, Flynn?"

Cesar catches me off-guard. I forget to manufacture

something generic, like world peace or a million dollars.

"That I could go back to the army."

"Interesting…"

Cesar shoves his empty beer bottle aside and gestures at the bartender for another.

"You wish they hadn't caught you?"

"No. I wish it hadn't gone down the way it did."

"They just discharged you, right? Clean break, get the hell outta here, that kind of thing?"

"No. It was…unclean."

"You're so ambiguous, Flynn! I thought that the first time I met you. You're honest—open like a book. But I just can't pin you down. Can't figure you out. There a—an enigmatic sorta androgyn—"

Cesar is intrigued, which is not good. I have no desire to talk to him about myself.

"Was it hard having your house built out here? Was it very expensive?"

This does the trick.

"Hell yes, it was expensive! I had it designed by Beckman and Associates. You heard of them? One of the biggest architecture firms in Seattle. They did the Museum of Native Culture. I wanted clean lines and the best wood you can build with. I love what they did with the house. Took for-fucking-ever, though. Anna and I had been married three years by the time they finished. I got sick of waiting and just moved her and me out here after the first year. We had clear plastic for walls. I felt like I was living in a glass house."

I manage to keep Cesar distracted with semi-coherent reminiscences of the house in its nascent stages through three more beers and final shot of tequila. Finally, at 11:00, Cesar stumbles to his feet and shoves at his sleeve to peer at his watch.

"Damn—goddamn! It's late! Anna's gonna be so pissed. Come on, want me to drive?"

"No."

I succeeded in nursing the first beer all evening, in spite of

Cesar's frequent attempts to force shots and Coronas on me. I'm stone sober to his sloppy drunk. Cesar slides off the barstool unsteadily and slumps against me.

"Getting old, can't stay up past my bedtime!"

I put an arm around him, wishing he wasn't taller and heavier than me.

"Just a couple blocks, Mr. Ortiz."

"Cesar, Cesar, you call me that!"

Cesar is jolly as he shakes his finger at me.

"And I'll call you 'Flynn.' Coz it's your name."

Such fun.

I lug Cesar two blocks downhill to the ferry parking lot, where I left the Jeep this morning. I cram Cesar into the backseat in case of vomiting and get into the driver's seat.

The drive home is dangerously dark and plagued with jocular, incoherent observations from the backseat. Five miles from the farm, I give up humoring Cesar and firmly snap, "Be quiet, sir! And sit still!"

Cesar finds this hilarious. He spends the rest of the trip with his finger pressed to his lips, hissing like a teakettle. We pull up in front of the house, and I pour Cesar out of the Jeep. His legs flow and slide like oil. I jam my shoulder under his armpit and heft him to the door.

"Shhh! Don't wake Anna. She'll be so pissed!"

Cesar fumbles in his pants pocket for his house key, looking like a pervert with his careless groping. The front door swings inward on its own. In the doorway stands Anna. She glows with terror, just like the day I met her. A shriek of outraged abandonment is roosting in her upper throat, waiting to fly out at Cesar.

However, she takes in her husband's condition, and her expression of hysteria smooths to dismay and shock.

"Oh, good Lord, Cesar! What on earth did you two do?"

Cesar lurches at her, grinning messily.

"Tequila, my heart, mi corazon! Don't yell."

She wisely steps back, leaving it to me to keep him on his feet. He's very heavy and I've lost much of my grappling skill since the discharge. I struggle to keep both of us on our feet.

"Let's get him upstairs. I'm sorry, Flynn. He never does this, really."

"Nooo, never, never, soy un hombre como caballero, como—"

"Cesar, pipe down, for God's sake!"

Anna gingerly takes his other arm and we lug him up the staircase.

"I can't imagine what got into you."

"Tequila, by the quarts! Flynn here liquored me up. Wanted to hit me up for a raise."

Cesar winks hugely at me, tries to kiss Anna, and nearly pitches the three of us down the stairs. We drag him down the hall, Anna opens the door to their bedroom, and we toss him shoes and all onto the bed. She closes the door softly behind us and crosses her arms over her chest.

"I apologize, Flynn. Cesar rarely gets drunk. It's been years since I last saw… *that*. What happened?"

"He wanted to get a drink at the bar in town. It turned into several."

"Just where did you two go today?"

I shrug. I'm not sure if the trip to Seattle is supposed to be kept secret from Anna.

"Seattle. We met with some men your husband wants to cut a deal with, and we had coffee with Antonio. Then we visited your mother-in-law."

Anna blanches.

"God, Cesar. No wonder," she murmurs.

She glances at me and her face becomes guarded.

"What did Cesar tell you about his mother? Specifically."

"I don't know. Not much. Just that she doesn't speak English, and she's been sick for a very long time."

"Did he mention Avalon? Her old hospital?"

"No, I don't think so. What—"

"Flynn. Some aspects of life are very painful, you understand? So painful that it's better to just bury them so deep that they don't affect your daily life. That way, you have

141

to fall very far before they affect you. That's healthy. Despite what the psychologists of the world say. Don't talk to Cesar about his mother anymore, promise me. Promise?"

Her face flames from within. Her features rear out, sculpted and man-made, like a Madonna in a chapel. She's being driven hard, yet tries to hide it beneath the beauty of her manufactured exterior. She's frightening to look at. Something very important is passing me by right now, as I stand befuddled in the hall with her.

I wish my CO were here. He would know how to guide the truth out into the open. I'm easily confused; easily thwarted.

"Okay."

Anna leans close to me and tiptoes to reach my ear. Her lips radiate warmth, though they don't touch me. I can feel their after-burn on my earlobe as she whispers,

"I'm trusting you, Flynn. It's so important. To me."

Thursday, September 17, 1998
8:25 p.m.
Ortiz Farm

"Flynn? Could you come in here for a moment?"

Anna's voice carries to my desk within the security nook off the kitchen without shouting. I can't raise my voice elegantly like she can. I'll have to shout my reply. Instead, I step tentatively into the living room.

The room is bathed in light: tiny beams directed on the paintings, fat pottery lamps squatting on end tables, track lights housed high above in sleek European fixtures. The enormous floor-to-ceiling windows are unshaded and flat black, like clean chalkboards. The room is homey in such warm light. I am soothed just being in here.

"Yeah—yes?"

"Do you have a few minutes?"

Anna is seated in a peach easy chair, her legs crossed, a pad of heavy cream-colored paper from a stationer in Seattle on her lap. She's making delicate notes with a fountain pen. Her body is diet-slender under her pale skirt and thin white sweater. Her makeup is subtle, her features too perfect underneath. She's Jackie O planning a soiree with cameras from *Life* magazine on her. I've never used a fountain pen in my life.

"Cesar is having some business associates out to the farm for the weekend. Did he tell you?"

I nod.

"Good. He's having Antonio sit in throughout, and he'll want you to participate as well. He'll explain specifically what he wants you to do later, but for now, can you free up the entire weekend? Evenings as well."

"Okay."

Anna glances down at the pad, as if checking for the next item of discussion. She bites her bottom lip, forces a smile, and looks back up at me.

"So! Tell me. What would you like to wear this weekend?"

She has nearly flawless charm as she asks me, yet a bit of embarrassment slides in under the words. I'm at a loss.

"What would you like me to wear?"

"Something…cashmere or wool? Maybe slightly tailored?"

She studiously does not glance at my body when she says this.

"I've got jeans. T-shirts and sweatshirts. That's about it."

Anna unfolds her slimness from the soft chair and steps over to me, rubbing her pale hands together, as if they're cold. She forces lightheartedness.

"Let's see…hold very still, now."

She presses her back against mine and measures with her hand.

"Not quite as tall as Cesar, a bit taller than me. Well, okay! Let's take a look through the Ortiz Collections from seasons past, shall we? We never throw anything out, Cesar or me. It's a bad habit. We've got literally closets and closets full of old clothes that we've barely worn."

She smiles, walks out of the living room, and puts her foot on the first step of the spiral staircase in the foyer. She curves her hand at me to draw me after her.

I follow her, mildly surprised that I'm not humiliated by this suggestion that I borrow used clothing to make myself presentable. I ought to be ashamed of my slovenliness, but instead I'm rather intrigued. I've never known anyone with tons of clothes that they don't wear. Except old uncles with leisure suits hanging like shameful dreams in the backs of their closets; cousins with

limp, butterfly-shaped bridesmaid dresses in horrid hues. I'm unfamiliar with true fashion; a collection whose season has passed. Anna's thin mules clack up the stairs like spoons on good china. "We ought to send some of it to the Salvation Army, I guess, but it seems such a sin to donate designer one-of-a-kinds to be sold at the same price as polyester pantsuits from a dead grandma's closet."

Anna's lips quirk up mischievously, wickedly. She looks as if she knows that she's being arrogant, and revels in it. I wonder if she didn't have money before Cesar.

We walk down the hall past the master bedroom, past Cesar's office. She opens the door to one of the spare bedrooms.

"I'll have to get the staff to clean this place very thoroughly before our guests arrive. Cesar said we'll need four of the rooms. And Antonio's room, of course. We'll be almost at full capacity: a little more crowded than I'm comfortable with. I don't mind hostessing, you know, but when there are more than four people, I get antsy. It becomes hard to keep up with the group mindset, especially when it's a bunch of Cesar's business acquaintances. Couples are easier. Couples tend to come to consensus. They can amuse themselves. They like to go for walks, take coffee alone on the deck. I can just be in the background. Not quite so center stage, if you know what I mean."

Anna tugs on a set of double-doors. As she promised, I'm greeted by the sight of racks upon racks of clothing within a vast walk-in closet as large as my bedroom. Anna flicks on the light and disappears inside.

Unfathomable numbers of Cesar's fine business suits, Anna's pale dresses, and line after line of shoes cram the space. Casual clothing lines one wall. Full linen shirts such as I've often seen Cesar wear around the house; light sweaters like the one Anna is wearing. Strangely, near the back, I see several hangers draped with slim jeans and bright tank tops like teenage girls wear. I frown and lean in closer to look. Anna begins to weed through the clothing, blocking my view.

"Let's see…subtle fabrics. Nothing constricting. Have you ever had your colors done? Analyzed?"

"Like…you mean, some kind of new age thing? Like an aura?"

Anna laughs.

"No, I mean having someone at a nice boutique tell you what colors look best on you. Maybe an upscale department store like Nordstrom's. Sometimes they'll do it right, but it's usually just a gimmick to get you to buy whatever they couldn't sell from last season."

"Is that why you wear white all the time?"

"Pardon?"

"Did they tell you it's your color? White?"

"Oh, no. No, Cesar just likes it on me. Light colors. He prefers them."

She steps out of the closet, her arm draped with sweaters and trousers that she fingers critically.

"Actually, he chooses almost all of my clothing. He started right before we got married, and he's never gotten tired of it. Do you find that romantic?"

I suppose it's meant to be romantic, her husband swathing her in creamy medieval fabric, like an immured princess in a fairy story. I'm not a good judge of such things.

"Maybe. I don't know. My mom was the last person to pick out my clothes. Then the army did it."

Anna giggles. She moves to the bed and lays the clothing out into deflated bodies: headless, handless, and compressed. She stares at each outfit, frowning.

"For the formal dinner on the first night, Cesar will probably wear one of his Egyptian cotton shirts and Caronti slacks. Very L.L. Bean, but higher end. Relaxed rural host, but not outdoorsy or too casual. Antonio will wear one of his everlasting Armani suits, of course. I'll wear a linen dress. It's cut like a sundress, but in quite an elegant material, like silk. You ought to be in between all of us. Not as casual as Cesar and me, but not in Antonio's corporate fantasyland. Slacks and a good Irish wool sweater, I think."

She reaches for a pair of pants that look very comfortable and very expensive. They're almost satiny, but not in a tacky way. She hands them to me. I've always worn jeans since I was five years old. The softest pants I've ever worn were sweatpants, and they seem scratchy compared to the richness of this cloth. I have no idea what it is.

"This is fun. Like playing dress up," Anna comments, as

she touch-tests several thick sweaters. She settles on one the color of overcast sky at dawn. She turns to me expectantly, holding it out.

"Want to try this outfit first? See if it fits? I think it will."

"Okay. Um, is there a bathroom, or whatever…"

Anna rolls her eyes and makes a face.

"Don't be silly, Flynn, I won't peep at you. Just do it here. This will take all night otherwise."

Pointedly, ending the discussion, Anna turns her back and elaborately covers her eyes.

I'm not bashful. I lived in a huge barracks with one-hundred fifty other people for over ten years. The bathrooms had stalls with no doors. We had to dress standing shoulder-to-shoulder every morning. We showered together, exposed under industrial steel showerheads, as the Drill Sergeant stalked back and forth calling out each body part we were supposed to be soaping and rinsing. I don't care if she looks. Even if she is my boss's I strip off my sweatshirt and toss it on the floor. Then I remember that this is a tidy house, and pick it up. I fold it neatly and lay it on the edge of the bed.

"When I was in college, nothing could make me get dressed up. I said fashion was bourgeois, but really I couldn't figure out how to get paint stains out of anything besides denim."

"Where did you go to college?"

I pull off my jeans and lay them on top of my sweatshirt.

"Eastern Washington University. It's east of Seattle. Almost in Idaho. There's just the college out that way—nothing much else. It's a very good school, though. Highly ranked."

"What did you major in?"

Anna's easy to interrogate when I'm half-naked. Cesar would have dodged and evaded me just from raw habit if I asked him anything so directly.

"Art history. Very useful major, huh?"

I slip on the pants. They're heavenly soft.

"I don't know. Did you work before you married Cesar?"

A chill descends. I work my head through the tight neck of the sweater in time to see Anna's back tense up.

"I didn't exactly graduate. And I didn't work after I left school."

"How come?"

I straighten the sweater over my body. It fits fairly well, bunching in a few spots it shouldn't, but otherwise feels luxurious and wonderful.

Anna's arms are crossed, white as china and just as stiff, over her chest.

"That's personal."

"Well…what do you think?"

Anna turns slowly. Her skin glows with heat and should be red, but there's absolutely no color. She's drained of blood. Her cheek and chin and forehead shine like carved quartz. Her face quickly snaps back into its usual remote, calm expression. She eyes me up and down, pursing her lips

"Here. Try this. Keep the slacks on."

Anna tosses me a gray button-down shirt. She is slow to turn away, and doesn't cover her eyes. The way things are going, loosening up between us, she'll soon be sitting on the edge of the bed, giving me the eye as I change. I'll be mostly naked as she chats. Cesar will walk in. We'll have a hell of a time explaining.

"This island has changed so much since Cesar and I first moved out here. I hope the city people aren't put off by it. I think Cesar promised them a remote, private island atmosphere. There are so many people here these days."

She smiles. I can see it in the long mirror across the room. Her lips are like the inner folds of polished shells.

"At least, it seems like so many to me. I liked the loneliness quite a bit when I first came here. It was refreshing. So safe. So far from the world."

I remove the sweater and slip my arms into the shirtsleeves.

"There was nothing here when we built the house, except the Indian reservation. A couple fishermen were living in absolute hovels along the western coast. Nobody ever visited the National Forest. Now…we've been discovered. We're not the only rich people on the island anymore."

As predicted, Anna sits on the edge of the bed, not looking at me exactly, but no longer averting her eyes. Cesar is definitely going to catch me half-naked and alone with his wife. I'm not concerned that he'll think we're up to any sexy-business, but I'll certainly look undignified. How can I ever seem professional if he's seen my in my skivvies?

"That sounds elitist, I suppose. I should be glad to have neighbors. There's a retired judge over on the east side, and an architect and his wife with eighty acres at the interior of the island on the edge of the National Forest. They're stranded in the woods; no view whatsoever. They had us out to their place for dinner last year. His wife served Dom Perignon with the salad course—how nouveau riche is that? Cesar checked him out. He's designed nothing in the Pacific Northwest. Just ghetto apartments for illegal Mexicans down in Nevada and New Mexico. His house was quite nice, though, I have to admit."

Ghetto apartments, like I had to drive by yesterday with Cesar. I can't imagine living like that: ten people crammed into a one-bedroom unit, cockroaches and rats roaming freely around the crawling babies. The barracks were crowded, but always sociable and sterilized three times a day on our Drill Sergeant's orders.

"Did Cesar teach you Spanish?"

I work the wrist buttons swiftly and I check myself out in the mirror over Anna's shoulder. She sees that I'm clothed and turns to get a better look. She has been watching me, after all.

"Very nice! That'll do perfectly. No: Cesar never tried to teach me Spanish. I took it for a couple semesters in college, but I've never had a great gift for languages. Cesar doesn't really use it that much anymore, except with his mother. His brother doesn't speak it at all."

"Doesn't, or can't?"

I hope my voice isn't too accusatory. I haven't done a true informational interview, an informal interrogation, in so long. I'm out of practice. But I'm curious.

Anna shrugs, a bit stiffly.

"I don't know. Antonio and I have never really…we've never gotten into that. Cesar spoke nothing but Spanish for the first five years of his life, till he went to school and learned English. But as far as I know, Antonio never learned more than Spanish baby talk. That's what he says, at least."

Anna studies the rug, her hands jammed between her knees. She clears her throat, straightens her spine, and folds her hands lightly in her lap.

"I'm not really comfortable talking about my brother-in-law. Just one of those boring, everyday family issues. You understand."

Her voice is steady and sanctimonious. She wants me to assume they've simply never gotten

along. Maybe he disliked her from the start: a barely-legal, unemployed Art History dropout that latched onto wealthy, middle-aged Cesar and seduced him until he married her. She's a lot shrewder in her aloof, rich matron mode than I realized. She's slippery.

"Is this all I need? Two outfits?"

"Yes, that should be enough."

I undress so that I can resume my former clothing. I keep my eyes to myself; Anna does not.

She smiles at me: a helpless, appealing smile that I can't prevent myself from liking. It's the studied smile of a little girl who just ruined dad's rug with poster paint, but tried real, real hard to clean it up. She's so very slippery.

"Thanks for being a good sport, Flynn. Can I tell you something?"

"Sure."

"I feel really comfortable with you. We've had a few other security officers before. Cesar probably told you. I feel like you're part of the family. I like you."

I'm supposed to turn all blushing aw-shucks at this. I'm supposed to be drawn in. I can tell, however, that hers is not a simple statement. I smile, neutral and gracious, as I skin my jeans back on. Anna rises and her smile becomes mischievous.

"Don't tell Cesar that we borrowed these outfits from the

old clothes. I'll bet he won't even recognize them. In fact, keep them, if you like them."

She wants me beholden, but not to realize it until later. She wants me to feel an obligation toward her. I'm not sure that it's for any malicious reason. I almost think she just wants me to like her as much as I like my real boss. She wants to ensure that I'm as loyal to her as I am to Cesar. If I don't agree, things will become awkward between us.

"Okay, I'll keep them."

She steps close to me. She lays her finger over my lips so gently.

"Now we have a secret to share."

Friday, September 18, 1998
1:06 p.m.
Ortiz Farm

"Oh, God, where's the wine? Kell!"

Anna, scowling and bristly haired, steps into my little security station off the kitchen. Her eyes whip the small space, then whip me.

"Flynn, did Kell come by here with a case of wine, by any chance?"

"I don't know. I don't think so."

"You've got all those—those cameras and scanners and things! How could you not know?"

She turns, on the cusp of storming away. She beats back her fly-away hair, forms a ponytail with her fingers, then shakes the strands free. She turns back to me wearing an apologetic smile that may or may not be genuine.

"Flynn, I'm so sorry. That was rude. I'm just very stressed-out right now. The caterer is trying to duck out of doing the dinner at the eleventh hour, and I can't cook to save my life, and our cook can't possibly pull off a dinner of this level. Kell was supposed to pick up a case of shiraz that we ordered weeks ago, but it's nowhere to be found. You're sure you haven't seen him?"

"Not in the house. Some of the cameras are still a little dicey out in the stable. I can go check there for you."

"Thanks, that would really help."

"No problem."

I rise, logging out of the computer surveillance system. I'm glad to get out of the house for a while. I finished surveying Ortiz Farm from the Jeep, as well as on foot, weeks ago. Now, I'm tied to the computer all day as I attempt to link the security terminals that I set up at key points around the farm. I have to work with what had been purchased, then abandoned in the garage, by the previous security officer. My raw materials consist of motion sensors with clunky software and outdated video equipment. All of it is so very Radio Shack. My predecessor didn't have a clue about how to establish electronic surveillance. This kind of low-level system debugging has always been the part I like least about security work. I love skulking in person; I hate doing it by remote.

I stroll through the crisp, early autumn sunlight to the rambling stable. The dry smell of horses, hay and mud fills my head, distracting me and making me twang with instinctive nervous energy. Thankfully, the outdoor pens are vacant. I step into the shadowy stable with reluctance, fearing the equine biomass within.

On all sides, hulking, glossy forms whicker and slam against stalls as thin as crates. My heart beats a jittery tattoo against my sternum. I truly don't like horses. We never had to train with them in the army. I can ride a motorcycle and drive a tank, but I dread getting near a horse, much less mounting one. I don't know how Kell does it. He's braver than me.

I walk carefully between the murky ranks of stalls. I have a vague terror that a horse will reach out its long neck and take a bite out of my shoulder if I deviate from the very center of the aisle. I keep my hands locked against my jeans seams.

A tinny radio at the end of the long row of stalls is playing 1970's rock. I aim for it. I won't call out for Kell: That would make him laugh at me.

I arrive after a sweaty century at a cramped, closet-like enclosure. The walls are hung with saddles, bridles, detached stirrups, odd bits of leather, pliers, awls, and horse brushes. A battered radio roped to an iron hook on the wall is scratchily playing Island County's only local radio station. At chin-level, a bare light bulb swings from the ceiling by its wiring. I poke my head inside tentatively.

Kell is sitting on a rickety wooden stool in the middle of the room, directly under the light bulb. He has a saddle draped over his lap, flat like a vacant turtle shell. He braces a boot against it while holding a strip of leather in his teeth to pull tension. He strains hard at a circle of silver metal with a pair of pliers. His arms and chest jump with impressive cords and tendons under his tight white tank top. I appreciate hard-won work muscle.

I don't want to startle him. Kell tugs at the pliers, grunting. The metal gives too much, throwing his grip off. The pliers jump out of his hand, pinging to the stone floor.

"Dammit!" He murmurs, shaking his hand out.

As he reaches for the pliers, he notices me. A smile, a genuine one, curves his lips up.

"Well, hey, Flynn. I didn't know you were there. What's up?"

"Mrs. Ortiz wants me to ask if you've picked up a case of wine for her yet."

Kell rises, sucking on one of his fingers ruefully and shaking his other hand out.

"Nope. Tell her I'll get around to it."

"Well...she's pretty worried about it. It sounded important."

Kell rolls his eyes. He sits back down on the stool, rubbing the saddle with an oily rag.

"She'll live. She and Cesar have big shindigs like this all the time. They're old pros."

He pauses and glances at me. He seems to reconsider.

"Oh well, I gotta do it sometime, I guess. I can't get this damned thing to tighten, anyway. Wanna come with me?"

I have nothing pressing to do right now. Nothing I'm eager to do. A break from the computer would be nice.

"Okay."

"Great."

Kell grabs a worn flannel shirt from a hook on the wall and uses it to towel his face. He stops abruptly when he sees that I'm watching. He grins sheepishly and pulls it on. He tosses the Jeep keys to me.

"You drive. My hands are killing me. I had to shoe a couple horses yesterday. The farrier from the mainland needed help. He only swings by twice a year, so it's not like I could say no."

We walk through the sunlight to the Jeep. Kell jumps in, light and easy. I slide into the driver's seat.

"Where are we going, exactly?"

"Just to town. The liquor store next to the ferry docks."

I start the engine and pull out of Cesar's long and winding driveway. I'm glad to drive. The wind is cool and pleasant on my face. Kell leans back in his seat, one arm draped out the window.

His head is angled casually against the headrest, a relaxed expression on his face.

"The farrier said his assistant was stuck back on the mainland. Sick. Pneumonia, or something. Pretty suspicious for September, huh? I think he was hung-over. Or still sloshed. That guy's got a major touch of the Irish, you know what I mean?"

"Mm."

I turn off the driveway onto the main road that circles the entire island. Kell rolls down his window all the way and leans his arm out, fanning his sore hand through the wind. He's like a large dog in the passenger seat, tipping his face out occasionally to take hits of the crisp, sun-brightened air.

"Did Anna want anything else while we're out?"

"I don't know. She didn't say."

I don't hang my elbow out the window or recline like Kell. I was trained in the army to sit upright and proper at the wheel. I can't break the habit.

Kell rubs his palm with his thumb, massaging deep into the flesh.

"So…how's your day going?"

"Okay."

"I'm so sore! I oughta be at home taking it easy. But El Capitan decided he wants to start harvesting the damned potatoes on Monday, so I gotta finish up all the stable work earlier than I

wanted. God, I hate harvest time! I get no sleep for weeks. The damned Mexicans do nothing but bitch at me and drag their feet, and Cesar always ends up nosing around at the worst possible moment, then he hollers at me for not, like, motivating them better. In front of them. In Spanish. Jerk."

I flinch instinctively at the open criticism of our boss. I've never been comfortable sharing grievances about the higher-ups.

"I mean, if ol' Cesar had told me that I have to get the stable work done early just because he wants it done, well, sure, no problem. But it sucks having to babysit those damned wetbacks. They can't stand me. I didn't used to have to do it. There used to be this guy from, like, San Diego or somewhere that did it. Then he quit, and Cesar's too cheap to hire someone else. He came at me one fine day with a Spanish phrasebook and that oh-so-jovial gleam in his eye. 'Hey, Kell! So! Gonna put you in charge of the field workers! Step up in the world, supervisory position. Great opportunity for you!' Bullshit."

Kell imitates Cesar disturbingly well. I have to bite hard on the insides of my cheeks to keep from smiling. I drive more precisely, my eyes locked on the road.

"Do you speak Spanish?" Kell inquires.

I shake my head.

"Ha—neither did I when he drafted me. That first day, Cesar taught me three phrases, then booted my ass out into the fields. I'm serious—just three. 'How's everything going?' 'Come with me,' and 'What're you people doing—get back to work!'"

Kell tallies his knowledge on his fingers, raising his eyebrow at me when a laugh escapes my mouth unbidden.

"I'm not kidding. That's all I say to those people, every damned day. '¿Cómo va todo? Venga conmigo. ¿Qué hacen ustedes? ¡Vueltan para trabajar!' Impressive, huh?"

I can't help myself. I laugh again, rubbing a hand over my forehead. I should have more self-control. Kell smiles broadly, seeming pleased that he's made me laugh.

"You better watch yourself. Cesar knows how much I hate that job. He might try to make you do it. If you ever see him coming at you with a little orange book and a big grin, run."

Kell's smirk fades as he squints into the wind.

"What I really ought to do next week, what I'd like to do, is work on Zapato. Get him to take the bridle. He's so stubborn! You gotta be consistent with 'em after you break them. Horses can tell when there are, like, loopholes to the rules. You gotta show them that you're the boss, and there's nothing they can do about it. I got him saddle broken finally, but we'll lose ground if I can't get him to accept the reins in the next few weeks. I hate harvest time! Sixteen-hour days in the hot sun with those bellyaching pendejos. Mexican torture."

I know that horse. I'm profoundly scared of him. He's the pinnacle of all that is alarming about horses.

"Mm," I say, since I don't want Kell to know.

"We got him wild—fully feral. Do you know how rare that is in this day and age? He came from off a ranch in Montana. Big ol' place, hundreds and hundreds of acres, real remote. The owner was, like, ninety years old, and he'd let his horses run free all over the ranch for the past fifteen, maybe twenty years. Zapato had never had any contact with humans before we grabbed him. I'll never get the chance to break and train a wild horse from scratch again. I wish Cesar would let me do it right! He's an amazing animal."

"Mm," I say.

"I heard about him from my cousin. He lives out in Montana; works the horses on a breeding ranch about one-hundred-fifty miles outside Helena. When the old guy died, the government started selling off all his property to pay the back taxes. It took weeks of badgering Cesar, but he finally agreed to buy one of the wilds. I drove out there by myself to get him. Great road trip—it's really gorgeous out that way. I got to spend a week helping my cousin and the other hands from the breeding ranch round up all the horses, just to get a feel for it. There must've been seventy horses—it was incredible! At the end of the week, me and my cousin nabbed Zapato and crammed him into the horse trailer before he knew what was happening to him. Poor bastard! He got massive bruising from slamming himself into the sides of the trailer all during the drive back to Washington. It was almost impossible to keep from swerving off the road with him crashing around back there in the trailer. I was totally worn out by the time I got to Seattle. The ferry trip freaked him out utterly. He almost broke his leg kicking the trailer door. I'm surprised he's not lame now."

Kell's expression is gentle and warm. It's so tender. This must be what he looks like when he's in love.

"Breaking him was one of the best things I've done. He fought hard as sin, then finally broke just like a fever: frothing and sweating and totally wrung out. He's been like a cat ever since: sometimes all sweet and timid and glad to see you; sometimes turning on you with a big swipe. He's amazing."

I shudder, then hide it quick with a phony yawn. Kell grins at me antagonistically.

"We've got to get you up on one of the horses pretty soon. Gotta teach you how to ride."

"What makes you think I don't already know how?"

Kell shakes his head and laughs. He's not fooled in the slightest. He'll torment me forever.

"You know, it would make your job a lot easier if you used the horses. I've seen you walking the farm all hours of the day—that's a lot of leg-work. The farm's too huge to go tramping around like that."

"I'm used to walking long distances."

"You'll change your mind come fall. The rain'll start and every inch of ground'll turn to sucking sludge, and you'll be miserable. It's a whole different world up on a horse's back. You're above it all. Lofty, like royalty."

I shake my head. Hard.

"I'm used to wet conditions."

Silence hangs in the air for a moment.

Kell is looking at me more intently than is polite. My skin tingles as goose bumps rise.

"I'd hate to see you get sick from all the wet. Or fed up with the whole Ortiz security guard gig. I want you to stick around for a while."

I glance at him. He hasn't lost his soft, horsey expression. I turn away and try to shake this uneasy feeling off. It's just that he's still thinking about that damned Zapato beast. He's hoping to get me to help him train it. He's trying to draft me for another job, like Cesar did to him. That's all.

"How come Mrs. Ortiz needs a whole case of wine? What's that, like a dozen bottles?"

"I'd really enjoy teaching you how to ride. It would be fun. It's been so long since I got to teach anyone. Anna was the last one. She didn't like it. Nobody rides the horses except me these days."

I stare fixedly out the windshield at the dusty brown road.

"Mrs. Ortiz seems very concerned about the party they're having this weekend. It's a big deal, right?"

"It'd be fun to have someone to go riding with. You're good company."

I'm done with subtlety. The subject must change.

"What do you know about the people coming out for the weekend? Who are they? Where do they work? How long have they been doing deals with Cesar? I'd appreciate it if you could clue me in a little."

Kell mercifully rolls his sun-spattered face away from me.

"Cesar didn't tell you?"

"I'm just wondering what you know."

Kell laughs.

"Oh, God, you're so careful, Flynn! Dry as the Sahara Desert! You were in the Marines, right?"

"Army."

"Same thing. Come on, don't be like that—we're on the same side, right? Us against Cesar Augustus. It's been a long time since he hired anyone new. What do you think of him? You've been here about a month and a half now. What's your opinion of the Ortiz family so far?"

Maybe I misread Kell. Maybe he was just trying to be friendly; trying to be a good coworker and make me feel at home on the farm.

"Why do you ask?"

Kell grins.

"Just curious! Okay, okay, I'll throw you a bone. Cesar

wants to buy this old steel recycling plant in West Seattle that's been shut down for environmental pollution or whatever. So he'll

have to bring it up to code first, which really means he'll do absolutely nothing to it—just drop some dollars into a few key pockets. He's having some investors that he's scrounged up come out here so he can convince them that this turkey can fly. He's done this kind of thing about a hundred times since I've been working here. He always manages to pull it off. Bulletproof son of a bitch."

I feel that I owe Kell now. Camaraderie has been established. But I'm not sure that I can trust him. "I like Cesar fine. He's a good boss. Mrs. Ortiz…she's nice."

"I've been working for them for years. I've got my own opinion. But I'm glad you're liking them so far. It's important."

I drive in silence for a mile. Kell grows stiffer and stiffer in his seat. He seems to be struggling with something.

"However," he finally blurts out, "Antonio…Antonio is another story. I hate that prick! You know what? One time, like a year ago, that miserable motherfucker threatened to sue me for scratching his car! His goddamned car! And I hadn't even touched it. Asshole."

"The Aston Martin?"

Kell snorts.

"No, he just bought that James Bond piece of crap. Naw, it was some kinda, like a—a Ferrari, I think. He buys a new car every six months. I'm not kidding. He always trades up. He's gonna show up here in a Lear Jet one of these days."

"Is he married?"

Kell shakes his head.

"Never been. He dates extensively and well. Nothing but rich, socially mobile women. Corporate lawyers at competing firms. Lady violinists in the symphony. Some Russian dancer for a little while. Antonio is a three date wonder. No women gets beyond the third date with him. Ever."

"But, he…"

"Well, of course he fucks them! He's the kind of guy that

wouldn't even bother to take his clothes off. Just unzips it and goes for it, I'll bet. How did he think I'd take it, hearing he was gonna sue me? He's a goddamned trial lawyer—was I supposed to think he was just kidding? That bastard freaked me out for three goddamned months, till I totally lost it and told Cesar. He made Antonio quit hassling me. Cesar was really pissed at him. I could see it. That was the only thing that kept me from quitting."

I turn onto Main Street. The town is tiny; barely a dozen businesses and trailer homes, all of which seem to rush downhill toward the ferry dock and the hope of escape from the island.

"Well, Mrs. Ortiz seems to hate him, too," I comment as I pull the Jeep into the parking lot of the liquor store.

I feel Kell's eyes on my face, searching and incredulous. He shakes his head, opens his door, and jumps out.

I trail Kell into the liquor store. The shelves overflow with an abundance of hard liquor in big, sun-glinting bottles: whiskey, gin, cheap scotch. The clerk finds the cardboard case shipped from Seattle easily and charges it to the Ortiz account. My throat closes when I hear that the wine costs thirteen-hundred dollars with tax. Kell hefts the box onto his shoulder and carries it nonchalantly out to the Jeep.

We get in and I start the motor.

"Hey, drive to that little park over there."

Kell points at the quaint, weathered cottage that houses the island's only school. Beyond it, at the edge of the bay, is a handkerchief park with a single picnic bench. I stop the Jeep by the water. Kell hops out and walks to the back. He pops the trunk, tears the packing tape off the box, and pulls out a bottle of wine.

"What…"

To my horror, he whips out a pocketknife and begins to peel away the neck wrapper.

He digs the knife's corkscrew attachment into the cork, strains, and yanks it out. He twists the cork off the corkscrew and throws it at the water. It lands a good way out with a little splash. Kell climbs onto the picnic table and sits atop it, his feet resting on the bench. He gazes out over the shimmering water and takes a long drink from the bottle.

"Relax, I've been doing this for years. They don't notice, or they don't care. Try it: ninety-five bucks a bottle, all the way from Australia. It's not bad."

I resist. This is like the transgressions that my fellow grunts would try to entice me into when I was in the army. They were forever drinking a little forbidden rum in the mess hall after dark; wandering off during midnight guard duty to peep at our Drill Sergeant lounging on a bunk, unscarily reading a gardening magazine.

I was always the straight arrow. I always refused. At first, for fear of being caught and drummed out of the army. I'd had enough trouble making it so far, given my natural physical specifics. Then later, the thought of my CO learning that I wasn't just misbehaving with him always brought a burn of shame to my face.

But now, I have nothing to lose.

Just this job.

If I don't drink with Kell, he'll probably tell Cesar that I did, if he's ever caught. It'll be his word against mine, and he's been with the family a lot longer than I have. They trust him. The bottle's already open. It's already too late.

I might as well.

I climb onto the table and sit next to Kell. He passes me the bottle, feeling around his shirt with the characteristic gesture of a man searching for smokes. He finds none. He leans back on his hands and gazes out over the water. I tip the bottle for a tentative sip. It's tangy. It puckers me. I pass the bottle back to Kell.

"It's beautiful, huh?"

Kell has dreaming eyes and a Buddha smile as he swallows the ninety-five dollar wine. I haven't spent much time with Native Americans. Kell looks remote and exotic. He's very handsome. He makes me nervous when he looks at me.

"Hey, Flynn. What you said about Anna and

Antonio…were you serious? Or kidding? I can't tell with you yet. We don't know each other well enough."

I look out over the sparkling water and reach blindly for the bottle. I feel Kell put it in my hand. I drink, to give myself time.

"I was serious. Mrs. Ortiz…Anna said that he makes her very mad sometimes."

I don't mention what Cesar said about them. I don't yet know how far I'm willing to go with Kell.

Kell turns to me, and again I feel that grip of unease as his dark eyes slide softly over mine.

"Just watch them. When they're together. You'll see it."

"See what?"

Kell's smile morphs into something specific and significant. I've seen this smile before on other people's faces. People in bars, buying drinks for each other. People thinking about things to do together, with their bodies, once the drinks are gone and the bar closes. Only one other person has ever directed such a smile at me.

"You're supposed to be the super-star security officer. Watch them. Then we'll talk."

I sit silent next to Kell, my mouth anesthetized and burning slightly from the wine. The sunshine is warm and generous on our faces. Kell swings his worn vaquero boots from side to side, the sunlight reflecting off the shiny leather in blunt patches of gold.

"Anna's a very strange person. I don't know if you've picked up on that yet. Cesar's got himself a thin sadistic streak like all the rich people I've run into—all the ones that made it in a cutthroat business on their own steam. Antonio's his own unique version of a heartless lawyer asshole. But Anna…"

Kell bites the inside of his cheek, toys with the half-empty bottle, then takes a drink. I don't think he'll say any more. He sets the bottle between us. It thunks nearly hollow on the wind-worn wood.

"Anna, though…she's bizarre," he says slowly. "I've met some odd people in my days, but I've never known anyone as…as *off* as she is. She's beyond the pale."

He hesitates.

"I mean, I'm sure Cesar told you already, right? What to be careful of with her. Know what I'm talking about?"

I shake my head.

Kell fingers the open mouth of the wine bottle. He shouldn't tell me; not if our boss hasn't entrusted me yet.

"You know that she doesn't deal well with being alone at night if Cesar's not home, right?"

I nod.

"Do you know what happens if she's alone for too long?"

"No."

"She…well….she's very unstable. Let's just say, she can't be trusted with sharp objects if Cesar's not home."

Kell straightens abruptly and grabs the bottle.

"I'm not gonna get into it. Cesar'll tell you when he thinks you're ready. He'll turn the job over to you pretty soon—keeping an eye on her at night when he's away, I mean. Cesar drafted me when the last security officer left. Maybe you'll do better than me; she seems to like you. I hate doing it. You have to spend hours trying to calm her down, struggling with her. You have to hear her tell you the same horrible story…horrible…"

Kell closes his eyes.

"You'll never, ever get it out of your head. You'll have nightmares for the rest of your life. She was so much worse before, when Cesar first moved her out here. She couldn't stand to leave the island, the farm, the house, even. But lately—"

Kell opens his eyes and shuts up so resolutely that I hear his teeth click together.

"I don't know what you mean," I begin, then I close my mouth, closing off my thoughts from Kell. I need to think for a while. I must ponder the evidence, sort the subjective from the verifiable facts.

Quiet stretches between us.

Kell drinks, then I do, then the bottle is empty. He lets out a slow, deep sigh. The sun spangles the water with a million sparks, and it gets to feeling peaceful here on the picnic bench. It's so serene, sitting and watching the broad, gleaming slat of water and the diving birds. Kell picks the bottle up by the neck and lobs it out into the water. He leans close to me, swinging his boots in to angle toward mine. He smiles his new, too-warm smile, his eyes very full on my face. I'm uncomfortable, but I don't dare scoot away from him. It would be rude.

"Do you like live music? Rock?"

"I don't know."

"My cousin's band is playing Sunday night. At the bar up north. Wanna go with me? They need all the support they can get."

"Um."

"Come on, it'll be fun. They really suck, but the beer's cheap. And it would be nice to get to know each other, away from work. Don't you think?"

I reply, "Uh," and Kell takes this for agreement, and his smile becomes radiant.

Somewhere back, when I wasn't paying attention, a line was crossed. I don't know how it happened, and I don't like it. But I don't have the least idea what to do about it.

Saturday, September 19, 1998
8:08 p.m.
Ortiz Farm

"Oh, no, no!"

Cesar laughs, pouring a bottle of wine with odd, oriental writing on the label.

"It's been years since I contributed to the symphony. Not for lack of appreciation, certainly. Anna's just sidetracked me into more socially responsible causes. I'll blame her."

The four wealthy men seated around Cesar's elegant dining table laugh on cue. The lighting in here is soothingly dim, like at an intimate restaurant. The stained-glass chandelier traces delicate filigree patterns over our plates and hands. Cesar passes a crockery-style cup filled with wine to the corpulent man on his left. I eye mine, striving to imitate the calm, neutral expression that Anna is wearing.

"It's a rather obscure rice wine from Thailand. Cesar and I discovered it when we were briefly obsessed with Thai food."

Anna speaks to the entire table, but I know this comment is for my benefit. I appreciate it.

The gray-haired man seated on my right smiles at Cesar, lifting his cup of rice wine. I'm afraid to taste mine. I'll watch the reactions of the other diners before I touch it.

"So, you don't find supporting the arts to be socially responsible?"

The rich men groan appreciatively at the jab. The man makes a toasting gesture at Cesar and sips his wine. He's the nearly elderly businessman we met in Seattle. He looks grandfatherly and twinkly-eyed in this pleasant light, but he radiates implacability.

Cesar laughs and raises both hands, palms out.

"Okay, okay, you got me on that one. Maybe I've just become lazy, or…all right, fine, I'll admit it—I never liked the symphony! I'm a jazz man. Sue me!"

Everyone laughs, and so do I, tentatively. The men seem to be enjoying their wine. I tap my fingers against my cup, then quickly raise it and sip. It tastes like soy sauce mixed with mineral water.

I clench my throat and force a hard swallow. I put the cup down, all the muscles in my face straining to maintain a blank countenance. I have to continually monitor myself during this meal. The warm light from the chandelier draws all focus to the faces and hands around the dining room. Every minute gesture, every flickering expression is easily noticed by all. I'm supposed to be a statue of dignity and veiled menace. It'll be so hard to pull off if I gag on something.

"Of course, I'll always retain a nostalgic fondness for the symphony. Anna and I met at one of their donor events, back…oh, God, how long ago? Years and years and years!"

Anna is mock-horrified.

"Please, Cesar! I'm not aging that rapidly, I hope."

The guests laugh, mirror images of each other with their dark business suits on both sides of the table.

Anna raises her hand and indicates our plates.

"Please, everyone, let me know what you think. It's a selection of sashimi and carpaccio. The salad is one of Cesar's favorites. The baby spinach and miniature squash are from the farm."

"Grew 'em my own damned self," Cesar quips.

"The goat cheese and olive oil are imported from Greece. Don't let Cesar take credit—he's never been to Greece."

"Never milked a goat, either. I swear."

As one, the four rich men hoist gleaming forks. They seem to know what they're being served. They seem impressed. The finger-sized slices of fish have a suspiciously raw look to them, as does the lunch-meat-looking circle of beef. I won't eat any of it. I will watch the rich men with an inscrutable face. That will please Cesar.

On my left, at the head of the table, Anna plies her fork like an actress manipulating a complex prop. At the other end of the table Cesar, too, is dexterous with his cutlery. I could never be rich. I can't eat elegantly.

"Now, I don't want to give the impression that the Ortiz family's a bunch of uncultured boors. Antonio here's a season ticket holder and board member of the symphony and the ballet. Isn't that right?"

Antonio's black-within-black eyes glide slowly around the table, skewering each face in turn.

"Guilty," he pronounces, producing menace rather than lighthearted jocularity.

As I watch Antonio precisely stab the raw fish, I'm struck with the absolute certainty that Cesar would have done better to designate him the hired gun at this dinner. He sits at Anna's left, directly across from me, chilling the air around him like an ice carving. I can't pull off such a subtle sense of threat. I look like a cheap army grunt, even in my borrowed sweater and slacks.

"Ah...yes, I think I remember seeing you at the symphony. Donor's lounge, opening night of Mahler's Fifth. You were with a...well, an oh-my-God beautiful lady. Tall, blond. Like a model. Anyone special?" Inquires the old man.

Antonio's mouth quirks up at one corner.

"That was Natasha."

"Wife? Girlfriend?" The man next to Antonio pipes up, his head as bald and shiny as an Easter ham.

Antonio continues to half-smile at the men.

"A very charming and fascinating ballerina. Principal dancer. We'd met at a fundraiser for the ballet a month earlier."

Anna glances at the guests' plates.

"Shall we have the fish course? Is everyone ready?"

"Wow. Lucky man," the bald man shakes his head, grinning broadly.

"I'll introduce you, if you like. I'm no longer escorting her."

The man grins and holds up his left hand, pointing at his wedding ring.

Antonio raises his eyebrow.

"Christ, John, she's a dancer! They don't talk."

Everyone breaks into loud laughter, especially this John.

Everyone, except Anna.

She glares darkly at Antonio, her face displaying unfiltered disgust. Kell was wrong about her. She can't hide her distaste for her brother-in-law at all. She really does hate him.

Her hands squeeze her napkin a little too hard as she adjusts it in her lap. Cesar sees and hastens to rise slightly.

"I think we're ready to move on, aren't we? You're all going to love this fish. It's absolutely amazing. It's local—it passes the island every year on its way to spawn. And the sauce...Anna discovered the most incredible caterer a few years ago, and we've been using her for everything since. If I can ever convince her to move out here to the sticks, I'll have her as our

private chef at any cost."

The fish is laid out on each plate. Cesar obtains clean, classic glasses and a new bottle of pale wine. The label is in English this time, to my relief.

Anna studiously does not look at Antonio.

Cesar clears his throat.

"The wine is local, too. Now, before any of you drink, please let me deeply and sincerely apologize for it."

Anna rolls her eyes elaborately. Her smile is indulgent.

"Cesar detests sweet wines. I adore them. This is a very dry mead. It's brewed at a winery on one of the islands just offshore from Seattle. It pairs extremely well with the fish. Though certain people will tell you otherwise. Deeply and sincerely."

Everyone chuckles. It's obvious that this wine bit is a routine Cesar and Anna have done many times, for many visitors. It's well-rehearsed and crowd-pleasing. It opens the door for conversation. Cesar pours the wine and raises his glass.

"To the future. And unsweet wines."

Smiles flash, glasses clink, Anna leans over and whispers in my ear, "It's a honey wine. It's not as weird as the rice wine."

I take a chance and taste it. It's easy on the mouth, like wine cooler. I can handle it. Maybe the fish will be all right as well. I glance at the many forks, pick one at random, and begin to eat.

The bald man leans over his food, arching his face up from his plate with the air of someone trying to be coy.

"So, tell me, Cesar. How's the market been treating you these days?"

Cesar keeps his eyes on his fish.

"How's it been treating you, John?"

The bald man glances at the man next to him.

"Okay: the curiosity has been eating me up for weeks. Why steel?"

"My God, what a direct question!"

Cesar gazes across the table with a forced smile. He doesn't direct it at the bald man or at Antonio as I expect him to, but at me.

"Well, we've all been wondering why, after all these years, you're choosing to diversify so far from your…usual areas of interest. Anything going wrong in the ol' portfolio?"

Cesar peers down the table at the bald man. His eyes have become light-swallowing black holes, like Antonio's.

"How are you liking that fish?"

The man's gaze rides Cesar's.

"It's outstanding."

Cesar lets out a tight laugh.

"And I thought I could distract you with an impressive dinner! Let's save this for afterward, shall we?"

"What do you think of the wine? Think very carefully before you answer," Anna interjects with a crafty, Cheshire Cat smile.

The bald man chuckles, then shakes his head.

"All right, all right. If Cesar can plead the Fifth, I think I'm going to, as well. So, Antonio, how do you like *Coppelia* this year? What do you think about Darcie Duncan in the lead? Think she can handle Swanilda?"

Antonio takes a sip of wine. His eyes land briefly on mine. Not inclusively, as Cesar's did; cautiously, watchfully.

"I think she can handle it. She's been dancing with the

company for a few years now."

"Yes, but she's only nineteen."

Antonio shrugs.

"She's a grown-up. Legal."

The men glance at him, then a backroom masculine snicker circles the table. I let my eyes slide over to Anna. She is very focused on her plate. Her body curves subtly away from her brother-in-law. Toward me.

Cesar raises his glass to Antonio.

"Life of the Seattle power broker, right? Must be hard. But, the thing I worry about, is Antonio's lack of—no, not lack of experience! Lack of real estate. The man's got no property. Renting is for idiots."

Sounds of assent come from half the men at the table. The others appear pricked.

"Now, not when it's for business."

"True. Property taxes'll eat you alive everywhere except in the boondocks."

"Well, obviously—most of the time. But I'm talking about your residence. Your castle. Gotta have a place all your own. It's the American way," Cesar takes a bite of fish and nods in a matter-settling manner.

Antonio swirls his wine glass, making a whirlpool of the pale wine.

"If I wanted to put down roots, I would."

The pudgy man cocks his head at Antonio.

"Bachelor life's treating you too well, my man."

"I just don't like changing the locks every time I forget to ask for my keys back. When I can't remember which women besides the maid can get in, I'll move. It's the American way."

"God, Cesar—did I tell you? Nina caught our maid stealing from us last month," the bald man drums an indignant finger on the tabletop.

"Money?"

He nods.

"Can you believe it? She dug through the closet, found one of my jackets with a money clip in it, and pocketed it."

"Sign of the times. Can't get anything but El Salvadorians and Jamaicans these days."

"Ah, for the days of the French maid."

The rich men smile at this, their eyes going unfocused. I take the opportunity to eat. The fish is very good. Anna was right: It goes very well with the wine. I decide to tell her so, very quietly. But before I can finish my drink and figure out an inconspicuous way to lean toward her, everything gets cast askew.

I happen to look over at Antonio. I try never to do so, since he scares the hell out of me, and I don't want him ever to realize it, or he'll be able to do me like he did Kell. But as I lower my wine glass, my gaze easing over the rim, I see his eyes cut to Anna. Unmistakable tenderness thaws the frost that clots his pupils. He seems to be straining himself out from behind the prison of his eyes, like a man struggling to see through blurred glass. Anna's neck tenses slightly, and she raises her face. Her gaze connects with his. Her scowl fades. A delicate look of awareness washes her face, then she carefully lowers her eyes to her plate.

That's all. It's something infinitely easy to miss. It's careful; something that no one at the table would have noticed. However, I have been watching for just such a thing. I'm going to have to reassess my initial analysis of their relationship.

When everyone finishes eating, Cesar tosses his cloth napkin onto his plate and lets out a heavy sigh.

"Well, was I right? Did you all enjoy it?"

"God, yes. Everything was excellent, Cesar."

"What did you say the name of that caterer is?"

"Oh, no, no, no, you don't! You'll steal her away from us. Promise her a professional-grade kitchen, dinners for the mayor and city counselors—she'll swoon. Don't tell him, Anna."

Anna smiles at Cesar and presses her finger to her lips.

"Trade secret."

He winks at her. He rises, glancing expectantly around the table at each face bleached pasty by decades beneath the corporate sun of computer glow.

"Well! Port and cognac?"

"And tokay," Anna adds.

"Oh, Jesus! Tell her no, if you don't like that sweet stuff. Don't humor her."

Cesar holds out his hand toward the door.

"Shall we? The living room's amazing—you've got to check it out. Most of you haven't had the grand tour yet."

We all rise and follow Cesar into the living room. I keep my eyes pasted on Anna, hoping to discover something more, but she is latched onto Cesar's arm, her back to me. Antonio waits until everyone, including me, has risen, then he trails us out of the dining room. I can feel his eyes freezing my skin on the back of my neck. Ahead of me, breath catches in lungs and footsteps slow on the plush carpet.

"Holy—"

"My God, Cesar!"

Softly, the men approach the massive wall of floor-to-ceiling windows. The stars have come out, spattering the deep blue waves with cracked silver. They stand, all four of them men of great wealth and experience, and gaze silently at the ocean.

Cesar hovers at the terminus of the windows, his arm around Anna's waist. He looks proud. He whispers something in his wife's ear, then steps away to the ornate liquor cabinet.

"Okay, we've got twenty-year-old port, we've got scotch, a very nice cognac—Anna doesn't know about that one. All right, all right, and tokay. Ugh. What's your damage?"

Cesar plays bartender, pouring rapidly and accurately into an array of creatively-shaped glasses. He and Antonio hand them around. I take a glass of the tokay. If Anna likes it, it's probably drinkable. I sit in the remotest chair, then move in closer when

Cesar subtly beckons to me. Anna settles into the soft, peach-colored chair that I've seen her reading in so many evenings. The guests sit on the couches. I realize that we have formed a circle. It's superficially not us-against-them, but it very much feels that way. Cesar doesn't sit. He stands, vigorously swirling his glass of cognac and pacing before the windows. He gives the impression not of nervousness, but of being goaded by such enthusiasm that he can't sit still.

"I'm telling you, there's nothing like fresh king salmon. If you liked that fish tonight, you'd die for the king. Fred, you fish, right?"

"Only for compliments."

"That settles it, then. I'm taking all of you out tomorrow morning on my yacht. We'll catch a bunch of salmon. Fry 'em up on the beach right down there. I've got a great fire pit. Italian tile, gas powered, plenty of tables and chairs. You've never lived until you eat freshly caught wild salmon. It's impossibly delicious with nothing but a little bit of lemon and a dusting of dill. Fantastic stuff!"

"Sounds good, but exactly how early will this little fishing trip be launching?"

"Oh, nine, ten. I'm not an early bird, believe me."

A silence, filled with palpable thought, descends over the living room. Cesar's pacing increases. He takes a deep drink of his cognac. The dark ocean surges behind him. Anna cradles the fragile glass of tokay in her hands as if it were an eggshell, placid and half-smiling, the perfect rich wife. I can't guess what's in her mind. Antonio is a deadly razor in his chair across from mine. Creases like a paper folds run down his trousers; his tie gleams like molded brass. His hands are templed at his chin, the fingers pressing together so hard that his nails are the color of sleet.

"So, is fishing a big industry here on the island?" the bald man inquires, ever-so-casually.

"No, not an industry. There are a few local pros. They make a little money off the salmon during the fall run. There isn't any industry on the island in general."

"No steel?" The elderly man seated next to the bald man inquires, taking his cue. Cesar pauses by a painting that looks like an accident of color. A crucial mark has been hit; the one everyone has been waiting for.

"No, Bailey. Nope."

The man leans forward, rolling his glass of cognac back and forth between arthritic hands to warm it.

"In that case, let me ask you something we four have been asking each other since we became involved with this deal: Why in hell did you decide, out of the blue, to get into steel recycling?"

"Good question, Bailey. Very good."

Cesar jabs his glass at the old man. He lets out a tight chuckle. I can tell he's forging a credible façade. I can tell he will lie.

"Have you seen my holdings lately? The real estate in the south end of Seattle?"

"Cesar. You know we've checked that out. Let's not play."

"Well, I've had massive demolitions in the last year and a half. All old stuff. Turn of the century buildings. Steel girders up the ass. I finally figured, why lose money disposing of them? I own them, so why not recycle them and sell the steel on? Recycle—socially responsible, right?"

The bald man shakes his head.

"Cesar, that's utter bullshit. You've got barely three-hundred tons of steel, at most. At most. After it's gone, where are you going to obtain more? The costs of acquiring and bringing Andresan Steel back up to code would bankrupt you. You couldn't even cover the cost of cosmetic landscaping with your old steel."

"Have you looked into my brother's financial statements, John?"

Antonio's voice is flinty. I wince. The bald man does not.

"That would be illegal, Antonio. You know that."

His voice is solid and without chinks, like Antonio's.

"Let's not get into all that shit. I put up half, you people put up the other half. Profits go fifty-one, forty-nine. Holdings the same. The offer hasn't changed since I put it forth to you all seven months ago. What I want to know is, what's the problem?"

"Cesar, it's not that we think you're not good for the initial investment—" the obese man begins.

"Oh, thank you very much. So much. In my own house."

"But we're still unclear about this profit sharing plan of yours. If the place tanks, then we're left holding the bag—"

"Not true! Jesus, how many times have I laid this out to you people? If—"

"What we are proposing here is a clean investment and profit share structure. If the concern fails, you recoup your losses; either through the profits made during the start-up, the sale of the business, or through insurance."

Antonio's eyes are diamond-tipped drills. They puncture each man clean through. In the silence that his gaze brings, the anemic blond man, who hasn't said a word all evening, turns eyes like Norwegian lakes on me. They are so like my CO's eyes.

"So...Flynn, is it? What's your role in this? Cesar mentioned you've been hired as a security consultant, is that right? What exactly is your role in this deal?"

Everyone turns to me expectantly. I grow numb and faint.

I open my mouth, and automatically, I hear myself reply, "That's classified."

Oh, God, I've made a mistake! But it was uncontrollable.

A flashback to my army days.

The faces of the rich men register surprise. They glance at each other uneasily.

"Okay. Well. In any event, you've hired in a security consultant on this deal, which is something you've never done with any of us before—am I right?"

The other men agree.

Cesar sips his cognac, soaking up their accusing stares.

"That's true. Wonder why?"

The bald man fingers his glass, pressing his lips together so tightly that I can see the outline of his teeth through the pink flesh.

"Will you tell us if we ask?"

Cesar glances elaborately at Antonio, then smiles.

"Hell no. That's my business. But, let's just say...maybe I

don't trust you people. Maybe I'm starting to think you're trying to screw me. Maybe I decided that I need to gather a little private information about what's going on at your end of the table."

The men recoil visibly. I glance at Antonio and see him shake his head very slightly at Cesar, just like at the café before Cesar and I took our unpleasant trip into South Seattle.

"Cesar. Be very careful here," the plump man's voice is ragged at the edges.

"Makes you feel a little paranoid, huh? Well, taste it. It's how I've been feeling lately. Not one of you has ever tried to stall me when we had a one-on-one deal going. Now that you've got a group thing, you're acting like the goddamned Gang of Four. I don't feel like playing your game by your rules anymore."

"We don't play games with the amount of money you're asking us to put up. Now, that business plan that Antonio prepared was tight, but it just doesn't quite add up. Fiscally. Long-term. Understand?"

"There are too many market variables at work here, Cesar. You've got to understand our position. If you fail, then we're—excuse me, Mrs. Ortiz. But we're fucked. Royally."

Anna's lips spread into a drowsy smile. She eases herself gracefully to her feet, smoothing her skirt with both hands.

"No offense taken. I think, however, that's my cue to

head off to bed. Thank you all very much for dining with us.

Don't stand—good night."

She crosses the room to Cesar and kisses him on the lips very lightly. Her gaze does not alight on Antonio for even the briefest instant as she moves out of the room. Cesar watches his wife go. He takes a final sip of his cognac, draining the glass. He sets the glass down too hard on a nearby end table. The thunk is resonant, like a judge's gavel.

"Well, Fred, that's an interesting way to look at it. I, however, see the situation much differently. I see myself utterly ruined if this venture fails, so if you really think I won't give it my all—"

"My brother is speaking figuratively. In terms of professional reputation; not in terms of finances. His assets are extremely well protected. Even if Andresan Steel failed eight times over, his holdings would barely be diminished. We have excellent shelters."

Antonio has never cut Cesar off in such a contradictory way. Not that I've ever seen. Cesar draws himself up short.

"Yes, yes, that's true. True, Antonio. I apologize, gentlemen: I get overly enthusiastic and speak from a position of emotion. But the point is, I'm not going into this as a hobby investor. I have more experience in industrial ventures than you may realize. Reread Antonio's business plan. Please. And…perhaps it's getting a bit late. Let's get some quality sack time, okay? Unwind a little with some yachting, some fishing tomorrow morning. I think we'll all be a little looser afterward."

Antonio rises, audibly snapping his jacket lapels straight.

"I'll show you gentlemen to your rooms."

The businessmen rise as well and bid Cesar good night. With the lurking posture of a murderous butler, Antonio guides them out of the living room.

Cesar grabs his empty glass and walks to the liquor cabinet. He reaches inside for the decanter of cognac. His shoulders sag momentarily. He wants to mutter "cocksuckers." I can smell it on him

He turns his head hard over his shoulder and locks eyes with me.

"Flynn."

He crosses the room and grasps my shoulders. He squeezes down hard, like a pleased coach. A huge grin blooms bright on his face.

"Classified! Brilliant! Absolute goddamned genius!"

Sunday, September 20, 1998
10:34 a.m.
The Pacific Ocean

Cesar stands motionless at the outermost edge of his yacht's bow. The morning sun spills lemon brilliance over his graying hair and the shell-white deck. An all-pervading freshness, and the odor of primordial salt, saturates the air. Cesar's casual boating clothes snap and ripple in the breeze, as he smiles calmly into the sun. His face is like a saint's in the stained-glass window of a church. Cesar watches the far horizon bob up and down in a perfect blue line that threads out infinitely far. We've been out of sight of land for far too long. We're completely isolated in this

unreachable patch of the Pacific.

Across the deck, safe within the little pilothouse, Antonio stands fixed at the wheel. His clothes, like Cesar's, are casual, though I find them barely less formal than his usual dark and dangerous litigator suits. Charcoal trousers, black deck shoes, a very pricey looking golf shirt. His forearms are bare and heavily coated with black hair and gym toned muscle. I can picture him at an exclusive sportsman's club in downtown Seattle, doing the circuit with some complicated, spidery machine. In the army, we had free-weights.

His expression is watchful and cautious. His eyes are wired to Cesar. I've seen his eyes like this when they were directed at me. I've never seen him look at Cesar this way.

I stand between Antonio and Cesar in the middle of the deck. The high wind buffets me. I have no idea where the land lies. I can't see anything beyond the vast, blue wetness that swells

and dips on all sides. This isn't like riding the ferry. This is sea-level and pitchy and alarming. Waves reach up to snatch at the deck, wetting my shoes. My hands are crammed in my jacket pockets. I'm desperately trying to keep my balance without holding onto anything. I must not let anyone know the struggle I'm having. I must stand stoic and immobile.

Cesar inhales deeply, then lets out a luxurious sigh.

"Smell that! Absolute salt purity! The smell of oblivion. Just look at all this emptiness! It's good to get away from civilization sometimes, isn't it?"

The rich men line both sides of the yacht; two on the left, two on the right. They, like Antonio, gaze hypersenstively at Cesar. Their fingers are knit into the navy-blue cushions on which they sit. Their faces ineffectually hide their fear.

"Antonio, as much work as you and I have put into this deal in the past months, isn't it good to get back to basic, primal things?"

"Yes."

Antonio's low voice makes the businessmen flinch. Their eyes never leave Cesar, however. Antonio may be manning the wheel, but Cesar is the one controlling this boat. Their anxiety is palpably mounting.

"See, there are so many ways to get a deal moving, and we've tried just about all of them, haven't we?"

Cesar's face remains ecstatically tranquil, pointing toward the sun and the undulating sea.

"At a certain point, one wonders…is this deal really worth it? It is to me. Even with all the work I've had to put in. Needless fucking work."

Cesar inhales deeply again. He doesn't look back at his guests.

"Did you ever hear what Johnny Brewster used to do when deals weren't getting cut in a reasonable amount of time? You know about him, Fred, don't you? He was a union representative, like you. Teamsters, I think. When he found that feet were being dragged needlessly during a negotiation, he would take those unwilling to deal out to his cabin for a hunting trip. Very rugged place, with lots of trophies on the walls. Elk heads, bear skins everywhere. He'd give everyone shotguns, but guess what he did first? He unloaded all of the shotguns when no one was looking, except his own. They'd all head out into the woods, and he'd take them into a clearing. Then he would fire a shot right over their heads. That ballbuster! Shake those city folks up. 'It's just us you've got to deal with now: me and a double-barrel shotgun.' That sure helped get negotiations going, you better believe it."

Cesar turns his head ever-so-slightly to look over his shoulder at the businessmen.

"I'm starting to think I need a shotgun. Metaphorically speaking, of course."

I want to glance back at Antonio, to see if he's as scared as I am. I've never felt afraid of Cesar before.

"Because, if you continue to fuck with me…oh well, let's not talk about it. You know, sometimes I worry about this boat. The ballast is absolute awful. I worry about someone going overboard. I ought to get around to buying life jackets someday. Don't you think?"

The boat pitches very gently. I clench my abdominal muscles and my quads to avoid being thrown to the deck. The men let out audible gasps, their fingers grasping for purchase.

"All right, Cesar. You win, we'll sign. All right?
Cesar?"

Cesar smiles into the sun.

Sunday, September 20, 1998
9:17 p.m.
Indian Mary Bar

I feel vulnerable, because I'm not driving. Kell sits confident and relaxed behind the wheel of the Jeep. He insisted; he thinks I will get us lost. Kell lacks faith in my navigational abilities.

"They're kind of a heavy metal band, I guess. Or grunge. I can't really tell. My cousin always spews this impossible to follow spiel about AC/DC and Dio and Nirvana whenever anyone asks. They're pretty good, though. My cousin's a great drummer."

"How far is it?"

"Oh, about another eight miles. It's up by the reservation."

I want to ask Kell if he lives on the Indian reservation. He doesn't live at Ortiz Farm like I do. Would it sound racist if I ask?

I sit quiet for a moment, letting the subject fall. Then, causally, I inquire, "Where do you live?"

Kell grins at me.

"On the reservation."

My train of thought must have ridden visibly right across my face. I hope I haven't been offensive.

"Ah."

"Most of my family's there. All my uncles, all my cousins. Except my mom. She's in California."

"Ah."

I look out the window, feeling awkward as silence eases in and takes a seat between us. It's perfectly black out. It's been miles since light from the windows of a house last spilled in a tawny patchwork across the road. Tall pines loom and whoosh invisibly above the Jeep. The wind sings through the undercarriage.

Kell glances at me and I feel a change in the air.

"So…how about you? Where's your family?"

"Ohio."

"All of them?"

"Uh-huh."

"How did you end up in Washington?"

Kell is prying. He's fishing for something.

"Army."

"Mm."

Kell drives in silence for a few minutes, but I can tell that he's not done. He's tying threads between us; seeking to make connections where none exist.

"Did you like the army?"

"Yes."

"Really? Wasn't it hard for you?"

He's referring to my build. It's a valid question.

"Only at first. After a while, you get fit, get good at stuff, and people start respecting you."

"Yeah?"

"Yes. Once I made it on my company's sniper competition team, things were fine. You get automatic respect if you can make it there. We—they compete against the Marines and the FBI every spring."

"Wow. Sniper, huh?"

Kell smiles at me for a bit too long.

"What did you do in the army? Like, what was your area or whatever?"

"Intelligence."

"What, you mean spying, or something?"

I don't answer. I smile vaguely.

"Very cool! Did you get files that actually said 'Top Secret' on them? Special pens that shoot bullets?"

"That's classified," I reply, since it worked last night.

Kell raises his eyebrows, then he laughs.

"So…did you leave anyone behind in Ohio? Other than family?"

"High school friends. I enlisted when I was eighteen."

"How about in the army? Did you leave anyone there?"

Kell is trying to discover something specific about me.

I'm growing uncomfortable.

"Did I leave behind friends, you mean?"

I could swear Kell has begun to blush, though it's hard to tell, what with his dark skin and the dimness of the car.

"No, not friends. You know. Anyone…special?"

I feel my own face grow hot. I wish he hadn't asked me this. It makes it harder to pretend that he only feels a coworker's

impersonal goodwill toward me.

"Anyone special?"

I speak slowly. My voice sounds metallic and unnatural.

I'm trying to stall.

"Yeah."

Now Kell's tone is deliberately neutral. I can tell that he's afraid I'll say yes; say that I'm spoken for. I wish he would stop thinking of me in this discomfiting way. I've never sought closeness with him.

"I. Someone. Yes. I was—there was one person."

"Oh yeah?"

Kell audibly forces an even voice. He drives with a tight spine and rigid, chauffeur arms. He is dancing with disappointment.

"Who?"

It's none of his business. I don't have to tell him.

"My…my CO. Commanding Officer. We became close."

"Really? Close friends, you mean?"

"No."

"I get it."

Kell maneuvers the Jeep through the thick darkness in silence, watching the black windshield too intently. Two minutes pass. We both breathe carefully. I wish the radio was on; just some jabbering noise I could pretend that we're listening to. I can't reach for the knob. It would bring more awkwardness; it would call attention to our painful silence. Three minutes pass.

Finally, Kell coughs.

"So. You ever see your CO now?"

"No. Never."

"Never?"

I shake my head.

"That's hard."

Kell's voice has a bright, unmistakable note of optimism in it now. His body relaxes, melding into the worn curve of the upholstery. He turns to me and smiles. He casts his eyes like dark nets, trying to draw me in.

"We're almost there. This is gonna be fun. The bartender knows me; maybe we can scam some free beer."

After several more miles of dark travel, Kell pulls us into the gravel parking lot of a very shoddy, shack-shaped bar at the northern end of the island. The poor end of the island. I've never been this far north. We're miles from Cesar's green, velvety fields and soaring house of clean glass and polished wood. I step out of the Jeep into an ankle-deep sludge of muddy gravel. On the other side of the Jeep, Kell's cowboy boots gnash on the ground as he surreptitiously knocks the driver's side ashtray clean against the front tire.

There's a dull taste of rain in the air. A lick of damp fog around the treetops warns of wet times to come. I've been told by Anna that once it starts raining here, there will be nothing but an oblivion of perpetually dripping white skies, and I'll be seized by Seasonal Affective Disorder, and will wallow in glum depression until spring. I wonder if it was the rain and dreariness that drove off my predecessors.

Kell thuds the driver's door closed. His shoulders puff up beneath his flannel shirt. He's eager. He seems filled with possibilities; swirling with them. He shakes his long hair smooth. He has let it hang loose tonight, parted in the center like a young girl.

"All set?"

I study the exterior of the bar before me. I shrink back.

"Yeah…"

The bar hunches rickety and squat at the darkest corner of the gravel lot. There are no windows. I spy a stove pipe jutting up into the night at one corner of the tin-and-moss tiled roof. The exterior walls have never been painted. They warp inward like a woman's corseted waist. I'm pulled toward the memory of the time my unit-mates and I went to a hick bar outside Tumwater. Just to laugh about it later. I rode the mechanical bull.

Kell is unperturbed by the trashiness. Fortunately, he doesn't notice the pinched expression on my face. We enter through a clunky door and are instantly hit full face with the smell

of cheap beer and mildew and sweaty men. The walls are crumby like old cork, and cluttered with neon beer logos and broken dart boards.

Kell moves with purpose and a little too much familiarity over the rough, tree house style floorboards. He calls hellos to the bartender and a few of the hunkered, swarthy customers at the bar. At the back of the room is a small platform. Three Indians are standing on it, setting up drums, guitars, and flimsy mikes. They wear torn jeans and concert T-shirts. AC/DC and Nirvana and Black Sabbath. Their hair hangs long like Kell's, but stringy and unwashed.

"You're drinking beer, right?"

Kell leans his elbow on the end of the bar. The surface looks as sticky as flypaper. I stand at attention. Kell is making too much eye contact with me.

"Sure."

"Great, why don't you grab us a table—somewhere up front. I'll get us a pitcher."

I wend through the mushroom patch of tables, aiming for the instrument wielding Indians. I sit at an empty table close to the platform. A few of the men at the nearby tables are speaking Spanish. I wonder if they are field workers from Cesar's farm. They glance at me, then studiously ignore me. Like Anna did to Antonio last night.

I've never met any of the Mexicans on the farm. Kell has never introduced me, and Cesar seems too lordly to know any of them by name. Anna probably doesn't even notice that there are actual humans employed to keep the farm tilled and planted. My CO knew every grunt's first name, middle name, nickname and mom's name by the end of the first week of boot camp.

"All right, here we go."

Kell plunks a sloshing pitcher and two mugs onto the gummy tabletop. He sits next to me, his chair aimed at the inadequate stage.

"It's Pabst—that's okay, right?"

"Sure."

Kell fills both mugs, pushing one at me. It's all head.

"They should start at ten."

I wish that Kell hadn't pitched me into thoughts of my CO; sad thoughts that drag at me and make the deep parts of my lungs ache. My breath condenses all thick and cottony whenever I think about him. I try not to think about him, but it sneaks up involuntarily sometimes.

I watch Kell's cousin adjust his drum kit, banging randomly, then practicing riffs. The bar is gradually filling up. Mostly Indians; women as well as men, their voices rising, the din growing dense. Kell sips long and full at his beer, drawing it in like an efficient hummingbird. Thank God he doesn't talk.

I think of the CO's arms as I watch Kell's cousin hammering on the drums with his sticks. They were lean, pale arms with slabs of hard muscle layered over the bone. He always rolled his camo sleeves up over his elbows, folded neat and crisp into two and a half inch cuffs at the exact middle of his upper arms, no matter the weather. He had two tattoos. One was on his left forearm, and everyone in the company knew about it. It displayed his squadron's name on a furling banner, walled-in by eagle wings, with *United States Army* forming a curved roof over it all. It looked like a solid, patriotic house on his arm.

The other tattoo wasn't on his arm. It was very low on the small of his back, and only I got to see it. It said, *Jordan, Tyler, Becky*. If I had been properly curious, I would have asked. I would have wondered who these three people were. Then maybe things wouldn't have ended so badly.

"Kell! Hey man, glad you could make it!"

A thirty-something woman plunks herself down across from us at our table. She looks an awful lot like Kell: pureblood Indian with lots of tossy black hair and a fringy leather jacket. She has lined her eyelids with heavy black makeup on top and on bottom. I guess it's supposed to bestow a haunted look, like the Indian maidens in the cheap paintings I've seen being sold with fake Persian rugs along minor highways. She has three men in tow: chunky, silent Indians with bulging flannel shirts and painful mullet haircuts. They smile shyly and avoid eye contact. Kell scoots closer to me to make room.

"Hey, Shawna. This is Flynn. We work together on the farm. These're my cousins. They're Jerry's brothers and sister."

Shawna and the brothers say hi, then immediately fall into familial talk with Kell. I drink. I grow less tense within the smothering chatter. My eyes follow Kell's cousins; the musical ones onstage. They practice chords semi-poorly.

I keep on drinking the Papst, and Kell keeps on filling my mug, and cousins keep on arriving. I can't keep track of them all. They draw up chairs, squeeze in at our table, yell greetings over each other's heads. I'm unremarked; merely waved at and then gently ignored. I like this. I always feel better in a group. A group is like the army: it's anonymous but inclusive.

I like this, except for one thing.

Kell keeps squeezing in closer to me.

I shake it off. It's just my imagination. It's just a problem of too many cousins and too little table. The Indians onstage take a hard stop on a sour note, then confer. Shining black hair eclipses their faces.

The band stops tuning and abruptly begins to play. Very loud, very heavy. The unholy offspring of AC/DC and Dio and Nirvana.

"So, Flynn," Shawna shouts across the table at me.

"What's the deal with those aristocratic assholes Cesar brought over from the mainland?"

"Shit, yeah, one of them almost ran over Jack Eastley's kid at the gas station in town. BMW driving prick—what the hell's his problem?"

The formerly-silent brother's voice is gentle on the cusses, his face as fat and sweet as a toasted muffin.

Kell takes a long drink of beer to empty his mug, then pours himself another from Shawna's pitcher.

"Just another of the Big C's business hustling parties. They're a bunch of investment bankers, or something. One of them's with the Steelworkers Union. Like a union rep, I think."

Another of the brothers, indistinguishable from the others in his teddy bear chubbiness, shakes his head.

"That man's gonna wind up in jail one of these days."

Shawna eyes Kell significantly, then me, over the rim of her beer mug.

"If there's any justice."

I am jabbed by a curiosity that I'm not sure is appropriate. This is gossip about the boss, after all. Loyalty precludes gossiping.

"What do you mean?" I ask.

Shawna quirks her lips and licks off beer foam.

"Hell, all those people that work his fields are illegal."

Kell leans back dismissively in his chair. He crosses one leg over the other, making a triangle of his knees manfully. My CO used to sit like this.

"Come on, everyone in agriculture does that."

"Yeah, but not everyone's using their farm as a goddamned tax shelter."

This is interesting. I sit up. I slosh slightly. I've already had more beer than I should, and the night is young yet.

"Where's his money really come from?"

"Real estate."

Kell untriangles his legs and stretches his boots out long in front of him. He's getting comfortably buzzed on the beer, I can tell. I hope he doesn't insist on driving us home. He will crash the Jeep. Oops. Now we gotta sleep it off together in this here field.

It would be awkward.

Kell slings his mug hand to hand over the grubby table top.

"He owns something like sixty-eight percent of the land in South Seattle. You know, the ghetto, where all the illegal Mexicans live? Not just the land, though—he's got a bunch of apartment buildings."

"Slums. They're total slums. My sister's stepdaughter lived in one of his places for a while. Nothing but cockroaches and rapists and midnight drug raids. Gunshots in broad daylight. Whenever someone didn't pay their electric bill on time, they'd shut the entire building's power off."

"Sounds nicer than your place, Kell."

Kell's youngest cousin, a man-boy of about seventeen in here against the rules, grabs Kell's mug and grins at him. He takes a drink. Kell snatches it back, taking a good-natured swipe at him across the table.

Cesar mentioned none of this when we made our trip to South Seattle last week. He ought to have. Riding in the cab through the sheets of rain, he should have pointed out one of the decaying apartment blocks as we passed, saying 'See that? I own it. Total piece of crap structurally, but it brings in good coin.'

I give Shawna the eye to see if she's exaggerating or fabricating. She doesn't stutter or amend. She nods importantly, her eyes all horizon-gazing and Trail of Tears profound.

"Well, nothing'll ever happen to him. Not with that damned brother of his. He's gotten him off so many damned things, I've lost count."

Another of the brothers, stoic in his chair, meets Shawna's eyes across the table. He's saying less than he's thinking.

"I swear, every time Cesar's ever been sued or fined by the city or, like, cited for violations, Antonio's managed to get him off clean and clear. Wish I had me a lawyer in the family."

"I heard Cesar got sued just last March by some construction workers or electricians or something for working 'em in unsafe conditions. Violating the, like, those OSHA laws or whatever. He was totally guilty—he pretty much admitted it, and there was tons of documentation and all. But his brother just went ahead and countersued on total bullshit charges—illegal stoppage of work, I think. He just kept on hammering them until they dropped the suit. Antonio shits fire, I swear to God."

"Fuck Antonio—can we please not talk about that son of a bitch tonight?" Kell snaps, startling me. I've never heard his voice sound so harsh.

Kell's youngest cousin, the teenaged Keanu-looking boy, smirks at him.

"Kell's scared of him. How's the lawsuit going? You gonna lose your awesome flannel shirt?"

Kell sits up slowly, his neck curving at his cousin in a deadly arc, like a snake coiling to strike. Around the table, the conversation dies suddenly and thoroughly. Kell digs his elbows hard into the tabletop. He leans and leans and leans until his face is so close to his cousin's that it looks as if they're about to kiss.

"That was over and done with a long time ago, so fucking stop bringing it up. It's not funny."

Cutie-boy cousin loses his smirk. He looks very high school, very mom-still-does-my-laundry.

"All right."

Kell's brown skin is flat and tense. It twitches across his cheekbones and in the lines of his forehead.

"I am not scared of that asshole."

"Okay."

The boy scoots back from the table, out of reach, glancing around at the unhelpful faces of his cousins. Everyone avoids his gaze.

"Sorry. Okay? Okay, Kell? I was just playing."

The band grinds on, loud and erratic. We all pretend to listen to it, an uncomfortable chill blowing in swirls around the table. Kell glares at his beer, his forehead all crumpled, his eyes narrowed.

The fattest of the brothers squeaks his chair back and hefts himself to his feet.

"Well…I'm gonna grab another pitcher. Anybody else want one?"

Another brother rises.

"Yeah. I'll come with. You want anything, sis?"

Shawna jumps up like a prairie dog coming out of its hole.

"I'm gonna get another hard pack."

Most of the cousins stand and depart to acquire more beer with the brothers, smoke a few outside, say hi to a bud they spy across the room. Those who remain around the table begin to chat tentatively. Gradually, laughter resumes, drinks get drunk, and Kell eases out of his broody scowl. He mutters something at the offending young cousin that makes both of them grin slowly. The cousin flips Kell off, and Kell good-naturedly shoves him in the shoulder.

The brothers return, each brown, meaty hand bristling with three pitchers of beer like German barmaids at Oktoberfest. Shawna flows abruptly back into her chair, refueled by nicotine and a choking spritz of cheap perfume. In my rickety chair, I ease into a slouch that gives the appearance of relaxation. I watch Kell as unobtrusively as I can. I can be very unobtrusive.

"I broke him about a month and a half ago, but he's still nearly wild. Too much juice, know what I mean? We need to geld him, I think. But Cesar wants to sell him as a stallion."

Kell traces circles in the beer sweat that coats his mug, as if he's outlining the stallion's offending balls for the offing.

"What, he wants to breed him?"

Kell's cousin, relieved to be off the hook, is very obviously forcing down his revulsion at the mental image of Kell castrating a wild horse.

"Nah, Cesar thinks he's worth more money if he's a stallion. I keep telling him, the way that horse is now, he'll be lucky to sell him for a grand to some rancher for a stud. Geld the bastard—he'll bring in at least fifteen thousand. Maybe more."

"Like upgrading a crappy Honda into a street racer, huh?"

"Yeah, it's exactly like that," Kell's tone is lightly mocking.

He bounces back easily. I can tell that anger is not a natural state for him.

"I thought Anna is the one who keeps track of that sort of stuff. About the horses, I mean."

I affect a casual tone, but it's been a long time since I went out drinking in a crowded bar. My voice comes out strident and accusatory, like a cop's, and stops the conversation. Kell's teenaged cousin stares at me. A gloss of horror makes his irises shine in the low light. Kell shakes his head at me, just like Antonio did to Cesar. I've been drinking, so I'm imprudent. I raise my voice even more.

"So, just what is the deal with Mrs. Ortiz, anyway? What's wrong with her?"

My voice hangs in the air. Everyone at table goes silent. So terribly silent. I am pinned in my chair by dozens of black eyes. I've asked something taboo. It's not the reaction I expected. I assumed they'd have some ready, bitchy complaints about her, just like they did about Antonio.

"I mean, I hear…I hear there's more between her and Antonio than just…just brother and sister-in-law."

The eyes blink, soften, and relax. Smirks bloom on all faces. Knowing snickers leak out around cigarettes.

"No shit, Sherlock. Everyone knows that."

"They've been going at it for years. Cesar's either an idiot, or he doesn't give a good goddamn."

"I'm surprised he's never walked in on them."

"I hate to think how much Antonio must be paying the Mexicans to keep them from tattling to Cesar. He's at the farm constantly when Cesar's out of town."

"Kell here's got himself a nice little sideline income off those two, don't you?"

"Oh, come on! I never asked for anything. If they wanna give gifts, hell, I'll keep my mouth shut. They're waiting for you to get settled in, Flynn, then they'll start up again like normal. They're getting all antsy, all pent-up, I can tell. Opt for a hundred-twenty-five a month, minimum. Don't let that cheap prick shortchange you on sixty bucks. That's what he tried on me when I first started working on the farm."

I'm confused. Here's my eager, gleeful gossip. What could possibly have upset these Indians, if it wasn't the idea that Anna and Antonio might feel things they shouldn't for each other?

"Where's she from? She's not Hispanic, like Cesar. Is she from around here?"

Again, the dull-edged silence. Eyes glance at eyes across the table.

It's Anna herself.

Kell turns to me. His neck has become the same dangerous, curving snake it was for his cousin.

"Ask them."

His eyes are not the warm ones he's been showing me since we met. They are the Indian eyes I see all around the table. They're the black, lightless openings to caves that conceal a terrible thing within.

"Have you tried to ask them?"

I shake my head.

"Well, don't bother. Everything Cesar, Anna, and Antonio ever say is bullshit. She and Cesar didn't meet at some charity ball for the Seattle Symphony. They didn't get introduced by mutual friends at some breast cancer benefit. What's the other one?"

"Business associate of her uncle," Shawna's voice is small, her shoulders pinching up to cradle her dangling silver earrings.

Kell shakes his head. Strands of black hair float over his nose and adhere to his lips.

"I know so much about that woman. More than Antonio knows. Maybe even more than Cesar. She's told me things; such grotesque things. She gets into your head, puts nightmares in there, and they never, ever go away. Her voice is so soft when she tells you her stories. You'll never stop hearing that voice when it's dark. When it's night and you're all alone."

"She's a witch," one of the brothers murmurs.

"She isn't supposed to be here. That's what we believe. People are supposed to stay gone when they're taken, but sometimes, one of them comes back. They're not fully human anymore. They bring bad luck, ruin your life."

Shawna's black-ringed eyes give me the creeps. Disturbed, I drop my gaze to my beer.

Coughs and awkward murmurs bloom around the table. Requests for more beer, a cigarette, should we get Jerry to play "Free Bird?" The music drones on. The table is pounded when one of the brothers tells a good one. No one will look at me anymore. I'm glanced at, like a sting, and then I'm unseen.

Except by Kell.

"Hey."

He leans close to me. His eyes are lit from within, like two lamps in a dark house.

"You wanna go outside? You smoke?"

I shake my head.

Kell runs his eyes up my face, then down it. He takes a swift glance around the table. No one is looking at us. He inhales, mustering within himself.

Under the table, I feel his hand slide warm onto my knee.

"I like you," Kell's voice is so quiet I can barely hear it beneath the noise. "You know that, right?"

My mouth is desert-dry. This has happened to me once before, in almost exactly the same way.

The CO's rock-hard hand was on my knee as he wrapped the elastic bandage around my ankle. I reclined on my bunk, aching from the shin down, annoyed with myself for turning wrong on the deck of the close combat training course, and spraining it swift and hard in front of everyone.

The grunt quarters were quiet, the walls tinted with warm brass by the sunlight pouring through the low windows. I could hear the CO's breath, light and even, as he wound the bandage around my ankle. His eyes were numbingly blue. His eyes were as remote as distant mountains.

'I'm very proud of you, Flynn. You took it like a soldier.'

He tucked the end flap into the tight wrapping, and his hand remained on my knee, the fingers firm and cool. It was so still in the barracks. We were completely alone, and things felt different than when we'd been alone before. It wasn't like when I screwed up, and he had to administer one hundred push-ups in the rain to help me remember. It wasn't like when we went over the results of my Military Intelligence Aptitude Test behind the closed door of his office.

My CO's face hadn't changed. He still wore the untouchable veneer of command. But there was something else there, just beneath it. I could feel it with every nerve. His hand stayed on my knee.

'Would you like me to sit with you for a while, Flynn? I'd like to.'

Kell's eyes probe my face softly.

"I don't know how you feel about hearing that—does it bother you?"

I can't find words. I shake my head. It doesn't bother me. But I don't like it. I don't want it.

Kell's face slowly melts into a smile. He squeezes a quick, hot pressure onto my knee, then removes his hand. He doesn't want his cousins to see and know.

I'm glad he's not touching me anymore. I'm glad he's happy. Just like I was glad for the CO's satisfaction; glad to fulfill his expectations. I never liked it with him, but I couldn't bear to disappoint. It's so much easier to be passive than to struggle to put a stop to things.

Kell refills my beer mug, and I drink long, long, draining it in one swallow.

Friday, September 25, 1998
8:47 a.m.
Ortiz Farm

I shouldn't be listening to Anna and Cesar, but it's unavoidable.

They are out of sight in the foyer. I'm waiting in my security nook to receive final instructions from Cesar before he leaves for Seattle for the week. The acoustics are like a concert hall at the foot of the spiral staircase, and their voices carry to me as if I'd bugged the room. I stare fixedly at my computer screen as Cesar's voice comes to my ears with a naked vulnerability that I never thought I would hear from him.

"Please, Anna, you've gotta pull it together. I can't stand leaving you when you're like this. You know that."

Anna draws in a breath so sharp that it sounds as if it flays her windpipe.

"Don't go, don't leave me here. I can't handle it without you, I can't."

"Sweetheart, it's just for a week. You'll be safe, I promise. Flynn will be here with you the whole time. Or maybe…Anna, do you want to come with me?"

I can hear the hope that forms a scaffold beneath his words.

"It'd be great—they've set me up in a really nice suite downtown at the Hilton. You can relax the whole time, go to the hotel spa, maybe do some shopping with some of the other wives. I'm sure if I called John, his wife would—"

"Oh God, Cesar, I can't do that! You know I can't!"

Her voice slices to the bone, twanging the marrow.

"Baby, don't make this hard for me. I have to go. It's business."

"Please, don't go! Please don't leave me, please Cesar! I can't breathe."

She begins to sob brutally, with the dark, unlovely tone of

real agony. She's not the dainty, rich wife anymore.

"Anna. Sweetheart. Let Flynn take care of you this week. And Kell. Okay? Anna?"

Anna's sobs sound flatter, closer to the floor, as if she has fallen to her knees.

"Baby, don't get yourself all upset. I can't have it. It won't make me stay home, but it'll make me screw up this deal. Please, Anna?"

Abruptly, footsteps pound up the spiral staircase. Somewhere deep upstairs, a door slams. There's a pause; a gathering. Cesar's expensive dress shoes come clacking toward my nook.

I feel awkward. How can I believably pretend that I heard nothing?

Cesar steps into the doorway. He looks exhausted and deeply unhappy, and accustomed to it.

"Okay, I'm off. Here's the phone number of the hotel I'll be staying at. I'll be back next Friday. Saturday at the latest. Those ass-jacks better not try to drag this out. I'll strangle those motherfuckers."

I pin the slip of paper to the corkboard over my desk.

"Kell's on the ball with the crops, so there shouldn't be any problems with the field workers. Try not to bother him this week, okay? He's gonna have his hands full getting the harvest in."

"Okay."

Cesar's frown slides to purse-lipped worry. He looks over my head at the corkboard; at the paper pinned there.

"Look after Anna for me while I'm gone, okay Flynn? She never does well when I'm away. She's all right when it's just for a few hours, but overnight..."

Cesar sighs with a depth that seems to deplete him. He glides his eyes over my computer screen.

"Try to cheer her up. If you can. Distract her. You understand?"

"Yes. I think so."

He almost doesn't say anything more; he almost leaves it at

that.

Cesar starts to turn; starts to go. He hesitates. He brings his eyes heavily to mine, as if lifting boxes filled with sand.

"Flynn. One more thing."

"Yes?"

Cesar inhales sharply, his eyes growing icy and intimidating. They become Antonio's eyes.

"I need you to do something else for me. About Anna. Something extra. I want you to really keep tabs on her while I'm away. I want to know what she does while I'm gone. Everything she does. Watch her. Use the security equipment if you need to. Don't let her know, though. Okay?"

I should have seen this coming. It was inevitable. He's heard things, just like I have.

"You don't have a problem with that, do you?"

His eyes and voice accept no refusal. His face is a harsh-edged, unreadable glyph he never shows Anna.

"No. Not at all."

"Good. See you next week, Flynn."

"Good luck on closing your deal."

"Thanks. Okay, Kell, let's go," Cesar calls.

Kell wanders in from the kitchen, hefting Cesar's luggage. He drops me a wink, and I know he was listening in. I've been spied upon. So this is how it feels. I don't like it. I feel stripped naked, exposed down to my bloody core.

Saturday, September 26, 1998
4:01 p.m.
Ortiz Farm

I'm in the hall, lurking outside Anna and Cesar's bedroom. The door is closed, as it has been since yesterday morning when Cesar left. However, instead of the worrisome silence of the past day, I can hear Anna hurrying to and fro behind the door. Skittering, mousy footsteps trace an erratic path from one end of the room to the other. Drawers and doors open and close. Something is brewing.

I pretend to measure the outer wall, a stud finder in my hand as a prop. I will tell Anna that I'm planning to install wiring for a new security gadget, should she open the door and demand to know why I'm hanging around her room. I will make up a name—Infra-Trek Readout System. Something like that.

I hear light feet take the stairs, curling up to the hall with soft, purposeful taps.

"Hey, Flynn."

Kell steps into the hall and gestures with his head for me to follow him. I move away from the bedroom door, aiming for a noiseless passage over the thick rug. We step around the corner to stand just outside Cesar's office.

Kell glances over his shoulder in the direction of the master bedroom. A smile pulls one side of his mouth up, forming a crescent moon of his lips.

"You really want to find out Anna's big secret?"

"Yes."

Kell takes a step away from me. His eyes sparkle.

"Go to the ferry dock. Right now."

I nod, making a small smile of thanks as an afterthought. Kell walks away from me. I hear him knock on the door to the master bedroom, as I hurry down the staircase to get the Jeep keys. I roll down the driver's window as I start the engine. It's beautiful out; warm and bird-ridden. Overhead, a hundred dark shapes are twirling and swooping in a narrow circumference over the half-harvested fields. Sea gulls and crows gleam and fight in the sunshine, bombed by starlings and blue jays. The migrant workers, toiling for days to get the crop in before frost or rot claims it, periodically wave cowboy hats and shovels at the birds, as they swoop in deadfalls at the stacks of unearthed vegetables.

I pull out onto the main road, kicking up a wave of gravel. I speed down the dirt road to town. I must get there first; I must hide the Jeep at the far end of the parking lot where it won't be noticed. My heart is going fast. Sour, bright adrenaline burns my guts. For a gorgeous instant, I can't remember that I'm not reporting to the CO anymore, but to Cesar.

I pull into the ferry dock's small parking lot. I scan. There aren't many inconspicuous spots to be had. I hesitate, then I slide the Jeep in between an abandoned van marked with neon paint for towing, and an RV that I suspect is being lived in by one of the ferry workers. If the person arriving on the ferry looks for the Jeep, they'll see it. If they're not feeling suspicious, however, it will go unnoticed.

I get out and walk past the ferry dock down to the beach. At the water's edge, I squat down behind some World War II military artifacts that have historical significance, but no discernable purpose. I can see the entire parking lot and the ticket stall from here, but I'm difficult to spot and impossible to identify. My appearance helps with that: from afar, I become utterly generic. My CO had great hopes for my career as a field operative. The parking lot begins to fill with cars loaded with people escaping the island for a Saturday night of cosmopolitan thrills in Seattle. There's no movie theater on the island; no restaurants, no arcade, no bowling alley. Just two bars, the liquor store, and poor, rural solitude between the houses.

It's dank and cold down on the beach. The sand wicks salt water up my jeans. The sun drips into the ocean, thickening the twilight and making it hard for me to see. I've lost my knack for outdoor surveillance. I never used to notice such things as wet, or cold, or failing light.

I wonder how Antonio, or whoever is coming, will react to me. Should I jump out and confront him as soon as he debarks? Or return unseen to the farm and obtain video evidence to show Cesar? My CO would have opted for the latter option. It's cleaner. There's reduced chance of personal injury. There's less plausible deniability.

Then again, maybe it's not a lover that's coming. Maybe Anna is into drugs, and her dealer is on his way with her monthly supply. Or perhaps a disgraced relative of hers that Cesar won't allow in his house is surreptitiously visiting.

Finally, as my knees are cramping and my neck is growing stiff, I see Cesar's tasteful, dark blue Mercedes roll slowly into the parking lot. It stops in front of the ticket booth.

Anna steps out.

I'm shocked. I nearly stand and give away my position.

She is wearing tight jeans, her hair sleek in a ponytail. A very low-cut, very red tank top peeks out from beneath a paint-stained jacket. Her face is bright with drugstore makeup.

My CO would have kicked my ass for reacting to this change in the game. Intelligence operatives never react. They respond. Reaction is a delayed response.

Beneath thick smears of blue, Anna's eyes cut from side to side like straight razors. She fishes in her purse and pulls out a bill, maybe a twenty or even a fifty, and hands it in to Kell. He stuffs it into the pocket where he keeps his cigarettes, then jacks the Mercedes into reverse and zooms out of the parking lot. I would bet my life that he's smirking right now.

Anna shoves her hands deep into her jacket pockets, then draws them out and crosses her arms over her breasts. She seems to be horribly nervous. My eyes strain through the orange half-light at her. I've never seen her out in the world before. She's hasn't set foot off of Cesar's property since I started this job nearly two months ago. She perpetually lounges in the house. She strolls to the stable to bother Kell. She reads in the living room. She is always dressed in flowing, Grecian goddess white. She is always aloof and pure, like a virgin queen.

She's tiny out here. So bright and juvenile in her tight, teenager clothes. She looks infinitely rape-able.

Of course I will follow her onto the ferry.

I wait until Anna hurries, with many fearful glances around her, to the ticket booth. She buys a ticket, fists it, and nearly runs to the glassed-in waiting area for walk-on passengers. I climb up the footpath from the beach and wait near some smokers, in case she chances to see me emerge from my hiding place. I rummage in my pockets and count out exact change so that I can acquire my ticket fast. I wait several minutes, then walk briskly—but not too briskly—to the booth. I buy my ticket and move directly back to the smokers.

The ferry, lit up with glaring white at every window, glides across the water like a tall office building tipped on its side. The sun is lost behind the horizon, and the sky is turning from citrus to deep denim. The ferry plows through the water and hits the dock gently, making a subtle boom. The cars that are going to ride across begin to turn on their engines, their headlights blooming bright to dazzle me.

I see Anna's dark ponytail sway up the passenger ramp with the rest of the crowd. I make my way to the waiting area, count to one hundred and forty as the CO taught his troops to do when following a target, then I step up the ramp and onto the ferry. I ease into the crowd and scan for Anna. She must not see me. I have to find her and set up a bunker from which to observe her.

I grab a free Island County newspaper as I slide through the main deck, my head down, praying Anna won't look my way. I exit swiftly out onto the aft smoking deck. It's chilly and damp; not somewhere Anna would go. I move into the farthest corner, close to the railing and unprotected from the sky. It's so dark out now that I can see in through the scarred Plexiglas windows, but the passengers sitting inside under the bright fluorescent lights shouldn't be able to see more than their own reflections gazing back at them.

The ferry has two small indoor decks where passengers can sit. Also this exterior smoking deck. Then there's the car deck below. I doubt Anna will go down there. It's dark and uncomfortable, blasted by sea and wind. Some drivers remain in their cars for the entire hour and a half ride, but no one ever stands around outside the cars. It would look strange, and be a cold and miserable ride. Anna doesn't prefer to be cold or miserable. So, Anna is either on this level, or the one above. The tiny galley is on this level. I scan the people waiting in line for oily burgers, dry donuts, and cooked coffee. Anna won't eat anything like that. She's probably up on the second deck.

I'm mistaken. There she stands, waiting in line. Her body language sings of fear. She radiates vulnerability to attack. She watches everyone.

I shiver in the cold as the ferry engines kick volcanically to life and we slide out into open water. The spray and wind are wretched out here, but at least I'm not alone. A few pathetic souls are huffing on cigarettes near me, looking longingly through the windows at the yellow warmth.

It's quite crowded inside. It's hard to keep track of Anna. I can't recognize her in such a riot of color, with her legs all bifurcated, and her features disfigured by cosmetics. She steps to the cashier and flashes green stuff. She receives change, and her hands shake so badly she almost drops it all over the floor. She takes a plastic cup with beer in it and moves uneasily across the room, her eyes switching back and forth as if she fully expects someone to pounce on her.

She sits in a corner booth, isolated from all the other passengers. She sips at the beer. Her eyes whip the room, slashing at everyone. She doesn't relax. It's apparent to me that she's not fearful of recognition, or of whatever it is she's heading toward in Seattle. I feel certain that it's simply being off the island, alone in a crowd of strangers, that scares her. She's almost cowering.

Now that she's stationary, I can sneak back inside. I ease the door open, then ooze along the wall behind several children who are perfunctorily fussing at each other. I make a determined circuit of the deck so she won't notice me. I park myself on a bench across the room from her, raising the newspaper like a sail to hide my face. It's a cheesy, 1940's detective movie maneuver, but it works.

Anna remains huddled in the booth, urgently watching those around her and sipping at the beer, for forty-five minutes. Halfway across the water, she furtively takes a brown prescription bottle out of her purse. She shakes a pill into her hand and dry swallows expertly. Then another. Then another. The ferry lands in downtown Seattle at 6:30. The islanders are eager, like dull cows at the milking gate, as they push toward the debarking ramp. They will blow so much money tonight. Eight-dollar hotdogs at Seattle Center, hundred-dollar lap dances down by the pier, stolen wallets on their way to the one a.m. ferry home.

Anna rises, teetering slightly on her cheap high heels, and crosses the deck. She tosses the empty plastic cup in a trash can. Her arms cinch her breasts with choking tightness. Her entire body quakes. I follow her at the back of the press of passengers. She moves with sharp speed down the walk-on ramp and rushes though the Seattle ferry terminal. I have to nearly jog to keep up. She pushes out the doors to the street and stops at the curbside passenger pickup area. Cool night air hits me hard, washing my nose clean of the gummy ferry odors. I jam myself into a dark doorway about half a block down from Anna.

Her face swivels fast to the right and left. She looks utterly panicked now. Her chest is going up and down so hard that her breasts bounce. She flinches brutally each time someone passes her. Two minutes pass. She looks ready to bolt at any moment. Then her face turns to a slowing car. Unmistakable relief glosses her features.

A phantom-silver Aston Martin pulls into the passenger pickup area and stops directly in front of her, its wheels nearly grazing the curb.

I am frozen. I can't feel my fingers or my feet. I recognize the make of the car immediately. I've seen many a James Bond movie. This is the first time I've ever seen one in real life. Nobody else in Seattle drives this type of car.

Kell and his Indian amigos were right about Anna and Antonio.

Anna hurries to the Aston Martin, opens the door, and gets in. I scout for a cab to follow them, but none are free. The three standing parked nearby are waiting for passengers who called them from the ferry. The drivers are dryly unimpressed with my attempts to bribe them into taking me instead of their legitimate customers. I step back and stare out at the crowded street, clotted by traffic glowing with white and red lights.

I've lost them.

I wander down the block, dodging jolly drunks and homeless vagrants. I don't know where Antonio lives. Some penthouse downtown, but how would I find it? He's not the type that would allow himself to be listed in the common phone book.

I stop at a seafood stand on the waterfront. I order clam chowder in a paper bowl, sit at one of the chilly iron tables, and ponder what to do.

There's always such intensity between Anna and Antonio. They are always alert to each other; always watchful, hanging on the other's words, anticipating their reaction. I just assumed it was due to distrust. I misread them badly.

I stare out past the high rises, past the little pleasure boats and barges jammed tight in repair docks, to the glossy water of Puget Sound. Skyhamish Island lies far, far out of sight. Even on a sunny, smog-free morning, it's lost in the distant sea. I don't know what to do. Did Cesar really suspect this? Did he want me to confirm it? To catch them in the act?

I turn away from the water to the tall buildings of downtown Seattle. Thousands of windows are staggered dizzyingly on top of each other, some lit, some dark. Antonio and Anna are probably in one of these windows by now. Cesar is in another, wheeling and dealing with the rich men. Closing deals, providing for Anna.

I finish the chowder and I can't help but sigh. This is a bad business I'm mixed up in. I don't want to involve myself further. I don't want to tell Cesar what I saw tonight. It makes me feel desolate. The situation can't help but decay.

I should go back to the island. Back home. I don't want to. There's nothing waiting for me there but a night of fretting about this discovery. And Kell.

He's watchful of me, like Anna and Antonio are. I wonder if people think we're up to such carnal mischief. I hope to God not.

I walk reluctantly back to the ferry terminal to buy a return ticket.

Wednesday, September 30, 1998
5:03 p.m.
Ortiz Farm

The sun slides perpetually downward as I walk, the landscape growing dimly blue and hazy all over the farm. Glittering clouds of gnats begin to mass up as the air grows cool and gentle. The sky is an immensity of navy with the bare hints of stars just beginning to poke out. I walk the circuit of the property, wrapping up the afternoon patrol that Cesar likes me to make. I'll do another sweep later tonight, then it's up to the computerized security system I installed to keep the peace.

Out in the fields, the illegal migrant workers are harvesting the last of the vegetables. They hack at the soil in the semi-darkness with hoes, shovels and small machetes. They toss armfuls of mostly-ripe produce into piles at the edges of the long rows. They'll be at it until it's too dark to see. They've been working from sunup to sundown every day for nearly a week and a half. This is the big push before the cold season sets in and rain washes everything out. Cesar will be royally pissed off if the year's crop is lost while he's away in Seattle.

Kell has been out in the fields all day, riding on horseback from the carrot patches, to the spare squash plantings, to the vast plots of spinach and romaine. He's off-horse now, striding wearily from hunched person to person, yelling at the driver of the loading truck in a mangled alloy of Spanish and English. He looks worn out. He had to fetch Anna home from the ferry dock on his lunch break. I would have done it, uncomfortable as it would have been, but they have an understanding. She slips him hard cash that he won't pass up.

Anna arrived home at noon with a whisper of soft shoes and a swish of light fabric. I was in my security nook at the time. I heard her pass a quick, quiet word with Kell, then she padded swiftly up the spiral staircase to the master bedroom. She didn't come out for hours. She probably ran a bath;

probably did her nails and her hair. Moisturized. Luxuriated.

I approach the house, whose blond exterior gleams like wheat. The flawless, old growth wood planks shoot straight up into the dark sky above me, like the façade of a cathedral. The house rides tall and dignified over the green fields, its architecture too impressive for this little island.

A white shape is floating like a great moth through the garden at the foot of the house. My stomach tightens immediately. It's Anna. I don't know what to say to her, given what I saw her do in Seattle.

The sun is nearly gone now, glazing the garden silver with a bare remnant of light. Anna's white dress drifts slowly against and behind her body, like seawater frothing around the bow of the ferry. She pauses and bends. Her arms are wrapped around a bulky mass shaped like a small baby. Something sharp and shiny glints in her hand.

She's cutting flowers. I want to be quiet; I want go away unremarked. Instead, I linger. I watch her from the edge of the garden.

I can just make out her face in the deep blue twilight. She's very pretty, but it's an impossible prettiness. Like a sculpture animated. Like someone carved her out of orchid-pale soapstone. Her arms dip into the thick greenery, pulling pastel colors out and bunching them into the crook of her arm. I don't like seeing her with the shears. It makes me nervous, and I'm not sure why.

I don't make a sound, I'm certain of it. Still, her face tips up and turns toward me. She stands up straight, slim without muscle beneath her white dress. She smiles at me through the starry blueness.

"Flynn. What do you think?"

She holds out the armload of flowers like an offering.

"What are they?"

I expect her to quip, "flowers." That's the sort of snide reply Antonio would make. Cesar might just grin, and that grin would let me know that I was a dumbass.

"Hyacinth. They're finally growing nicely. They looked

terrible for the first couple years. I almost had them pulled, but Cesar likes them. I'm glad they're proving out after all this time."

She shines small in the core of the dark garden. She looks like someone treading water in a dark lake.

"I grew bleeding hearts the first year we lived here. Dicentra. They bloomed very consistently; very vigorous foliage. But Cesar hated them. He said they looked like baskets of dead fetus hearts hanging everywhere. Maybe it's a Mexican thing. I thought they were pretty, like the Hanging Gardens of Babylon. Do you think it's a Mexican superstition?"

"I don't know."

She shrugs, bloodless and slim as a waning moon. I wait for her to make an excuse for her absence these past four days. A flower show. Buying rare roses in Seattle. Silence falls awkwardly in the garden. Does she think I didn't notice that she's been gone for half a week? I'm not stupid.

She's not stupid, either.

She begins to wend through the tall stalks of spiky flowers and blowsy country grass toward me. She stops within touching distance and looks up at my face. She smiles coolly. She makes eye contact.

"Would you like some dinner? Have you eaten yet?"

"I've got work to do."

"I'm going to make something. If you get hungry later on, feel free to use the kitchen. I gave the cook the week off. Cesar's not here to want anything fancy."

She's not reaching. She never reaches. She manages to draw instead. I don't know how she does it. I feel subtly compelled when I'm around her.

She turns away and glides over the dark, evergreen lawn to the deck. Warm light spills from the enormous windows, dyeing her dress golden and celestial. I don't know why I want to hurry after her. I don't care about her. She's no friend of mine. She betrayed my boss. I follow her inside, but I don't go into the kitchen. I sit in the security nook just outside the kitchen. I fiddle with the computer. I need to activate the sensors on the perimeter of the farm for the night. I'll walk the perimeter again around nine o'clock. I'll check the garage, wine cellar, and stable in person. Then I'll activate the alarms. Kell hasn't taken anything since I installed this system. We don't talk about it.

I hear Anna rustling around the enormous kitchen, picking through the many refrigerators and cabinets. Heavy objects are settled onto the marble countertops with bright clinks. She hums softly, contentedly. This upsets me. Things rarely upset me here on the farm. It's a calm place. I stand up and walk into the kitchen.

Anna is moving around the car-sized butcher block, wielding a knife and a redwood cutting board. She looks relaxed and thoughtful about the food she's preparing. She spent the last four days screwing her husband's brother—how the hell can she be so mellow and proprietary in Cesar's kitchen?

"What are you making?"

My voice is too tight. It clashes off the imported tile walls and tightens Anna's shoulders.

She looks up at me and makes her detached, wealthy smile.

"Huevos con chorizo. Cesar taught me how when we were first married. It's his favorite dish."

This incites me, making me indignant. Now I have to stay.

"It's very easy to make. I can't cook at all, to be honest. Would you like some?"

"No. Yeah. Okay."

Anna slices a fat, hand-length sausage on the cutting board.

"Cesar's tastes have improved over the years, but he's still got a weakness for weird Mexican dishes. Nothing normal—he hates tacos, enchiladas, fajitas. But if you give him a plate of churros and this god-awful hot sauce he gets in Seattle down in the ghetto, he'll die of happiness. And a Corona or a Dos Equis."

"Does Antonio like that stuff too?"

She ought to flinch. She ought to stiffen, glance at me, then rein herself in hard. Instead, she laughs. Very easily, completely unperturbed.

"No, God, no! He'd rather die than eat that sort of street vendor garbage. Cesar Americanized him from a very early age. He likes dark chocolate. Japanese-style salmon. Old port. Cesar's converting him to cognac these days. Ugh."

Does she think that I approve? She's so casual. Cesar must know all about them. Is this some sophisticated, rich people ménage à trois thing that I'm too naive to comprehend?

She leans across the counter with a sly smile that seeks to make me feel naughty and curious.

"Although, one time I found the two of them drunk as lords on Herradura tequila, out on the deck there."

She gestures with the knife beyond the kitchen, toward the deck as big as a concert stage, where I watched her mount golden with her arms filled with flowers. I won't be pulled into this confidence. I'm nothing if not loyal to my boss. She's undeterred by my silence.

"Cesar had received a few bottles of very expensive tequila from a client for Christmas. I think he and Antonio had closed some big deal—this was a few years ago, so I don't remember what they were optioning at the time. Anyway, Cesar had been working on it for months and months. He wrapped it up just in time for Christmas, so he was feeling very festive that year. Very jolly."

When she smiles about this, about her husband, her face is soft, and radiant, and utterly true. It's so obvious that she loves Cesar deeply.

So why does she fuck Antonio?

She opens a woven basket with a tight lid. I see a dozen richly brown eggs inside. I've only ever eaten white ones from a supermarket carton.

"He called Antonio and made him come out here a day early. Antonio usually spends the major holidays with us. Christmas, Easter, Thanksgiving. He works till the last minute, shows up just in time for dinner, then leaves first thing the next morning. Cesar harassed him until he agreed to come early in the morning on Christmas Eve. Cesar made him skip one of his donor events at the ballet."

Anna's mouth goes slightly sour. I should leave. I should stop listening to this. She cracks the eggs, two at a time, into a heavy iron skillet.

"It was very mild that year. No rain, not too cold. When the cook had the duck ready, I called them, but they weren't up in Cesar's office. I went looking, and…" her mouth arcs up into the first real grin I've ever seen from her.

I won't be drawn in. But she looks so young, so sweet, when she smiles like this.

"What?" I ask involuntarily.

"I finally found them because…"

She has to stop whisking the eggs to cover her lips with her hand, pressing back a giggle.

"I could hear the two of them singing 'Las Mañanitas' out on the deck."

She sees that I don't get it.

"That's what the Mexicans sing instead of 'Happy Birthday.' They were singing it to Jesus. I heard Cesar bellowing over and over, 'Feliz cumpleaños, Jesùs!' When I went out there, Antonio was weaving around the deck, singing and sort of waving an empty tequila bottle like a conductor. Then he tripped and fell into one of the lounge chairs. I remember that when Cesar saw me, he jumped about a mile in the air and yelled, 'Oh shit, I took His name in vain, and now here He is! Forgive me, Jesùs!'"

I can't believe it, can't even picture it. Antonio, his fine suit rumpled, stumping around like a wino with a bottle of tequila, singing a kid's song. I like the idea of him drunk. It makes him seem vulnerable and foolish, and any weakening of his intimidating aura is wonderful to me. I can't help the smile that hovers over my mouth.

Anna tosses the sliced sausage into the frothing yellow eggs and carries the skillet over to one of the complex, chrome-coated stoves.

"Cesar can hold his liquor quite well—he was just playing, you see? But Antonio was completely gone, totally intoxicated.

I remember when he saw me, he staggered up out of his deck chair and stumbled over to me. He put his hands on my face and stared at me for a moment. He said, 'Hola, mi salvadora.' Then he kissed me. Then he passed out.'"

My smile fades away completely. The eggs sizzle as she prods them with a wooden spoon.

"Cesar thought it was the funniest thing he'd ever seen. He teased Antonio about it for months. Years. He brings it up every Christmas."

I know why Cesar would have found such an incident pleasing. It would have mistakenly seemed to be just what he most hoped for. His greatest wish fulfilled. What a mountainous error.

Anna's smile eases down to a pretty softness about the eyes and lips.

"I never knew that Antonio could sing. He really has a very decent voice. I don't think I'd ever seen him that drunk before."

She clicks off the stove and hefts the skillet filled with steaming eggs to the counter.

"I left them to it, and ate with Kell that year. The boys ended up sleeping in the deck chairs all night. Lucky for them, it didn't rain. I woke them up for the presents Christmas morning. Both of them had crashing hangovers all day long, and blamed it on Jesus for having a birthday. Isn't that silly?"

She heaps the eggs onto two brightly painted, Italian-looking plates. Hundred-dollar-looking plates. I'm afraid to touch them. She picks them up, one in each hand.

"Let's eat in the dining room. It's so much nicer than in here. I always feel lonely when I eat in the kitchen."

I'm cowed by the dining room. I've only eaten in here two other times. I tiptoe behind Anna over the deep Asian rug. I keep my hands military-stiff against the seams of my jeans to avoid thumping against the little brass stands with their mounted bits of statuary. The extremely polished walls reflect my face vaguely, like wood grained mirrors. I sit gingerly on a velvet-padded chair. The flowers that Anna cut out in the garden are casually arranged in a frighteningly fragile glass urn at the far end of the table. If I breathe too hard, it will tumble to the ground and shatter.

Anna sets the plates on the creamy myrtle wood dining table. There are no placemats, no tablecloth to protect the wood. I must be exceedingly careful not to spill anything. She dims the sprawling stained glass chandelier, casting ruddy red and purple patches over our food.

The eggs are good. I eat intently to avoid saying anything. I don't know what kind of conversation we can have, given the images that are dancing unwelcomed through my mind.

"Do you like it here so far, Flynn?"

Antonio caressing Anna's face. Calling her his savior. Leaning down to kiss her. Their lips meeting as Cesar watches.

"Sure."

"Good."

She forks the eggs and sausage efficiently. She's not as artsy with her utensils as she was at the dinner party a week and a half ago.

I wonder what she and Antonio ate during the last four evenings. Would they have risked going out? Maybe to some intimate restaurant on Capitol Hill, where Cesar wouldn't go. Some obscure bistro with scattered candles, billowing gauze draperies, and discrete gay waiters. Some place where they could gaze at each other in their watchful way. In the candlelight, Antonio's skin would glow richly, like East Indian tea; while Anna's face would shine as smooth as wedding gown satin, her features so imperfectly perfect.

"I hope the field hands can get the crop in on time this year. Cesar was very upset when they lost an acre last year to frost. Kell was on his hate list for three months. I don't like it when Cesar's angry. He spreads it around."

Maybe they stayed in at Antonio's penthouse, and Anna cooked for them. Antonio would have black leather couches. A view of downtown Seattle sparkling in the night like sequins and burning cigarette tips. Chrome and glass décor. Very sleek; very cold and manly and impersonal.

"Would you like some wine?"

"No, thanks."

"I think I'll have a glass. White."

She rises and steps briefly out of the dining room. I can't take this. I'm not good at sharing a secret that's not military in nature. Am I supposed to wink and nod at all of this? Should I demonstrate my worldliness by dropping subtle hints that I know all about it? Or should I boldly accuse her and demand an explanation?

She's back within a minute, bearing an open bottle and two long-stemmed glasses. She smiles apologetically.

"Just in case you change your mind. You don't have to."

She sits, pours herself a glass, and sets the bottle and the empty glass neutrally between us. They tempt me and want me to pick them up. I eat and stare hard at my colorful plate. I must be careful. I'll knick the colorful Italian paint job, and Cesar will dock my pay.

"I hope Cesar's eating well this week. When he gets heavy into a deal, he tends to drink his dinners, if you know what I mean. But Antonio will be with him. He'll make him eat."

I wonder if Anna and Antonio drank white wine last night, when they sat close and all unbuttoned on his glossy leather couch. No, Antonio's the type of man who would have a mini-bar. He'd be adept at making martinis, as a sign of his worldly, modern maleness.

"I hope the hotel he's saying in doesn't have computer access. Cesar likes to pull all-nighters when he's at this stage in a contract negotiation. I've seen him go three or four days with no sleep at all. He always gets sick afterward."

She must have been coiled up on the couch with her shoes off, leaning against Antonio as they chilled their hands on his designer glassware. There must have been music on an unbearably expensive stereo system. He likes the symphony; maybe classical music. Something delicate and romantic.

"I hope you brought raingear, Flynn. It's going to be very rainy within a month. You'll be miserable if you don't have boots and a good raincoat."

I can't do this anymore. I need it—I grab the bottle and pour myself a very full glass. The wine is yellow-white, like baby pee.

"I've got an army field jacket. It's pretty waterproof. My shoes should be okay, too. They're sturdy."

"Good. If you need anything mid-season, feel free to take a day off to go shopping in Seattle."

Anna sips her wine reflectively, her eyes gazing over my right shoulder at the painting hanging on the wall behind me.

"Do you like the wine?"

She doesn't ask about the eggs.

I take a drink. I can't hold a wine glass the way she and Cesar do. I have to fist it around the stem like some drunken, medieval monk.

"It's okay."

"It's a Sémillon-chardonnay. I remembered that you didn't care for the rice wine at the dinner party, so I thought this might be milder for you."

How considerate. I can see her lying on Antonio's couch, beneath him, losing clothes. His lean body presses down on hers, his mouth is hard on hers. He must be skilled at undressing women, adroitly, with one hand. Pushing himself into her, with most of his own clothing still on like Kell told me. Does she like it with him?

Or.

I nearly drop my fork. Or is it like Antonio did with Kell and his car? Is it something cruel?

I rarely have such flashes of insight. My pulse ticks fast in my neck. Is Antonio making her? Is their time together arranged through threats? Does he know a secret about her that she must keep him from exposing?

"All done?"

It would explain so much: why she has always seemed to dislike Antonio; why she looked so frightened on the ferry to Seattle. If Antonio is forcing her, raping her, then I can fix it. I can investigate, I can find a solution. I can make Antonio stop. I can rescue her. Anna is a person who inspires strange, protective fantasies.

"Yeah—yes, I'm done."

Anna is polite; a hostess, even with me. She gathers up our plates and carries them into the kitchen.

I have to get her to talk to me. She won't trust me, since we're still fairly new to each other. But if I can get just a hint, a sense of what Antonio is threatening her about, I can dig and seek, and eventually I'll find the truth. I was very well-trained.

Anna returns and leans against the table, her sharp nails tapping the wood.

"Did you get enough to eat?"

"Yes. Thanks. It was good."

"So…you're not busy now, are you?"

"No."

"Would you like to have another glass of wine? Maybe talk for a while?"

"Sure. Okay."

Anna picks up the bottle and the glasses. She leads the way into the living room. The vast, profoundly aching beauty of the view through the massive bank of windows lining the far wall hypnotizes me. Rising out of the floor to grip the ceiling some thirty feet up, the windows gift me with the lusciously sweeping sight of the moon-brightened ocean, whose waves lift and drop in utter silence.

How can Anna casually wander in here, set the wine bottle on an end table, shove aside a throw pillow, with not a glance at such strength sapping beauty? It's the kind of loveliness that could kill you.

Anna flicks on a few lights, warming the room to mellow flesh tones. She sits in her soft, peach easy chair. She crosses her legs, tenting her long, white skirt up.

I sit awkwardly on the couch across from Anna. I clutch the wine glass tightly to keep from spilling a drop onto the embroidered upholstery. The walls behind her are covered with very good paintings. Even though I don't understand them, I can tell they're real art. They evoke.

"I rarely drink chardonnay. It's got too much bite for me."

I don't know how to do this. If I blatantly ask her where she was for the last four days, I sense that she will masterfully evade me. She's slippery.

"The last time I had a pure chardonnay, in fact, was this past Thanksgiving. Cesar insisted. We had quail that year, since none of us really like turkey. The sauce was quite strong, so it needed a wine with teeth to fight back, so to speak."

If I don't do this tonight, she will assume that we have an understanding, like she has with Kell. Then, nothing will ever be said between us again. She'll go to Antonio every time Cesar's out of town on business, and I'll be unable to question her.

"We haven't had quail since. It's just too much work for too little meat. Cesar was highly unimpressed with the end result."

I realize that Anna hasn't looked me in the eye since I began thinking these thoughts. My face is revealing too much. I have to control myself.

"Do you know how Cesar and I met?"

She toys with her wine glass and quirks her eyebrows at me. I'm puzzled. Cesar told this story already, at the dinner party.

"This."

She holds the glass out slightly. The wine tilts against the thin sides, but doesn't spill.

"We were at a breast cancer benefit several years ago. They were serving the most horrible chardonnay I've ever tasted, and I was having a very hard time keeping my reaction to myself. Cesar, from what he tells me, had been trying to think of some way to come introduce himself, talk to me...well, to flirt, you know. Anyway, when he saw the face I was making, he just walked up and commented on it in a very charming way, and we got to talking about wine, and then, well...sometimes bad wine is a good thing."

She lifts one shoulder, glancing around the wealth-soaked room. The story has changed. Drastically. Doesn't she remember that I know better? I have to tread very carefully. I force my face to show nothing but bland interest. Not watchfulness. Not curiosity. I inhale and open my mouth.

"You don't go to benefits with Cesar anymore, right?"

Clouds roll in, corrupting her placid expression.

"No."

"How come?"

"I can't."

She never leaves the island, never leaves the farm.

Except to go to Antonio.

I keep my eyes on hers.

"Cesar was very worried about you when he left."

Anna is alert. She couches it in a relaxed posture. Her eyes are vague and disinterested as they gaze into her wine glass.

"Yes. I know."

Neither of us speaks for many seconds. The room shrinks and closes in tight around us. I can hear her light breathing. She continues to stare without focus at her wine.

"He asked me to do something."

Anna meets my eyes.

She will beg for my silence now. Offer to pay me off.

"What?"

"He wanted to make sure you were okay while he was gone. He was very concerned. That you'd—"

"Hurt myself?"

She twists her lips into a wretched attempt at a smile. She makes a tiny exhalation that wants to be a laugh, turns her face toward the huge windows, and takes a swallow of wine that drains the glass. She doesn't speak for over five minutes. Her hand moves jerkily to bring the empty wine glass to rest on her crossed knee.

"I…"

She turns her face to mine, and she is concentrating very hard. She is not really looking at me, though her eyes are all over my face. She gropes at me with them, rubbing her fingers over the thin glass.

"Have you ever been married, Flynn?"

"No."

"It tears you to pieces. I've never loved anyone like I love

Cesar. I can't live without him. I mean that. No one else could ever…goddammit."

She fingers her upper lip, and her hand is openly shaking.

"I wish I could be better for Cesar. A better wife. I'm sure he thought things would improve over time, but, I don't know. Do you realize that I haven't left the island with him for over two years? That was just to go to the dentist. Cesar had to dope me up so heavily that I had to be admitted to the emergency room to have my stomach pumped. I'm really not what he deserves. He should have a wife who can go on business trips with him. Join the donor circles at the symphony and the ballet. Give luncheons in Seattle for the mayor's wife. Cesar is too wonderful to me. He understands me too well. He lets me, do you understand?"

I stay very still. Anna starts to lift the empty glass to her mouth, then sets it down sharply on the end table, nearly snapping the fragile stem.

"It's complicated. It's…there's too much that happened. Before."

Please. Please tell me.

I lean forward. I clench my fingers fiercely around my untasted wine glass. She curves her mouth up bitterly, sadly. She gazes out at the ocean.

"If I'd realized how much I love him, I wouldn't have married him."

All at once, like a punch in the gut, I get it.

Antonio has never raped her; has never pressured or coerced her. I've seen this delicate alertness, this unique expression on her face before.

I stare at her, punctured.

She reaches for the bottle of wine and her glass. She is pulling herself together urgently.

"More? This really tastes much better when it's kept chilled. We have a proper ice bucket somewhere. You know, when the caterer prepared our Easter dinner two years ago, she brought this very unusual chilling device for the wine. We had a straight Sémillon that time, which was quite bland—almost flavorless.

KATHERINE LUCK

She used a padded silver blanket to keep it cool. It had small batteries in it to keep a tiny refrigeration unit going. But it was so thin! Absolutely silent. Probably terribly expensive, but it would make a good birthday present for Cesar, don't you think?"

There's nothing for me to solve; nothing to save her from.

I'm disgusted.

"I wonder if Cesar will bring back any new wines to try. He usually picks something up when he goes to Seattle, or a client foists something on him. It's better when Cesar chooses the wine. He's got really excellent taste. Though that wasn't always the case. He learned the hard way. We drank some pretty awful stuff early on in our marriage. I hate to think what he drank before we met. Not that I had anything to do with improving his palate. Except that he started, you know, wanting to impress for the first time. He finally paid attention to varietals; asked advice from the sommelier instead of just opting for the obvious upper-priced reds."

How can she love Antonio?

"He's actually toying with the idea of planting a vineyard on the farm. Just a small one, of course, to see if anything will grow. It's very expensive to get into the wine making business. Just one oak barrel for aging can cost as much as a car, you know. If it's French oak, that is, and you really have to use French oak, or you'll never sell a bottle. Except to the wine cooler crowd."

Antonio's a very attractive man. He's cut from a block of cold pistol steel. He could seem sexy to Anna. But how can she love him?

"I think it would be wonderful if we made this place over into a winery in a decade or so. We could call it Chateau Ortiz. Except, that would seem confusing, wouldn't it? Mixing French

and Spanish. Maybe Casa Ortiz. Or Castillo Ortiz. It might be fun to run a winery. The vines would certainly be prettier than all those filthy fields we have now. We could lure *House and Garden* out here, finally. Cesar was terribly disappointed that they didn't take an interest in the house when it was completed. Well, you really can't blame them—they'd managed to get access to Stephen King's place that month. They'd been trying to get him to agree to do a photo shoot for years. It sold out all the newsstands, I heard. *Inside the Madman's Domain*, or something like that. Cesar was so put-out that he cancelled our subscription. Poor Cesar."

Antonio is a heartless, bastard, lawyer assassin. He's glacial hardness and utter dispassion. How the hell can she love him?

"In any event, I think that Cesar will be too busy this week to go to the wine shops. These particular gentlemen he's dealing with haven't shown themselves to be true partners at all. I hope Cesar's not having too hard of a time with them. It's so strange. We've known John socially for years. Cesar's had multiple business dealings with him and Bailey. I don't know why they're treating this investment so suspiciously."

I stand.

"I have work to do. I have to patrol."

Anna stops hard on her chat. Her eyes instantly become round and large within their finely cut lids.

"Can't that wait?"

"No. Nine o'clock every night. That's what your husband wanted."

"Sure, but…"

She's strongly debating grabbing my wrist. I can see it in the path her eyes dodge along; the way she shifts her wine glass from hand to hand.

"Can't you skip a night? I won't tell."

"It's not something I can skip."

"Flynn…"

She doesn't grab my wrist, but my sweatshirt sleeve. Lightly, like a cat snagging its claw by accident.

"I'd like…I'd like it if you'd stay with me a little longer. Please. Just to talk. I really don't…maybe Cesar told you that I don't do well when he's away for the night? It's something like a phobia. I really can't be alone."

Her voice is so soft.

I'm hard-pressed to be civil.

"Sorry."

I have no trouble loosening myself from her grasp. She gives off easily, but her whole body gleams with terror, like a slender stem of willow set afire, as I walk out of the room.

Thursday, October 1, 1998
7:14 a.m.
Ortiz Farm

I still dress fast in the morning, just like when I was in the army. I don't sit down at any point, not even to lace up my shoes. It takes me a bare two minutes to go from shower dampness to dry-brushed-deodorized-clothed action. I never primp.

I shut the door to my bedroom and walk down the hall. Even though there's a bevy of silent, rarely-seen Mexican maids who vacuum and dust, I never leave my room in disarray. I always make up the bed with sharply tucked corners. Every garment is hung, folded, or stacked in its proper place. My grooming supplies are in a ruler-straight line on my dresser. My quarters are inspectable at all times.

I'm hungry. I miss the huge breakfasts they served in the Fort Lewis mess hall. Biscuits and gravy and Cream of Wheat. Yogurt for the calcium. Gallons of orange juice for the vitamin C. Here on the island, I eat a quick cereal in my security nook, as I go over the previous evening's security tapes. There's been nothing of note yet.

As I reach the end of the hall, the door to Cesar and Anna's bedroom swings open. My legs seize and I pull up short. With all my heart, I don't want to encounter Anna. I can't look her in the eye after last night. Kell emerges, drawn and rubbing his eyes. His clothing is rumpled and creased in odd places over his body. He steps blearily into the hall and nearly walks right into me.

"Shi—oh God, Flynn. Didn't see you."

A weary but true smile forms on his earth-brown face.

"What's going on?"

Kell sighs irritably.

"Guess. No Cesar yet. She cornered me before I could go home last night. I don't need this; I've got so much work to

225

do! The damned Mexicans haven't gotten more than three-quarters of the crop in, and Cesar's gonna have a conniption if the fields aren't fully cleared when he gets back. I hate spending the night with her."

Kell rubs a hand through his hair, springing long strands free from his ponytail. His eyes are lined, making him look middle-aged. He grins with a quirk of sarcasm as he steps away from me.

"Nights like that, I actually start to wish Antonio was here."

Saturday, October 3, 1998
3:25 p.m.
Ortiz Farm

A loaded gun looms overhead, the barrel snug against my temple. Cesar is coming home today.

"Hey Flynn. You seen the Jeep keys around?"

I sit up fast, positioning my fingers over my keyboard. I look busy.

Kell strolls into my security nook, pulling off his work gloves, awash in casual indifference. He props one butt-cheek on the corner of my desk as I retrieve the keys from my jeans pocket. He's wearing his usual button-down flannel work shirt over a tight white tank top. He smells of horseflesh and fresh hay.

"Thanks."

He gathers up the keys unhurriedly. He leans over my chair, his hand resting on the back.

"Don't forget about tonight. It's gonna be great. I'm really glad you're coming. Do you want me to pick you up?"

I shake my head. I slide my chair back slightly, but Kell doesn't let go.

"I'll get there, thanks."

"Okay. It's gonna be fun. You'll like it, I promise. Don't be late."

He takes his ass off my desktop, and his hand off my chair. He moves past me, out of the nook, out of the kitchen. I hear the heavy front door shut, closing me in.

I'm trapped in the house with Anna.

I should warn her. I've argued extensively with myself about this. Even if she did wrong, I should give her a sporting chance: the opportunity to organize a cover-up. My CO and I never got such a chance. It might have helped if we had. Maybe things would have turned out better for both of us.

I check the status of the video monitors via the computer

hook-up. I research a security system for Cesar's steel recycling plant. I keep glancing at the ceiling, wondering what Anna is doing upstairs. Is she pacing? The house is built so solidly that I've never been able to hear a sound from anyone living here. I can usually hear everything: I was trained to. It made apartment life hell after the discharge. Coughing and TV and shoes thunking to the floor and pans rattling above, below, and on all sides. From the depths of my soul, I don't want to tell Cesar. I'm beginning to sweat icy down my back and along my forehead. I shouldn't know about the sexual habits of my boss's wife. It's dirty knowing; it turns my mind to swiss cheese, with dark pits and gaps to avoid. I should never have gone hunting for her secrets. I feel like I've stolen something. I feel shameful.

Cesar arrives home in slightly less than an hour. He must have been waiting at the dock, his ferry already landed. I can picture him standing in the too-warm sun with his luggage, impatiently checking his watch, debating whether or not to call home. Kell might be in trouble for this. I hear heavy suitcases clunk down in the foyer. I type quickly to save my report on the new security system. I need to seem as if I was up to something useful. Not fretting; not

concerning myself with a secret.

Light thunder rolls in a helix down the staircase. Bare feet pound through the foyer.

"Cesar, Cesar, oh God, Ce—"

I hear the impact of two bodies. I creep to the door to spy.

Anna is cocooned within Cesar's arms, his trench coat enveloping her from her feet to her hairline. Cesar says nothing as she holds tight to him, her toes barely touching the floor. She sobs brokenly, yet with such horrendous relief. Cesar's eyes are closed.

He looks so tired.

"I missed you so much! I can't handle it when you're away. I couldn't breathe."

Her voice is wooly under his coat. Cesar doesn't answer. He seems used to this, but no less agonized by it from experience.

She shrouds herself within his embrace, soaking him up. Finally, he pushes her gently away. Just an inch or so, but it causes her to gasp fearfully.

"Come upstairs with me, okay, amor? You're so upset, baby."

Anna clings to him like a kitten on a high tree branch. Cesar is large man, and I expect him to pick her up. Instead, he gently kisses her face many times, murmuring too quietly for me to hear. His large hands stroke her cheeks and his lips graze her forehead as he whispers to her.

God, he loves her so much. How can I tell him?

She hides her face against his neck and grips his lapels hard. Her tears begin to slow.

"Please come upstairs, sweetheart. You've got to lie down. You'll make yourself sick."

She digs her fingers through his hair, opening her eyes to him and returning his kiss.

"Don't leave me alone, promise? Please, I can't be alone! I can't stand it, it's been so long…"

She lets him guide her up the stairs, and I withdraw myself to my nook. I return to the computer and look up luxury cars on the Internet. I scroll through photos of Aston Martins. Just on the slim chance I was mistaken.

I sink. I wasn't mistaken.

Maybe I won't tell Cesar. What possible good would it? It will end his marriage. He will hate his brother.

Well. That I wouldn't mind. Not at all. Antonio could

use some agony. A little ruination in his smug, insular, arctic life.

He could use a disaster.

Besides, it's information, and I've been trained to report information. Without purging myself of it, I'm as faulty, as unclean, as guilty as Anna and Antonio. As guilty as my CO and I were. And I told then, when asked.

Only when asked: I volunteered nothing.

If Cesar doesn't ask, what should I do?

Cesar comes down the stairs an hour later, much cheered

and hearty. I can guess what happened up there to put a spring in his step. It makes this so much worse.

"Hey, Flynn, how's it going?"

He claps a paternal hand on my shoulder briefly, and I stop pretending to work on the computer.

"Hi. Good. How was Seattle?"

"God, almost a total disaster. Those damned ad hoc morons! I couldn't have thrown together a worse group of investors if I'd planned it. The whole thing almost fell through big time, but then Antonio joined us on Wednesday, and we hammered those cocksuckers till every last, piddling signature was on every damned dotted line. Then we got the hell out of there. I took Antonio out to dinner last night to celebrate, just us two. Usually I take my investors out as a show of goodwill and team spirit. Fuck 'em all."

Wednesday. I shift slightly. Just a movement of the foot; nothing more. Cesar is a wickedly perceptive man, however.

He sees.

He pauses.

He looks into my eyes.

He blinks, and things shift irredeemably.

"Say, Flynn. Let's go on up to my office, okay?"

"Now?"

"Yeah, sure."

There's a chill underpinning the jovial voice. I follow Cesar up the spiral staircase to his office. We step into the manly room exuding leathery power and brushed velvet sophistication. Sunlight speckles in and out of the clouds, pecking at the windowpanes. The rug is dappled with gold. I stand at attention. My hands are behind my back. I concentrate on breathing evenly.

Cesar glides behind his enormous desk, unmistakably setting the tone of this exchange. He doesn't sit, and neither do I.

"So! How did you like being head of the farm while I was away?"

He is forcedly jocular. I smile lamely. I have to humor him.

"How did everything go? Any problems?"

I hesitate.

"The farm ran fine. The workers got all the crops in on time. Kell had the load shipped off to market. The security system held up very well. There were no breaches."

"Good, good. So…what did Anna do all week? Did she keep busy? She wasn't too gloomy, I hope?"

Cesar has cut right to the chase. I eye the coolly accurate paintings of native ducks and fish which line the walls. All calm pastels, with perfectly drafted feathers and scales. I measure and weigh, but not for too long.

"She kept herself occupied."

"What did you two do?"

I hesitate again.

"Friday, when you left, she told me and Kell not to bother her. She locked herself up in the master bedroom until the next day. She gave me the day off Saturday."

Cesar watches me with mild eyes. It's worse than feeling suspicion in his gaze. I will start to tremble soon.

"What did she do on Saturday?"

"I'm—I'm not confident in my ability to report that accurately. Sir."

"Well, I seem to recall that I asked you to keep an eye on her the entire time I was gone. You didn't actually take Saturday off, did you?"

This is all Antonio's fault. Why couldn't he keep his damned dick to himself?

"Flynn?"

The CO and I never had a chance. We were never given one.

"Anna went to Seattle on Saturday. She had Kell drive her to the ferry."

Cesar flinches, then blanches very slightly. It's clearly not what he expected to hear. Not at all. He strokes a pen, a brass cigar ashtray, the desk blotter, seeking to maintain a casual equilibrium.

"Oh. Did you follow her there?"

"I followed her."

"And?"

Cesar's dark eyes dig deep into mine.

"She went to Seattle alone."

"Yes?"

"A car picked her up at the ferry dock in Seattle. I tried to follow it, but there weren't any cabs."

Cesar's eyes go unfocused. He stares at the sun-brightened window, not out it. The moment rings. It vibrates. I don't have to volunteer any more information. He isn't asking.

I never really decide. Antonio's face, hard-lipped and scornful, jumps to the front of my brain.

"But…"

Cesar's eyes slice to mine, burning black like smoke from an oil fire.

"Yes?"

"You should know…it was an Aston Martin she got into."

Saturday, October 3, 1998
9:14 p.m.
Skyhamish Indian Reservation

The stars hang high and bright above me, shining like the steel heads of nails in a dark roof. I walk off the main road, past a charred wooden sign stating that I'm leaving U.S. soil. I cross an invisible border and step into the Skyhamish Indian Reservation.

I inhale deeply, perceiving no difference. No earthy, foreign scent. No perfume of shamanistic mystery. It smells like the rest of the island: pine trees and salt water. Kell warned me that it was small, but I'm taken aback when I discover that the reservation is just an empty field of well-trodden dirt sprinkled with dead grass, and an adjacent trailer park littered with sagging 1970's era mobile homes and dogs. It looks like a poorly-maintained campground. It's smaller than Cesar's carrot patch.

At least it shouldn't be hard to locate Kell.

I walk into the thick of the reservation, past trailers smelling of Marlboros and macaroni 'n' cheese. Televisions jabber behind RV walls as thin as cardboard, flashing aquarium-blue against the windows. The ground sparkles with jagged bits of broken bottles beneath snapping bug lights.

I'm unimpressed with this quasi-country. I jam my hands into the warmth of my field jacket and drift. The air's crisp out here in Indian Country. No one accosts me, no one questions my white presence. There's a vibrating excitement here on the reservation. Indians are wandering purposefully to and fro in the night, their faces flashing eagerly when yellow light spills over them from dusty trailer windows.

A middle-aged guy dressed like a Hell's Angel biker shoves by me, throwing a bright red felt blanket dotted with tacky white buttons over his leather jacket. A couple teenage girls dart by, arcing red lipsticks in blunt lines over their

233

cheekbones.

"Flynn! Hey, Flynn!"

I turn to see Kell jogging between two rusting trailers. His face is warm with the smile he always gives me, and as usual, it's too warm and makes me uncomfortable. Kell looks interesting tonight. He has let his long, black hair hang loose and straight down his back. His too-tight jeans and migrant worker boots are typical for him, but he has topped them with a very large, very red Blackhawks hockey jersey. For the sake of the Indian-in-profile logo, no doubt.

"Hi! You have any trouble getting here?"

"No."

"Cool, good. Hey, wanna beer? Come meet my uncles."

Kell puts a guiding hand on my elbow, which is a touch too much. I start to wither away into my jacket, like a mollusk. I force myself to keep still and endure it, however. Maybe it's cultural. Like French people kissing when they meet. Maybe it's just a handshake to his people, dignified and reserved. We'll see: Kell has only touched me one other time, and that could not have been taken as a casual, collegial touch.

I am guided by the elbow through a boxy alley of trailers, forced to dodge scruffy, mid-sized dogs and little kids bent on running into my knees in their sugared hyperactivity.

"Hey, Uncle Billy! Uncle Ed, this is Flynn! Finally made it, as promised."

I force a fake, good-natured smile. It's quite a walk from Ortiz Farm up north to Injun Territory. There's no way I was going to drive. I plan to drink tonight.

Kell's Uncle Billy or Ed sits on the broken metal steps of his trailer, in splendid state with a mesa-shaped crew cut, gaudy red plaid shirt, and pumpkin-round beer gut. A dozen guy-Indians stand around him, ranging in age from a tender fifteen up to an old man who looks crinkled and bent past ninety. It's red T-shirts and flannels all around. Jeans topped with big ol' belt buckles. They eye me.

Eye me.

Finally, this Billy or Ed hocks a throat booger loose, spits, and intones,

"This here's Flynn, huh? The famous Flynn—heard you're Cesar Ortiz's new guard dog. Like it?"

He glances me up and down, wondering.

I shrug.

"It's okay."

"That a fact?"

"Um…yes."

The Indians are silent. They ponder me. I shift a bit, my hands in my jacket pockets. Their faces are awful, studied blanks, like still photographs.

Kell rescues me.

"Wanna beer? There's Corona, Bud…um…Coors. And Pabst."

Kell scrabbles around in a blue and white plastic cooler.

There's more water than ice in there, but plenty of beer.

"Whichever. Doesn't matter."

"You ever been to a pow-wow before?" a middle-aged man inquires, picking at his fingernails speculatively as a way to continue to look me while seeming to break eye contact.

"Nope."

Kell hands me a Coors. It's pretty warm, and fizzes chokingly in my mouth. I swipe at my chin with my sleeve.

"We're all real glad you agreed to come. Real glad."

A very handsome, very glossily black-haired young man speaks up from the edge of the group. His unsmiling coolness reminds me of Antonio, and I instantly hate him.

"See, we gotta sacrifice a whitey tonight, and the one we had lined up ran off."

"You crazed fucker, shut up!" Uncle Billy or Ed bursts into loud chuckles. The rest of the men snicker, fail to contain themselves, and fall into hysterical laughter. I can tell they've emptied that cooler between them at least twice already tonight. I can also tell, as they slice their eyes at oblivious, laughing Kell, that it isn't just my mysterious physique that is making them stare. They're wondering about us. What has he told them? I take another big drink of beer, wincing at the fluffy fizz on my tongue.

Kell leans in close.

"He's just kidding."

"I figured that."

"You hungry?"

Kell is still close. Too close. He's intimate by my ear, almost whispering. He, too, has had quite a few this evening from the smell of his breath as it traces my cheek. I ease a step to my right so I can see him, and fend him off, if necessary.

"Yeah, sure, I skipped dinner."

"Here, Token. Fry bread."

An extremely old man lobs a bag of tortilla chips at me. The Indians collapse with guffaws again.

Oh, hell yeah, I need to get very drunk very fast, or this I going to start to irritate me.

"Come on, let's go to the field. These guys are jerkoffs."

Kell gets empty beer cans slung at him by his relatives. We walk through the dimness, aiming for a patch of open ground. I clutch the tortilla chips and my beer. Kell's hand returns to my elbow, and I can't get rid of it because both my hands are occupied. I grasp awkwardly for conversation. Small talk. Nothing occurs to me except distressing Ortiz topics. Kell's fingers cup my elbow firmly. His eyes are locked on my face. He's watching me. He's enjoying it. It's as if he kept himself from doing so in the past, and is indulging himself now.

"They should get things started pretty soon. Everyone's getting cold. Are you cold?"

I shake my head.

"This jacket's very warm. Army-issue."

He looks at it; at my body.

"It looks warm. It fits you good."

I don't know how to respond to this, so I say, "Thanks."

We step out of the dark clot of trailers into the empty field. Several men are squatting in a half-circle, squirting lighter fluid and splashing gasoline over the ground in an inattentive and worrisome manner, while others struggle to get lighters and matches lit.

"Here, have a seat."

Kell plops down on the packed, scrabbly dirt and leans back on his hands. He looks up at me in that open, naked way of his. I avoid his eyes.

I sit carefully, arranging my sad picnic on the ground in front of me. I take a single chip, then flinch when the bonfire bursts into flame with an audible *whooom!* Everything is orange, a forest fire, an exploding star. Heat slaps me thick in the face.

Apparently, these Indians are fireproof. There are hoots and cheers, then the brightness and heat ebb down a bit. People begin to gather around the licking fire. Kell watches, his brown skin dipped in glowing gold as if by sunset. His dark hair reflects the firelight with impossible blues and silvers. His eyes have moons in their black cores. I look away since I don't want him to catch me staring. It would please him and give him hope.

"Hey, man, you're so sober!"

An incredibly fat man thuds by, dropping a liter soda bottle full of noxious-looking orange liquid into Kell's lap.

"Thanks! Awesome!"

Kell wrestles the plastic bottle open, flashes the departing man a thumbs-up, then gives me his face. His eyes dance too softly on mine.

"That was my Uncle Sully. He made this—want some?"

I don't inquire what it is. I take the heavy bottle and sip lightly, tasting it like a cat. I hope it's something exotic; I hope if ruins me. I want to leave my mind and my thoughts tonight, more than I've ever wanted anything. It's Tang and vodka. It's all-too-familiar to me. It'll do the trick.

I take a very large drink. Kell laughs approvingly. He wants to liquor me up, and I know why. I should leave. I could trash myself privately at the bar in town by the ferry dock. Or at the decaying shack in the woods Kell took me to.

"It's good to get away from the farm, isn't it?"

I nod vigorously. I have no desire to be there tonight. I don't know what Cesar's going to do to Anna. Or to me, for destroying their marriage.

"Just us."

I'm vastly alarmed by this, and Kell sees it. He hastily amends himself.

"I mean, no boss-man around. Christ, the mood he was in tonight—what's wrong with him? Do you know?"

I stare at Kell. I blink hard. My head's starting to drone and buzz from the booze. I'm slowing down.

"I guess he must've blown that deal in Seattle, huh?"

I tip back the bottle again, wishing with all my soul for Kell to shut up.

"I saw him sitting up in his office when I was heading out. He looked like hell. Looked like he was thinking about blowing his brains out. Probably lost a good half-million this time. I hope we aren't out of our jobs."

Kell sounds a bit anxious. I let his eyes drag mine to contact. I don't evade them like I usually do. I look long at him, and I think I can tell him what happened in Seattle last week. It might make me feel better to tell him. But I don't. I was trained in the army to keep things to myself. 'That's classified,' and all. It's none of his business. Besides, it could cause us feel close if we share a confidence.

I shrug.

"Dunno."

"But…I've never seen him so upset before."

Kell rubs his hand over his jaw, then suddenly freezes.

"Did you…Flynn, oh God. You didn't—"

"What's the fire for? Why do you guys have a bonfire?"

"Ceremonial. Like, tradition. I don't know."

I let uncomfortable silence fall over us and remain. I pass him the bottle.

The pow-wow still hasn't started. Or maybe it has. A few chubby Indians keep wandering out to the fire, where they hop around briefly as if testing out stiff new shoes, then they meander abruptly back to the gloom at the edge of the firelight to guzzle more beer and gossip.

Kell drinks and drinks, tipping his head back heavily on his brown neck. I can see his Adam's apple prod out sharp under the arch of his throat. His hair hangs stone-black and long like a woman's to kiss the dirt when he drinks. It's very beautiful, so I look away.

I haven't spent this much time alone with anyone since my CO. We were never in public, however. It wouldn't have looked right for him to be seen with one of his subordinates, socializing. Fraternizing. I never liked it with the CO, but I never hated it either. It was a vague discomfort. An uneasy forward march without bearings. Like it is with Kell.

The field grows crowded. Indians ring the sun-bright fire, drinking beer, wine coolers, and bottles of hard liquor sans paper bag of shame. Suspicious concoctions like Uncle Sully's orange brew circulate hand to hand. Limp cigarettes dangle from mouths. Everyone laughs loud and loose.

I drink more, then more. Kell wanders off somewhere, and I'm rather glad. He has left me the bottle. That's all the company I want. I gag a bit but keep drinking. I can feel it staining my tongue and teeth the color of a cartoon carrot.

I realize two things all at once: I'm very drunk, and the pow-wow has finally started. The hot space around the bonfire is choked with Indians: dozens and dozens of Indians. Craggy old men in red sports jerseys like Kell's; young girls with their black hair raked into perky ponytails; little boys in cherry-red T-shirts; women in full black skirts that threaten to catch flame. The red and black spins a drowning whirlpool, sucking down the firelight. The Indians stomp-dance, circling the fire with great deliberation and a sense of casual abandon. Their feet pound the dirt hard, throwing up round brown clouds. They stare at their feet or the star-dotted sky. No one smiles. They're perfectly synchronized, from old women gnarled with arthritis to large headed toddlers who can barely walk.

It takes me a while, but I gradually realize why. A deep, dull thrumming is coming from the other side of the fire. As the flames shoot to the sky and crash back to earth, I spy an enormous skin drum the size of Cesar's dining room table. At least fifteen men sit around it, whacking with sticks and singing in the flat, impossible tones that I've heard in a dozen cowboys 'n' Indians movies.

A hard hand suddenly grasps mine, startling me into executing an unstable counter attack with the other. There's no technique to my defense at all. My CO would have bawled me out good for it, drunk or not. Kell glows down at me, his face like a thousand candles.

"Come on, Flynn! Come on, get up! Dance with me."

"Nah, no."

I resist, but I can't pull my hand free from Kell's. He's stronger than he looks. He breaks horses.

"Aw, don't be like that!"

Kell pulls again, laughing. I resist again, putting dead weight behind my arm.

"Drinking, can't, don't wanna. You do it."

"Jeez, you whites really got no rhythm, huh? Thought that was just a rumor."

Kell rolls his eyes and cavorts away, smiling at me until he's back in the thick of the stomping circle. I can look openly at him now, since he's oblivious. He thrashes in his bright red hockey jersey, slamming his boots into the dry dirt to make his whole body shudder. His long, black hair tosses as coarse and wildly-arcing as the mane on the horse I saw him breaking so long ago. His back arches like the horse's did when it wanted to throw him; slow yet frantic. Violently ecstatic.

I don't want to experience Kell's body. I don't want him to want me.

I'm dizzy, almost spinning myself though motionless, as I watch the Indians grind their way around and around the bonfire. I feel vaguely sick and stained within. It's too hot by the fire. It's urgent that I get away.

I make it to my feet, pitch slightly, then wobble my way

into the shadows of the trailers. In the dark, away from everyone, I

can no longer avoid my thoughts. I have destroyed everything for

Cesar. I've shattered his world.

Maybe he'll forgive them.

Maybe he'll beat bloody hell out of Anna, and I'll have to call in a domestic dispute to Island County's boat-bound cops. Hell, maybe he won't care and will let them keep screwing each other. Maybe he knew all along, and I was just yet another security officer to report Anna and Antonio's affair in oh-so-serious tones to him in his impressive office. Maybe it's become a practiced routine for him, like his dinner party schtik. Pretend to care, nod a lot, then fire the security officer and hire a new, untainted one.

Kell is suddenly at my side, breathing hot, longing, whisky breath in my ear.

"Flynn...hey..."

His hand gropes over my lower arm, gaining my hand. His fingers braid into mine, seeking connection.

"Come on, please, Flynn. You want to? Please, I really want this. Will you?"

Before I realize it, before I'm aware that I'm on foot and traveling, Kell manages to propel me to a sagging, humpty trailer in a nondescript corner of the reservation. He clumsily unlocks the front door, tossing coaxing murmurs over his shoulder at me. I look down at my hands and realize that I've lost the bottle of Tangy vodka. Maybe I drank it all, or maybe a thieving Indian took it. I feel bereft.

Kell guides me inside. He doesn't force me, but simply aims me and lets my intoxicated, wind-up feet send me stumbling up the rusty steps. I shuffle through the door, tripping over piles of car parts and bits of trash in the dark. I stop to lean against a faux-wood closet door the width of a paperback book. Kell blunders past me and flips on a light.

I wince at the white flare of electricity. It's a truly pathetic trailer. I don't know if Kell shares this cramped, cluttered, velvet-painting-bedecked space with a few of his uncles, or if he lives alone. Either way, it's depressing to think of him making his home here. I expected pictures of wild horses in fields of emerald green grass in Kell's home. Instead, a huge poster of Dale Earnhardt leers at me.

"Come in, sit, sit."

Kell flops down onto the tiny built-in couch and smiles sloppily up at me. His body is too relaxed and puppet-limbed to be anything but profoundly drunk. This comforts me: we're both ruinously smashed, so I can't be manipulated. This seems logical right now.

"C'mere."

Kell leans forward, his legs splayed to make his crotch rear masterfully, and swipes at my hand. He misses by yards. I stub my way to the couch and sit on the floor. Nubby brown carpet, like in the Fort Lewis rec room, crushes beneath my hands. I watch the room spin, my head lolling against the couch cushions. Kell makes an effort and slides himself closer to me, reaching for my face. He gets my cheek with a passing bat of his fingers and seems content that this has been a sort of caress.

All smoothness and angularity and ambiguity, that's how I must strike him. No one can ever tell if I'm a man or a woman. I lack specificity, cues. Why does he like it?

"Flynn, jeez, can't tell you...I've really been thinking about doing this. With you. A lot. I mean, Christ, I've wanted you since we met. That time. C'mere, let's...y'wanna?"

I'm uninspired by his slurred wooing. I stare at the ceiling, trying to will it to quit rotating.

"Maybe, I dunno, maybe you don't, maybe this's not something you're into. But...I really like you a lot, Flynn. I can make it good for you."

Kell leans down and appears to be ready to make His Big Move. Instead, he touches my hair curiously. His face broadcasts his thoughts like a readerboard: *So that's what white people's hair feels like.* His eyes slide to mine very slight focus.

"It's so hard to meet someone on this island. I mean, I'm related to every Indian around here one way or another. Can't...y'know, that would be, like incest or whatever. Can't date someone from the same tribe. And the migrant workers— the Mexicans won't talk to me. I'm their boss on the farm, sure, but see, even the ones from the other farms won't. Like, not just a language barrier. They hate the Indios back home.

They're racist. And, like, the whites around here, they just always think I'm some damned alcoholic welfare Injin. But God, Flynn, you've always been so…nice. So open-minded."

Open-minded—that's his hook. Just try it; we'll stop if you want. The CO wasn't so ham-handed as to put that one out there when he made his move.

"It's always been like that, know what I mean? I—God, goddamn it all, you know?"

Kell leans away and his eyes go all fuzzy.

"I mean, I get shit wages on that stupid farm, but I can't quit. There's no work on this damned island. Half my uncles are on the welfare. Other half are working worse jobs than mine. It's so messed up, Flynn! It's a poverty job, and like, if the big Cesar Salad gets bored with the gentleman farmer bullshit game and sells the place, then that's it for me. Back on the welfare. Bureau of Indian Affairs office every week. No money for anything. No light bulbs. No freakin' telephone. Just…sitting. Waiting. For nothing to happen."

Kell begins to shake his head, his dark hair making a storm cloud over his face.

"And you've gone and told him, haven't you? It's all so damned *wrecked* now, Flynn! Why did you do it? You've ruined everything for all of us, you know that? So many things are gonna completely *end*, and…I just want the horses. That's all I've ever wanted. Just wanna break 'em and take care of 'em and—why the hell's that so much to ask outta life? Huh? Why'd you take it from me?"

Kell rubs his hand over his face, trying to contain things. He's too drunk to do so. He humps over and his body crumples into itself. He rests his head on the couch cushions and begins to weep softly. His chest hitches within his vivid hockey jersey.

I should do something. I'm the one who did this to him, after all.

I pat his hand.

It's more than I would ordinarily do.

KATHERINE LUCK

Sunday, October 4, 1998
1:01 p.m.
Ortiz Farm

I attain Ortiz Farm after three hours of weaving and stumbling along the road that encircles the island. I sneak, as well as I can when hungover-cum-drunk, into the echoingly silent house. The enormous front door snicks softly closed behind me. I feather-step my way through the deserted foyer and up the gleaming blond wood of the spiral staircase. It spins me dizzy, nauseating me.

I slide down the hall to my room. The door to Anna and Cesar's bedroom is closed, thank God.

I ease the door to my room open, slip in, and gently swing it shut.

I turn to the bed, and Cesar is sitting on it.

I let out a very loud, very shrill scream that sobers me and brings a humiliated, cherry-red burn to my face. Some stealthy soldier. Some self-contained security officer. A girly scream at
    seeing my boss sitting on my bed.

I grab the doorjamb, slam a hand to my chest, and pull in a steadying breath. I don't want Cesar to know that I've been drinking all night.

"Sorry. Jeez. I didn't expect…"

Cesar looks up at me, and I don't recognize him. He is profoundly silent; everything about him is submerged beneath a dark and wrathful stillness. His fingers are twined, the hands hanging ready between his knees.

My heart starts to go fast and urgent.

Cesar clears his throat. It's a rough sound, like stones grinding together.

He parts his lips slowly, and his voice freezes me.

"I called Antonio. I told him to come out here immediately."

I grope, lost and swimming, for the bedstead, the chair, the desktop. Something to steady myself with.

"Okay."

I don't feel alcohol-blunted anymore. I feel too present, too crucial. Time has sped up brutally. It has become an exquisitely conscious thing that chases me and will consume me.

"I want you to bring him here. He's coming on the next ferry."

I get my fingers around the corner of the dresser and cling with my nails.

"Where's Anna?"

Cesar raises soul-cleaving eyes to mine. His tongue rolls light and fast over his upper lip.

"Go pick Antonio up, Flynn. Now."

Sunday, October 4, 1998
3:25 p.m.
Skyhamish Ferry Dock

I veer the Jeep down Main Street, my heart jumping like a piston. The tiny town flashes by in a clotty smear of sea-faded pastel mobile homes, squat storefronts, and rust-webbed cars.

I swing into the ferry dock's small parking lot. I turn off the engine, my hand jittering the keys so hard they sound like Christmas bells.

I get out and lean against the Jeep, crossing my arms nervously over my chest like Anna did when she was here. The ocean is as flat as a bone china platter under the massive, blue sky. The last shreds of summer are gleaming off a dozen sea gulls' wings, tinting the dull sand silver at the water's edge. I can just make out the ferry in the distance; a pale flaw on the monochrome horizon.

I know how Antonio will come to me when he arrives: menacing as hell, striding cockily down the ramp as if he's packing an assault rifle under his power suit jacket. He will sneer at me. Arrogant bastard. He needs to realize how much trouble he's in.

The ferry slides fat and sluggish across the water; a great beetle with all the time in the world. I squeeze my arms tighter over my sweatshirt to keep my trembling confined to my innards. This time, I won't let Antonio intimidate me. I can stare him down if I really try. I'll summon the spirit of my CO. I'll become him; the epitome of control and veiled power.

A small crowd gathers around me to wait for the ferry. On this island, a crowd is ten people. They stand bored and probably as hungover as I am, watching the ferry slide closer and closer over the calm water.

The ferry eases into its landing. The wide prow bumps resoundingly against the rubber padded dock. Workers in orange vests take down the nylon barrier, and cars begin to roll off the drive-on deck. My eyes latch onto the passenger ramp.

Below, three beat-up pick-up trucks roll off. Two motorcycles manned by Indians heading home to the reservation. Some form of Volkswagen that looks completely corroded.

Then a ghostly, silver Aston Martin shoots out.

This viscous, luxurious drop of mercury makes every head turn. The engine guns as the driver shifts gears violently. It cuts off all the other cars, flies out of the parking lot, and grabs the road to Cesar's farm.

Antonio realizes how much trouble he's in.

Sunday, October 4, 1998
4:02 p.m.
Ortiz Farm

I follow Antonio up the grand coil of the staircase to the second floor. I barely managed to reach the farm ten minutes after he did. His car is a bullet. I nearly drove into the ocean three times, as I followed him through the winding curves of the main road. Something blew out deep within the Jeep's engine. The CO would have been pleased with my improvement in automotive pursuit.

Antonio is aware of my trailing presence as he steps off the staircase into the hall. He is ignoring me, as he has been since I pulled up behind him, tapped on the driver's side window, and asked him to come into the house.

His hair sparkles with pinprick rainbows as he passes beneath the tiny crystal chandeliers hanging from the ceiling. His shoulders are precisely horizontal, like shelves, beneath his navy blue suit jacket. His hands are unclenched at his sides. They don't tremble.

Antonio stops outside of the closed door to Cesar's office.

He doesn't hesitate. He raises his fist and knocks: three even, medium-toned raps. He doesn't pause or glance at me when his older brother's voice tightly tells him to come in. He enters and closes the door behind him firmly.

I stand alone on the swirly Turkish rug, doused by prismatic color from above, and stare at the closed door. When I hear a soft breath catch in a throat, I turn.

Anna is standing in the open doorway to the master bedroom. Her eyes are huge and blank with terror: hostage eyes. They are affixed to the office door. Slowly, they drift to mine.

My vague, shameful pleasure at Antonio's predicament rinses off like dust under a cool faucet. I take a step toward her, unsure of what I intend. I never gave her a chance. I take another step toward her, then another. Anna stands locked within the doorway, neither shrinking back nor stretching to meet me in the hall. She stares at me with her mouth slightly open. She gasps quietly, trying to ride her breath smoothly, but unable to. Her face, her skin, her features have never looked more wrong to me. The man-made perfection is bleached like the sunless belly of a fish. Every bit of her seems to tremble and strain, petal-pale and breakable.

"Flynn."

She reaches out abruptly and grips my arm with her long nails, digging them in to hold me in place. The doorway to the bedroom that she shares with Cesar is partially blocked by her thin shoulders and the fall of her dark hair. Just beyond her body, I can see the sun beginning to squeeze itself into the ocean. The windows behind her shudder with pure light, illuminating her like deadly heaven. She is a corpse made beautiful for planting six feet down.

I won't be drawn into the room. I root my feet into the soft rug.

"Please. Antonio's here. Cesar called him. He said. That he would."

She is close to hysteria and doesn't bother to hide it from me. She shakes my arm, hurting me. Her nails will break the skin soon. I pull my arm away and take a step back.

"Does Cesar know? Is that why Antonio's here? Please, Flynn—you have to find out for me. Please, Flynn, please! I feel like I'm going crazy. I can't breathe."

She looks so young, her face like a prepubescent girl's. Is this the first time she's felt the hideous, sour clench of being caught? I can never forget the singing burn, the acid floating that filled my head and guts when I was caught. I can never forget the voice saying, 'Corporal, an issue has come to the attention of your superior officers,' and the entire world crashing and burning around me.

I hate how she does this to me. She evokes protective urges. It's not manipulative. She radiates a dire vulnerability that I've never been able to pin down, but which I can't keep from responding to. She extracts instincts of heroism and rescue.

A dull murmuring of masculine voices is growing within the office.

"Please, Flynn. Oh God, please?"

How the hell does she do this to me?

Sunday, October 4, 1998
4:07 p.m.
Ortiz Farm

I'm smotheringly silent as I approach Cesar's office. The slickly polished door is shut as securely a medieval castle gate. I hold my breath and lean against the cool wall three feet from the door. The wallpaper is a silky pillow under my cheek, the rich carpeting like sun-warmed grass cupping my boots, as I press my ear to the wall. I concentrate.

At first, all I can make out is the indistinct, back-and-forth muttering of two male voices. I slide carefully down the hall, keeping my cheek pressed against the wall. The voices grow under

my ear, becoming a fluid yammering that stubbornly refuses to resolve into individual words. I frown, bringing my hands up to the wall to feel the vibrations.

There's no way around it. Anna has a way of making you desperate to help her; of making you do foolish, risky things.

Cautiously, so very carefully, I wrap first my palm, then my fingers one by one, around the gleaming crystal knob. I bite hard on the insides of my cheeks and squeeze down. I wait. Wait.

I begin to turn my wrist infinitesimally. It takes ninety seconds to rotate the knob fully. I wait another ninety, silent, perfectly still, clutching the knob.

Cesar's voice suddenly booms out, harsh enough to carry clear out into the hall. I want to flinch hugely, but I've been too well trained to do so. His consonants are in the wrong places. The vowels are blurred and stretched. I can't understand what he's saying.

I ease, ease, ease the door ajar. I apply my left eye to the crack. I don't breathe.

I see Antonio. He is standing by the river rock fireplace, beneath the painting of the dignified and unfilleted king salmon, scientifically sketched in pink and gray. He is pacing a small circumference very slowly, his fingers pinching and rubbing at his forehead. He looks edgy in his dark, corporate suit. He looks harangued by a judge in a courtroom. He looks trapped.

"Antonio. Antonio!"

Cesar's voice pierces the air, skewering the momentary silence. Antonio does not flinch, though I do.

"Este es muy serio, Antonio! Escúcheme!"

"Estoy escuchando! Te entiendo muy bien, okay?"

Antonio snaps, dropping his hand sharply.

Antonio told Anna that he can't speak Spanish anymore. They were both keeping secrets.

Cesar's voice mounts and expands with rolling Rs and flexible vowels that smear themselves into one impossibly long, breathless word. Antonio shakes his head and stalks out of view. I can't see either of them now, and this worries me desperately. I'm vulnerable. They'll become aware of me. They'll unite to attack me. My eye at the door crack keeps involuntarily winking closed. I am not helping Anna at all.

Suddenly, Antonio steps aggressively back into my field of vision, and suddenly it's all English as he shouts, "That's not true! Ask Anna—ask her! She wanted to. She was the one who started everything—"

"Shut up, I swear to God, I swear it, Papi, I don't want to hear anymore of your bullshit—"

Antonio's face is hot red, deadly red, like a devil mask.

"You don't really know her at all, Cesar. She's always hidden things from you. She's got so many secrets—"

"Ella no tiene secretos!"

All at once, I see Cesar. I wince and want to duck away into the hall as he comes at Antonio with the purposeful speed of my CO closing an attack in close combat training.

"Ella es mi esposa. Ella nunca me traicionaría. Never! She hates you!"

His hand is close to Antonio's face, the finger jabbing at his brother's eye. Antonio doesn't blink.

"It isn't like you think between us. We love—"

Cesar's hand ricochets off his brother's cheek so hard that his knuckles jounce against his own chest. The frantic clap echoes within the office and stops Antonio's words dead.

Cesar's hand drifts back into the air. It hovers, like a pale gull riding the wind currents.

Silence rings within the space between their bodies. Antonio stares at Cesar. I can see the whites of his eyes. This is the moment. This is where Cesar must decide to ease back, or else cross the threshold.

They stare so hard at each other.

Then Cesar's hand shoots forward, and he grabs Antonio's starched collar. He strikes out hard and erratic with his other hand, and it becomes a fist, and he's shouts, "No, no, goddamn you, Papi! You did this—goddamn you!"

Antonio wrenches himself free, and almost before I can react, he rushes for the door. My guts seize up—I should have been prepared for this. I dodge backward to the end of the hall. My CO taught all his troops how to back step with great speed, and I'm a sprinter.

I'm a secure fifteen feet away when Antonio shoves through the office door. His face burns an ugly, unnatural maroon. One cheek bears a purple print that is distinctly hand-shaped. His pace is razor-edged, steady, measured. He still hasn't lost control.

He rounds the corner to the spiral staircase and is gone.

I wait at the end of the hall.

Cesar doesn't come out of the office. He doesn't chase Antonio. He doesn't go looking for Anna.

I approach the open door slowly. I strain my ears. No sound comes from within. I slide along the wall and press my eye to the crack between the doorframe and the door, where the brass hinges gleam distractingly. I see Cesar leaning against his big desk, his stocky body sagging in on itself within his expensive cotton shirt and trousers. He slumps slowly into his chair. His hands rise to his face, covering his eyes, nose and mouth.

I wait. I don't breathe.

I hear the sound of rough male sobs; first soft and indistinct, then harsh and tearing.

I creep away.

Sunday, October 4, 1998
4:45 p.m.
Ortiz Farm

The setting sun gloams dense and brazen through the huge house. I sit in my security nook off the kitchen, staring at nothing. Antonio hasn't left his brother's house yet. For half an hour, he sat brooding in his Aston Martin parked out front. I watched him on a security monitor. Then he was gone. His car is still there.

A chaos of feet beats down the spiral staircase. Hard shoes cross the kitchen floor, then Antonio thrusts his head into my nook. His eyes are wild, like a bobcat's. He grabs the back of my chair. I brace myself against my desk.

"Flynn, where's Anna? Have you seen her?"

"I don't know. Her bedroom?"

Antonio lowers his head for a moment, his hand drifting to his mouth. His hand is shaking.

"She isn't there. I can't find her. I don't think she's in the house. Help me look for her."

I can't involve myself any further in this situation. I'll make it worse.

But then he says, "Please, Flynn."

Antonio has never used that word with me before. I rise. This is so unwise. If Cesar finds me helping his younger brother search for his wife, he'll kill us both.

I lock the handgun in the desk drawer. I don't want any weapons available to anyone, including me. I'm scared, and when I'm scared, I become trigger-happy.

I follow Antonio through the deserted foyer and out the front door. The sun is setting slow and thick over the water, turning things to brass and blood. The yard is radiant with autumn haze and early crickets. Motes of pollen and fluff blow in sleepy puffs of wind toward the ocean. I smell brine and fish and evergreen.

"Check around the house. I'll look in the stable. Maybe Kell has seen her."

"Okay."

I can feel myself slipping into obedient, army grunt mode.

Antonio's voice is as abrupt as my Commanding Officer's was, so it's comfortable to obey without question. I watch Antonio stride away toward the stable. Like my Commanding Officer, he has nurtured a secret that has ruined him. I'm growing sorry for him.

I walk through the golden yard, my eyes keen for signs of my boss's wife. The mucky fields are deserted. The harvest is in, so the Mexicans are off work. I can see for acres: a vast, denuded, coffee-brown desert. Anna is nowhere.

I veer toward the bullet-bright stable. Dust swirls up in little cyclones on the evening breeze, gently choking me. The sun glares off the corrugated metal roof, bringing a hard squint. I hope to find Kell in one of the corrals out front, but they're empty. The horses are locked safely away in their stalls. I'm relieved by the absence of horses, but disappointed not to find Kell. He might have provided a breath of sanity within this ruination. Some perspective, some reassurance.

Antonio runs out of the stable and skids to a hard stop by the breaking corral. He is panting.

"You didn't find her?"

I shake my head.

Antonio breathes unevenly into his tie, trying to pull himself together. He turns his head toward the inlet where Cesar docks his yacht. His face loses color. He puts both hands over his mouth for a moment, hiding it with a child's gesture.

"Oh, Jesus, no…"

"What?"

His body seizes up hard, then he takes off at a sprint toward the yacht dock. I shade my eyes and peer into the light wind gusting off the ocean, then run after him.

Cesar's yacht is bumping softly against its wooden dock, the hull booming low like a drum. We find Anna sitting a few yards away from the dock on the thin slat of gravelly beach at the water's edge. She is wearing the same milk-smooth linen dress she had on when I met her two months ago.

Anna sits inert like an ivory carving. Only her dark hair and the foamy hem of her dress move in the cool wind. Her bare feet are licked by the burbling water that stretches from the shore to the horizon. She doesn't turn when Antonio calls her name.

I come to a stop up on the dock and watch as Antonio, heedless of his pricy leather shoes, jumps down onto the damp sand beside her. He kneels by Anna and hesitantly seeks her hand, lost within the folds of her skirt. I've never seen the two of them alone together before. His eyes delve into hers, straining out to reach her.

My eyes drift to the point on the horizon where Seattle lies, unseen, beyond the waves. Just a ferry trip away from this catastrophe I created.

The wind kicks up a cold spray off the ocean. I glance back at Antonio and Anna. He sees it just as I do: the flash of wet red that has been hidden by her skirt. He grabs her arm and pulls it into the ebbing light. His eyes grow and grow, and his skin grays to a grotesque pallor.

Anna's arm is painted a bright, slickery red from her fingertips to her elbow. She jerks her it out of Antonio's grip and gets to her feet, weaving slightly. The sand beneath her is so thoroughly soaked that it looks black. The back of her skirt is a gaudy crimson. The front begins to redden as well, as fresh blood pumps freely from both of her wrists.

Oh God.

Antonio bolts at Anna. She dodges him and throws herself into the ocean. She floats red and white atop the water, pulled toward the setting sun by the current, her eyes open and dead to the sky above. Antonio dives in after her, his suit weighing him down as the wool takes on cold salt water.

He reaches her just beyond the dock and scrabbles at her frantically, trying to hook his arms around her waist. Her eyes click on and she begins to fight him, splashing up great gouts of water. She shrieks like something feral, her mouth straining open so wide it looks as though it will split at the corners. She is Kell's unbroken horse as she thrashes and kicks in the frigid water. Antonio's arms strain to hold her. Her blood makes a rusty circle in the water around them as he pins her arms by her sides and hauls her violently ashore.

He sloshes through the cold water; dragging her as the water drags at him. He throws her to the dry sand. He falls to his knees next to her, gasping hard, as she screams and wriggles her bloody hands free to push him away.

"Get me a bandage! Something!" Antonio shouts, as he wrestles her down to the sand.

I can't move.

Anna claws desperately at the sand as Antonio presses her flat with his body. His hands push her arms down as her bright blood runs over his fingers. He drips thin streams of water onto her face from his black hair and brown skin. This posture, this grinding of two bodies against each other: this is what caused all their trouble.

"Goddammit, Flynn! Give me a fucking bandage for her!"

It's the voice of my Commanding Officer, harsh and urgent. I react with mechanical army efficiency, stripping off my sweatshirt and baseball-arming it off the dock to Antonio. He snatches it off the gritty sand and whips it around Anna's wrists, as much to stop the blood as to restrain her. Bound, she begins to sob beneath him.

Such soft sobs; such a soft voice.

Antonio staggers to his feet. He picks her up and holds her draped over both arms like a baby. Anna thrashes once more, then goes limp. Her soft cries morph into horrendous animal moans that are muted by Antonio's wet chest. Twilight is turning the dock a deep blue. Antonio drops his face to Anna's neck for a moment. Slowly, he lifts his eyes, seeking me high above him.

His face is a supplicant's. His face is a little boy's.

"Please…please, will you …"

He's scared.

"Will you tell Cesar? For me? I can't. Please, I can't do it."

I finally see what Cesar sees when he looks at them. The torn and bleeding woman, the wet and shivering little boy. This is what he wanted to protect them from becoming. This is what he hired me to prevent.

I always was stupid.

THE END

www.ingramcontent.com/pod-product-compliance
Lightning Source LLC
Chambersburg PA
CBHW061956170626
46813CB00006B/2663